Amy Cross is the author of more than 100 horror, paranormal, fantasy and thriller novels.

OTHER TITLES BY AMY CROSS INCLUDE

American Coven
Annie's Room
The Ash House
Asylum
B&B
The Bride of Ashbyrn House
The Camera Man
The Curse of the Langfords
The Devil, the Witch and the Whore
The Disappearance of Lonnie James
The Dog
Eli's Town
The Farm
The Ghost of Crowford School
The Ghosts of Lakeforth Hotel
The Girl Who Never Came Back
Haunted
The Haunting of Nelson Street
The House Where She Died
The Night Girl
The Purchase
The Revenge of the Mercy Belle
Stephen
Strange Little Horrors and Other Stories
The Soul Auction
Ward Z

CONTENTS

CHAPTER ONE
page 17

CHAPTER TWO
page 19

CHAPTER THREE
page 27

CHAPTER FOUR
page 29

CHAPTER FIVE
page 37

CHAPTER SIX
page 39

CHAPTER SEVEN
page 47

CHAPTER EIGHT
page 55

CHAPTER NINE
page 57

CHAPTER TEN
page 65

CHAPTER ELEVEN
page 75

CHAPTER TWELVE
page 83

CHAPTER THIRTEEN
page 91

CHAPTER FOURTEEN
page 99

CHAPTER FIFTEEN
page 107

CHAPTER SIXTEEN
page 115

CHAPTER SEVENTEEN
page 125

CHAPTER EIGHTEEN
page 133

CHAPTER NINETEEN
page 141

CHAPTER TWENTY
page 149

CHAPTER TWENTY-ONE
page 157

CHAPTER TWENTY-TWO
page 165

CHAPTER TWENTY-THREE
page 173

CHAPTER TWENTY-FOUR
page 181

CHAPTER TWENTY-FIVE
page 189

CHAPTER TWENTY-SIX
page 199

CHAPTER TWENTY-SEVEN
page 207

CHAPTER TWENTY-EIGHT
page 215

CHAPTER TWENTY-NINE
page 223

CHAPTER THIRTY
page 231

CHAPTER THIRTY-ONE
page 239

CHAPTER THIRTY-TWO
page 247

CHAPTER THIRTY-THREE
page 255

CHAPTER THIRTY-FOUR
page 263

CHAPTER THIRTY-FIVE
page 273

CHAPTER THIRTY-SIX
page 281

CHAPTER THIRTY-SEVEN
page 289

CHAPTER THIRTY-EIGHT
page 297

CHAPTER THIRTY-NINE
page 307

CHAPTER FORTY
page 315

CHAPTER FORTY-ONE
page 323

CHAPTER FORTY-TWO
page 333

CHAPTER FORTY-THREE
page 343

THE HAUNTING OF HARDLOCKE HOUSE

AMY CROSS

This edition
first published by Blackwych Books Ltd
United Kingdom, 2020

Copyright © 2020 Amy Cross

All rights reserved. This book is a work of fiction.
Names, characters, places, incidents and businesses are
the product of the author's imagination or are
used fictitiously. Any resemblance to actual persons,
living or dead, or to actual events or locations,
is entirely coincidental.

Also available in e-book format.

www.blackwychbooks.com

CONTENTS

CHAPTER ONE
page 17

CHAPTER TWO
page 19

CHAPTER THREE
page 27

CHAPTER FOUR
page 29

CHAPTER FIVE
page 37

CHAPTER SIX
page 39

CHAPTER SEVEN
page 47

CHAPTER EIGHT
page 55

CHAPTER NINE
page 57

CHAPTER TEN
page 65

CHAPTER ELEVEN
page 75

CHAPTER TWELVE
page 83

CHAPTER THIRTEEN
page 91

CHAPTER FOURTEEN
page 99

CHAPTER FIFTEEN
page 107

CHAPTER SIXTEEN
page 115

CHAPTER SEVENTEEN
page 125

CHAPTER EIGHTEEN
page 133

CHAPTER NINETEEN
page 141

CHAPTER TWENTY
page 149

CHAPTER TWENTY-ONE
page 157

CHAPTER TWENTY-TWO
page 165

CHAPTER TWENTY-THREE
page 173

CHAPTER TWENTY-FOUR
page 181

CHAPTER TWENTY-FIVE
page 189

CHAPTER TWENTY-SIX
page 199

CHAPTER TWENTY-SEVEN
page 207

CHAPTER TWENTY-EIGHT
page 215

CHAPTER TWENTY-NINE
page 223

CHAPTER THIRTY
page 231

CHAPTER THIRTY-ONE
page 239

CHAPTER THIRTY-TWO
page 247

CHAPTER THIRTY-THREE
page 255

CHAPTER THIRTY-FOUR
page 263

CHAPTER THIRTY-FIVE
page 273

CHAPTER THIRTY-SIX
page 281

CHAPTER THIRTY-SEVEN
page 289

CHAPTER THIRTY-EIGHT
page 297

CHAPTER THIRTY-NINE
page 307

CHAPTER FORTY
page 315

CHAPTER FORTY-ONE
page 323

CHAPTER FORTY-TWO
page 333

CHAPTER FORTY-THREE
page 343

CHAPTER FORTY-FOUR
page 351

CHAPTER FORTY-FIVE
page 359

CHAPTER FORTY-SIX
page 367

CHAPTER FORTY-SEVEN
page 375

CHAPTER FORTY-EIGHT
page 385

CHAPTER FORTY-NINE
page 393

CHAPTER FIFTY
page 403

EPILOGUE
page 417

THE HAUNTING OF HARDLOCKE SCHOOL

CHAPTER ONE

A STRAY FLY BUZZED in the darkness as it flew through the railings and between two old candles, before swooping around the room and then making its way into another large, abandoned room.

The fly quickly landed at one end of a large, hefty oak table. Whether by accident, or due to some strange half sense, the fly stood now just a few inches from an old fruit bowl. By human standards, the bowl was long since empty, but the fly scurried to the edge of the bowl and made its way through the ornate patterned gaps, and then it began to search for scraps of matter that could not have been in the bowl in more than thirty years. The fly's antennae twitched as it continued its hunt, and then the insect stopped suddenly as if it had detected a possible threat.

All along one wall of the room, large windows were smothered by grime that let in only a fraction of the available moonlight.

Dust drifted in the air, hanging undisturbed.

Satisfied that it was in no danger, the fly returned its attention to the bowl. After so many years, there were no scraps of fruit left, yet something seemed to be of interest to the fly as it hurried across the patterned silver swirls. The insect's tiny brain had picked up on some trace of what had once been there, on the ghost of a long-gone orange or banana, or it perhaps merely recognized the shape of a fruit bowl and struggled to believe that there was nothing to eat. After all, in the two days since it had inadvertently entered the building through a tiny crack in one of the outer walls, the fly had found not so much as a scrap of food. Desperation was setting in. Without a change in fortune, the creature would be dead within another twenty-four hours.

Suddenly, sensing movement nearby, the startled fly took off and soared around the space above the table before buzzing back out into the next room.

CHAPTER TWO

"I JUST WANTED TO congratulate you on your retirement. Do you have any plans?"

As soon as those words had left her lips, Jessie winced inside. She'd worried so much about how to open a conversation with the great Doctor Diana Moore, and now she'd failed miserably by blurting out something so bland, so unmemorable, that she instantly expected a stinging rebuke. Doctor Moore was not known for her tolerance of fools. Then again, Jessie knew that getting verbally ribbed to shreds by the indomitable doctor was something of a right of passage.

"I'm sorry, what?" the doctor asked, turning to her.

Jessie opened her mouth to apologize, but

then she realized that she'd been given a second chance. Somehow, miraculously, the sharp-witted Doctor Moore had been off in a world of her own. Looking around the darkened garden, Jessie hoped for inspiration, but all she saw was an empty, moonlit lawn, and all she heard was chatter from the dinner party back in the house. So far, her parents' party had seemed very thin and pointless, and she was fairly sure she'd been the only person who'd noticed Doctor Moore wheeling herself outside a few minutes earlier.

"I was a million miles away," Doctor Moore continued, "and I'm afraid I didn't hear what you said." She looked past Jessie, toward the house, and she visibly cringed as she heard more music blasting from the stereo. "Have you ever noticed," she added, "how often people throw a party for someone without considering what that person might want? In all my life, I don't think I've ever indicated an interest in dinner and wine and bland conversation over canapes. I don't even know why I agreed to be brought here tonight. I suppose we all have moments of weakness occasionally, don't we?"

Jessie waited, not really sure whether Doctor Moore was finished. Someone laughed hysterically inside the house, but out in the garden the sound seemed much harsher.

"My name's Jessica," she said finally, realizing that she hadn't even introduced herself. "People call me Jessie, though. I'm Dom and Karen's daughter. They let me come to the party tonight. I'm just finishing school soon and I'm thinking of studying psychiatry at college."

"Is that right?"

"I just, uh, wanted to tell you that your work really inspires me," Jessie said, "and that I've actually been reading your book on suggestive psychiatry over the past few weeks."

"Really?" Doctor Moore hesitated for a moment, before taking a sip from her glass of wine. She adjusted her seating position slightly, sitting up a little straighter in her wheelchair. Blankets covered her lap to keep her warm. "Well, that's nice for you. How old are you?"

"Almost eighteen."

"*Almost* eighteen?"

"I'll be eighteen next week."

"What a difference that'll make."

"I don't know. Probably not."

"So you're a child. Then you couldn't possibly understand my work."

"I've tried my best."

"Oh dear."

"It's really inspired me to study hard," Jessie

continued, desperate to say something – anything – that might win her a modicum of approval. Above all, she wanted to seem smart. "I know Mum and Dad really respect your work. In particular, I liked some of your ideas on dominant susceptibility and I tried to think of them through a different lens in an attempt to demonstrate some new concepts. I... I mean, I wrote an essay on you for a school assignment, I could send it to you if you..."

Her voice trailed off as she realized that a genius of Doctor Moore's stature would never be interested in her pathetic scribblings. That second chance had been well and truly wasted.

"You seem enthusiastic," Doctor Moore muttered. "Congratulations on that, at least. I do hope you won't waste that enthusiasm by doing something as stupid as going to university."

"Well, actually I was hoping to -"

"University education is the greatest form of conformity in the civilized world. It should be outlawed. Young people should be forced to think for themselves, instead of being rewarded for seeking out the approval of a bunch of crusty old farts who never would have survived in the real world. And I count myself as one of those old farts, by the way."

"Oh, I'm sure you're not a -"

"And then you end up in all that debt. The whole thing is absurd."

"Mmm," Jessie managed in reply, before realizing that she'd already outstayed her welcome. "That was it, really," she added, taking a step back. "I just couldn't ignore this opportunity to introduce myself and tell you how much I like your work. I'm only at the start of my studies, really, but I'm already determined to pursue some of your theories. Not that I'd ever dare to compare myself to you, but..."

Again, her voice trailed off as she begin to realize that she was coming across as some kind of starstruck idiot. Then again, she figured that seemed somewhat appropriate, given that Doctor Diana Moore *was* a genuine star in her field of work. If anyone was genuinely interested in interpretative or suggestive psychiatry, or really in anything to do with the human mind, then Doctor Moore's work was hugely important. She'd been one of the biggest names in the field for more than half a century.

"I hope you enjoy your retirement," Jessie added finally. "I'm sorry, I'll leave you in peace now."

She turned to go back inside.

"*Enjoy* my retirement?"

Jessie froze, fully aware that those three

words had – in Doctor Moore's voice – been absolutely dripping with disdain and disapproval.

"You hope I enjoy my retirement?" the doctor continued, and somehow, impossibly, she now sounded even more irritated. "And what, young lady, do you think one such as myself should *do* in retirement, other than shrivel up and wait to die?"

Jessie turned back to look at the doctor, who stared up at her from her wheelchair, and frankly she wanted the world to swallow her up.

"I'm seventy years old," Doctor Moore pointed out, "and my retirement was always avoided while Professor Martindale was in charge of the faculty. Upon his death, and the arrival of that new young Professor Bollinger, I was forced out and effectively told that I could be of no further service. Even this party here tonight, which I was more or less forced to attend, is part of some devious attempt to paint my departure as an act of mercy. I have absolutely no interest in retirement whatsoever. Life without work is no life at all."

"Right," Jessie replied cautiously. "I mean, I get that. I guess."

"You *guess*?" Doctor Moore rolled her eyes. "Young people these days are so imprecise with their language. Then again, I shouldn't expect to be able to hold a conversation with you. You are, after all, more than half a century younger than me."

"I really didn't mean to disturb you," Jessie told her. "I guess... I mean, I think I just wanted to tell you that I admire your work and you've inspired me a lot. Your career is such a great example of success, and I really want to emulate that."

She paused, but the elderly lady said nothing in response.

"Some day," she added.

Again, only silence followed.

"So now I'll go inside," Jessie added, turning once more to return to the kitchen. "Mum and Dad probably need me to... do something. Thanks again."

"My career has been a lamentable failure," Doctor Moore said.

Jessie stopped in her tracks. This time she was closer to the kitchen door, but she knew she couldn't simply walk away from such a surprising comment. Turning, she saw Doctor Moore sitting slumped in the wheelchair, looking utterly defeated.

"Why... Why would you say that?" Jessie asked.

"Because it's true."

"No," Jessie continued, heading back over to her, "you've had the most amazing career of anyone I've ever heard of. Your papers on psychiatry are some of the most widely read and quoted of all time, you've received awards for your studies, you're regularly invited to conferences all over the world. Didn't someone name a library after you?"

"I'm a dismal failure. A wretch of the highest order. I'm feted everywhere I go, but only because people choose to overlook the fact that my entire body of work is fatally undermined by the one problem that I was never able to solve. I'm not exaggerating, young lady, when I say that this fatal problem towers above everything else I have ever done. When I am dead and buried, they should leave my name off the gravestone and merely inscribe the word FAILURE in big letters."

"Everyone knows you're a genius," Jessie pointed out. "How can you possibly suggest that your career has been anything other than a stunning success?"

Again she waited, and again Doctor Moore seemed unmoved. Just as Jessie was about to try again, however, Doctor Moore turned to her with an exhausted expression, and her lips moved slightly as if she was about to say something.

"Two words sum up my miserable failure," Doctor Moore managed finally. "Hardlocke House."

CHAPTER THREE

BUZZING THROUGH INTO THE next room, the fly once again made for the large oak desk that stood over by the window. Landing on a set of old papers, the fly scurried across the pages for a moment before taking off again.

This time, the fly landed on a second pile of papers that had been left open on the desk. For a few seconds, the fly merely sat on the papers with its antennae twitching, but then it crawled onto the desk itself and made its way through a thin layer of dust.

And then, as a floorboard creaked nearby, the fly took off, narrowly avoiding a dark, shadowy shape that hung in the dusty air.

CHAPTER FOUR

"I'VE READ YOUR PAPER on Hardlocke House," Jessie said as she sat on the edge of the rockery, looking up at Doctor Moore. "It was brilliant. I mean, I didn't understand it all, but I got some of it. You proved that the tenants were suffering from some kind of psychosis, that the supposed proof of paranormal activity was all bogus. It was one of your best debunkings of... well, of ghost stories."

"It was no such thing," Doctor Moore replied.

"The woman... I can't remember her name," Jessie continued, "but she claimed she'd heard a whispering voice in the house at night. And you proved that it was all in her mind."

"That doesn't mean anything."

"And the man thought he saw a figure on

the landing, outside the master bedroom, and he thought he saw a face in the mirror up there too, but you showed that he was extremely suggestible. His wife basically instigated the whole thing when she claimed she was experiencing things, and he was hooked on prescription drugs. They were, like, the least reliable witnesses in the history of anything."

"Those people were cretins," Doctor Moore said, nodding slightly. "Believe me, I interviewed them. I know this isn't going to sound very politically correct, but they were thick as pig shit. Especially the woman. How they ever managed to afford to buy Hardlocke House in the first place is beyond me."

"I read between the lines on that," Jessie said with a faint smile. "They got the money from her father, I think, and then they tried to convert that into some kind of weird ghost-chasing career. Didn't you find evidence that they'd been talking about ghosts even *before* they moved into the house?"

"I did."

"And they were aware of the house's history, right?"

"They were."

"So they basically moved in with the intention of experiencing something," Jessie continued. "That immediately undermined most of what they'd claimed. They were just hoping to hit the headlines. Didn't they initially deny that they'd had any idea Hardlocke House was supposed to be haunted? And then didn't they have to backtrack a little bit after the truth was revealed?"

"They claimed a lot of things that turned out to be untrue," Doctor Moore replied. "Andy and Lizzy Malone were a pair of chancers who thought they could achieve fame by moving into a haunted house and snapping a few photos of ghostly happenings. They'd tried it a number times before, but no-one had been very impressed by their feeble attempts, so they realized that faking it wasn't enough. They decided to move into a real haunted house and get images of real ghosts."

"And they failed," Jessie pointed out. "When you were hired to go over their claims, you picked it all apart and proved that they were lying."

She waited, but Doctor Moore said nothing and seemed lost in thought.

"You *did*," Jessie continued. "You disproved every aspect of that so-called haunting. The camera tricks, the made-up stories, you skewered the whole thing so brilliantly. They never tried it again at any other houses. You totally owned the pair of them!"

"Did I?"

"Andy Malone committed suicide a few years later," Jessie pointed out, "and Lizzy died of cancer a couple of years after that. It's a sad story." She paused for a moment. "But it's not your fault! I wasn't implying that!"

"The fate of the Malones is completely irrelevant," Doctor Moore replied. "Nobody cares about that soap opera rubbish. What matters is the fact that I failed."

Jessie paused for a moment, as she tried to understand what point the older woman was trying to make.

"Doctor Moore, I've read that paper several times," she said finally. "It's a classic. You listed every claim that the Malones made about Hardlocke House, and you explained why they were wrong. The whole thing was a perfect example of the way the human mind can start tricking itself when it's placed under duress. You ripped them apart completely."

"Every claim except one," Doctor Moore replied.

"What do you mean?"

She waited, but Doctor Moore sighed and looked down for a moment at her own hands.

"What claim?" Jessie asked. "I don't remember any loose ends in that report."

"I was a coward," Doctor Moore continued, "and a fraud. When I finished my investigation of Hardlocke House and wrote up my report, there was one incident that I was never able to explain. So I simply left it out."

"You mean..."

Jessie hesitated, unable to believe what she

was hearing.

"There was one moment that never made sense," Doctor Moore told her. "It occurred late in the investigation, while I was wrapping things up. I'd finished my research into the history of the house, particularly into the woman who ran the school there back in the nineteenth century."

"Sarah Clarke."

"Indeed. Sarah Clarke." Doctor Moore paused for a moment, as if she was struggling to get the words out. "I'd explained my findings to everyone, in the front room of the house as it happens. I was rather full of myself, and I used some injudicious words to describe Ms. Clarke. I explained that the woman had been a hypocrite, a hate-filled monster who enjoyed hurting the children at her school. I included a lot of that information in my report."

"I remember reading it," Jessie said.

"But what I didn't include," she continued, "is the fact that I had experienced something rather unusual. I had gone into one of the rooms of the house, I had just wanted to check a few things, but I wasn't in any way concerned. I was all alone. And that's when..."

Jessie waited for her to explain.

"A book flew off the shelf," Doctor Moore said finally, "and hit me in the face at great speed, before dropping to the floor." She reached up and touched the side of her chin. "It got me right here, and it cut me. Do you see that little scar?"

Jessie squinted a little, and she could just about make out a tiny white mark.

"And in the instant that I was struck," Doctor Moore continued, "I felt something that I've never felt before or since. I felt the most enormous sense of rage and hatred suddenly fill my body, as if I was about to be consumed. That strange sensation lasted for several seconds, until I took a step away from the shelves, and then do you know what I did?"

"Did you check for hidden wires?" Jessie asked. "Or some other mechanism that might have been used to set up the trick with the book?"

"I walked out of that room, and I never looked back. I never *went* back. I left that place, claiming that I had a train to catch, and I went home and I wrote up my report without any mention of what had happened to me in the library."

"Okay," Jessie said cautiously, "but that doesn't mean -"

"I ran away," Doctor Moore added, interrupting her. "Don't let your foolish hero worship blind you to the truth. I ran away and I concealed that incident. I pretended it hadn't happened." She took a deep breath. "In my entire forty-year career, I studied two dozen haunted houses and I proved every single ghost story to be untrue. Except that one at Hardlocke House. And ever since, for the past forty years, I have felt the guilt burrowing away in my gut. I am, indeed, a fraud."

They sat in silence for a moment, although voices and music could still be heard coming from the party in the house nearby. Someone was apparently attempting to start a conga line.

"Just because you didn't manage to explain what happened with that book," Jessie said finally, "doesn't mean it was a ghost. Your own research proves that point over and over again. You're not immune to the manifestations that you wrote about, Doctor Moore. The confusion, the exhaustion, the loss of perspective..."

"I never claimed to be immune," she replied. "You can't imagine what I felt in that house, young lady. It wasn't really the book that troubled me, it was the sense of fury. For a few seconds, I felt as if the most immense anger resided in that place, floating through the air like some kind of cloud of emotion." She sighed. "I know how utterly foolish this all sounds now, but I'm sure you understand how I can never view my career as anything other than a travesty. I failed, and then I covered up that failure."

"Doctor -"

"Unless," she added, "I fix my error."

"You want to admit that you left the incident

out of your report?" Jessie asked.

"That will be part of it, yes," Doctor Moore replied, "but there's something more important that I shall also have to accomplish." She took a deep breath. "You asked me what I intend to do in my retirement," she continued finally. "Well, I shall tell you. If I am ever to regain so much as a shred of self-respect, then I must, after forty years, do the one thing that I have avoided. I must go back to Hardlocke House."

CHAPTER FIVE

THE FLY SCURRIED UP one of the wood-paneled walls in the empty room, and then it stopped as it reached one of the ridges. Beginning to feel weak now, the fly was trying to conserve energy while it waited for some source of food to arrive.

A moment later, a floorboard creaked at the far end of the corridor, near one of the windows. Outside, trees were gently swaying in a late night breeze, casting moonlit shadows against the glass panels. In the room, meanwhile, nothing seemed to be moving, save for the fly's antennae as it remained in its place on the wall. Yet something was happening, something that the fly had never felt before.

Panic.

Fear.

Terror.

The fly knew something was wrong, that there was a threat nearby, but it could see nothing.

Setting off again, the fly crawled past another ridge on the wall and then made its way onto the gilt-edged frame of a large mirror. After briefly investigating the mirror itself, the fly scurried down the side of the frame and onto the lower corner, where it stopped for a moment. Unable to stay still, the fly still had no idea where the threat was coming from. Its antennae were twitching, and a moment later another floorboard creaked slightly, this time a little closer.

A shape, approximately human, was standing near the fireplace.

CHAPTER SIX

"OKAY, DIANA, HAVE A safe drive home," Karen said as she and the rest of the guests stood at the door and watched the elderly lady being carefully loaded into the back of a taxi. "I'll call you soon to talk about the investiture plans."

Doctor Moore glanced back at them all, her face filled with apprehension, but then the driver slid the door shut before going around to get into the front. The party was by no means over, but Doctor Moore had managed to stay for two hours and evidently that had been all she could handle.

"She's so amazing," Karen continued as she waved at the departing taxi. "Honestly, if I'm still half as bright when I'm her age, I'll be amazed. Did you know she still gets up at five in the morning every single day and starts reading? She has a phenomenal mind."

"I can't believe they forced her to retire," Dom added as they all stepped back so that Karen could shut the door. "The office isn't going to be the same without her, even if she could be grumpy at times. At least now we can get a proper coffee machine without her complaining, though. There are some upsides."

Still comparing stories about the 'cranky' Doctor Diana Moore, Dom headed into the living room with the rest of the guests.

"Are you okay?" Karen asked Jessie as the music was immediately turned up and the party moved into another gear. She reached out and put a hand on daughter's arm. "You seem a little... out of it. If you want to go to bed, that's fine. I'll make sure there's not too much noise down here."

"I was just thinking about Doctor Moore," Jessie admitted.

"I know you were really excited to meet her," Karen replied. "Was it how you expected? I know sometimes it can be a bit of a letdown to meet your heroes, and I know the old battle-ax has a reputation for being mean to people who try to praise her. She didn't say anything bad to you, did she?"

"Nothing bad," Jessie said, but then she stopped herself as she realized she could never tell anyone about the doctor's surprising admission.

"She just talked a little about her work, that's all."

"You got more out of her than most, then," Karen said as she turned and headed through to the kitchen. "Come on, I've decided to stop being mean. You can have one glass of wine."

"I'm okay, thanks."

Karen stopped and turned to her.

"Seriously? A daughter of mine is turning down the chance of a 1982 rioja?"

"Coming," Jessie muttered, although she loitered a little in the hallway as she found herself thinking back to Doctor Moore's comments about Hardlocke House. She wasn't sure what she'd expected Doctor Moore to say to her, but she certainly hadn't expected an admission of failure. Of academic fraud.

***

"I am *so* going to try to get her office," Sabrina Hall said a short while later, as she crashed down onto the sofa next to Jessie in the front room. "I want that view from the back window. You know how you can see the main campus square from there?"

"Uh, not really," Jessie replied, barely listening as she continued to scroll on her phone.

"Well, I want a perfect vantage point for when I go totally postal and start shooting everyone," Sabrina continued, before pausing again.

"Bitch, you're not listening to one word that I'm saying. And you haven't touched your wine. Are you *sure* that Karen's really your mother?"

"Sorry," Jessie said, turning to her. "I was listening, I swear. You were talking about Doctor Moore's office, and getting in there, and... shooting someone?"

She furrowed her brow.

"What are you reading about?" Sabrina asked, grabbing the phone from her hands and taking a look. "You sure know how to be antisocial, don't you?"

"It's nothing, I just -"

"Hardlocke House. Wasn't that one of Doctor Moore's big studies?"

"She wrote a paper on a haunting there," Jessie replied. "Back in 1980, or 1981, a couple moved into that place and started claiming that all sorts of things were going on. It had a history before, but they were the first ones to really go public. Eventually a TV company hired Doctor Moore to go and investigate the place. The paper she wrote as a result was one of her most important."

"I'm sure it was." Sabrina scrolled up to the top of the page, where a photo showed Hardlocke House nestled at the edge of a forest. "Man, if you wanted to build a creepy house, that's how you'd do it. It just *looks* haunted, you know? And why would anyone want to live all the way out there in the middle of nowhere? You wouldn't, not unless you were planning to get up to no good."

"It was built as an orphanage," Jessie explained. "It's something like two, almost three hundred years old, and it was supposed to be a place where orphans could be raised and educated."

"Okay, so that's even creepier."

"It wasn't an orphanage for very long," Jessie continued. "The headmistress, Sarah Clarke, had a bad reputation. She'd actually been fired from her previous jobs for... Well, there were claims that she hit the children, and whipped them. Obviously those stories might have been exaggerated. Somehow she got the money together to have Hardlocke House built, and she decided to set up on her own. She was the only member of staff. It was just her and the children there."

"What kind of person would send a child to someone like her?"

"I guess... I mean, I think it was easier to hide things back then," Jessie pointed out. "It was the eighteenth century, you couldn't exactly go onto Google and look stuff up. I guess people weren't really too worried about what happened to the orphans, either. They just wanted to dump them at Hardlocke House and forget about them. Even when rumors started again about Sarah Clarke, it was probably easier for most people to just ignore them."

Sabrina scrolled down the page until she came to a sketch of a stern-looking woman standing on the steps at the front of the house.

"That's supposed to be her, huh?"

"I think so," Jessie said. "She was from some family that had once been pretty important, but eventually she was the only one left. I guess we'll never really know the truth about why she started the orphanage, but when she died... Well, you know what happened to her, don't you?"

"I'm just getting to that section now," Sabrina replied, as she peered at the phone. "She was found stabbed to death in the hallway at the bottom of the stairs, in the house," she read. "None of the children at the school were tracked down and asked about what happened. They were never even found. Or, if they were, there's no mention of that in the records."

"She'd been stabbed twelve times," Jessie said. "There were twelve pupils."

"So you think they took turns?"

"There was always a suggestion that they'd taken revenge on her, for all the awful things she did to them," Jessie explained. "She used to beat them for the slightest transgression, and one of the theories is that they'd had enough. Whatever really happened, they took the secret to their graves. Not one of those boys ever spoke about Sarah Clarke's death, at least not as far as we can tell. In fact, we don't even know what happened to them. They were never heard of again after that night."

"That's pretty creepy," Sabrina admitted, before handing the phone back to her and getting to her feet. "Then again, I can understand it. If you're stuck in a creepy house with a monster, eventually you're going to fight back, aren't you? I guess it never occurred to the evil old bat that she was totally outnumbered. So, are you going to sit there being boring, or are you going to come through and join the rest of us? You're by far the youngest person at this party, Jessie, but so far you're acting like the oldest."

"Sure," Jessie replied, putting her phone away and hauling herself up off the sofa. "Sorry, I know you're right. I guess I just still find the story of Hardlocke House so fascinating. Especially since even Doctor Diana Moore was unable to -"

She stopped herself just in time.

"Was unable to *what*?" Sabrina asked.

"I guess it doesn't matter," Jessie replied, as she stopped in the doorway and saw her mother drunkenly dancing in the kitchen while all the other guests laughed and drank at the dining table. "I guess it's just history now. I just can't help wondering... Do you think Doctor Moore has any reason to feel dissatisfied with her career?"

"Are you insane?" Sabrina asked. "She's

done everything. She's won prizes, she's had buildings named after her, and she was a celebrated debunker of hoaxes and ghost stories along the way. I'd say that Diana Moore made the most of her life and career, and now she can afford to sit back for a well-earned rest in her retirement. Not that I really expect her to do any such thing, of course. Some people just can't ever stop, can they?"

"Jessie!" Karen screamed excitedly, running over and grabbing her daughter's hands and dragging her into the room. "You're here! Okay, now it's time to *party*!"

CHAPTER SEVEN

"I CAN'T DESCRIBE THE fear that I felt," Lizzy Malone said, as a line of static briefly interrupted the old VHS recording that someone had uploaded to YouTube. "It was like I just knew I was in the presence of a powerful evil force. I remember thinking that I was about to die."

"It was the same for me," her husband Andy said. The camera pulled out, a little jerkily, to reveal him sitting next to her in the hallway of Hardlocke House. "I don't think it can really be explained. I think you just have to experience it for yourself." He looked at the various people who were behind the camera. "Have any of you encountered it yet?"

Several voices murmured that they hadn't, as a boom mic briefly dipped into the shot.

"And how to you feel about Doctor Moore

coming to investigate your home?" a voice asked from off the screen. "As I'm sure you know, she has a history of debunking haunted house stories."

"We can't wait!" Lizzy said, although her wide, forced grin hinted at some degree of discomfort. "We know that there's something here, and we're sure that Doctor Moore will find it. And if she doesn't, then that just means that maybe she isn't quite as sensitive as she thinks she is."

"I'm not a psychic," Doctor Moore said, as the film cut to a shot of her in a dark corridor. She was standing up, and Jessie couldn't help but smile as she saw that although she was forty years younger on the tape, the doctor had the same irritated expression that she'd worn during the party the night before. "Please don't ask me questions about feelings or intuition or any of that nonsense. I deal in cold, hard facts."

"And do you think that there really *might* be a ghostly presence here at Hardlocke House?" the interviewer asked.

"I can't believe you asked me that question," she replied, casting a withering look at the unseen man. "Actually, ignore that. You're from the production company, of course I can believe that you'd be so stupid. I think the best thing might be for you people to keep out of my way as much as possible. If this investigation is anything like all the others I've conducted over the years, I should have proof of fraud by the end of the day."

She turned and peered at the Malones.

"Perhaps even within the hour," she added disdainfully.

Suddenly hearing a bumping sound, Jessie paused the video. A moment later she heard a distant groan, and she realized that finally – a little after midday – her mother had emerged from the master bedroom.

***

"My head feels like someone emptied an ashtray into it," Karen said, pale and queasy as she sat at the kitchen table, "and then topped it up with stale beer, and then stirred it. And then blew it up with dynamite. How much did I drink, again?"

"A lot," Jessie replied, glancing at the huge pile of bottles and cans in the recycling box, which was overflowing next to the door to the utility room. "But if it makes you feel any better, you definitely weren't the only one."

"At least we gave Diana a good send-off," Karen murmured, taking a sip from her glass of orange juice. "I mean, somewhere under that gruff and sour exterior, she must have enjoyed herself." She paused. "Mustn't she?"

"You know Doctor Moore pretty well, don't you?"

"As well as anyone knows her. She's always tended to keep herself to herself. No partner, no kids. As far as I know, she's never even had a pet."

"Apart from that chip on her shoulder," Dom muttered, stumbling into the room in his dressing gown and heading straight to the fridge. "I assume you're talking about our guest of honor from last night, aren't you?"

"Has she ever talked to you about Hardlocke House?" Jessie asked.

"Not that I recall," Karen told her. "We've discussed a lot of her cases over the years, but I don't remember any specific conversations about that place. Why?"

"I was just wondering," Jessie replied. "She talked about it last night when I was out in the garden with her, and I kinda got the impression that it was weighing on her mind. Like it was bothering her." She held back from explaining what Doctor Moore had admitted, but she was hoping that at least one of her parents might be able to shed some light on the matter. "I guess what I was really wanting to know," she added, "is whether anyone else in the academic community ever raised any doubts about the Hardlocke House story."

"I don't think so," Karen said. "If they did, old Diana would have given them short shrift. Let's just say that she never took too kindly to criticism or questioning."

"I saw you out there with her, Jessie," Dom muttered, carrying a cup of coffee over to the table. "What were the two of you talking about?"

"Nothing much," Jessie said, preferring to not get into much detail. "This and that."

"Damn it!" Karen hissed as the phone in the hallway suddenly started ringing. "Did someone turn that thing up? I swear it's not usually that loud!"

"I'll get it," Dom replied, hurrying out of the room. "If it's Karl about that bloody bike again, I'll strangle him."

"So you met your hero, huh?" Karen said with a faint smile, watching her daughter's expression.

"She's not my hero," Jessie countered.

"More or less," Karen continued. "I hope she didn't put you off too much. I can't imagine she's the type to give encouraging words to a youngster who wants to follow in her footsteps."

"She told me further education is a giant scam."

"There you go," Karen added. "Biting the hand that feeds her."

Now it was Jessie's turn to smile.

"Diana Moore is a perfect example of why you need more in your life than *just* your studies," Karen said, reaching over and squeezing her daughter's hand. "You need a life as well, but the two things go hand in hand. Everyone does. It wouldn't hurt you to rebel a little. Drink more than a sip of alcohol, flirt with some boys – or girls, if that's your thing – and just generally let your hair down. Honestly, if you want to go out occasionally and stay out so that your dad and I worry, that's absolutely fine."

She paused.

"Please," she added. "Just once."

Before Jessie could reply, Dom wandered back through with a slightly bemused expression on his face.

"It's for you," he told Jessie.

"Who is it?"

He paused.

"It's Diana Moore," he added.

"Huh?" Jessie paused. "You must have got that wrong. Isn't she calling for one of you two?"

"She was very specific," he replied. "Her exact words were that she wanted to talk to my, and I quote, annoyingly young and naive daughter. Although she added that you were far more interesting than anyone else she spoke to at the party last night." He turned to Karen. "By her standards, that's almost a compliment."

"This has to be a mistake," Jessie said, getting to her feet and heading to the hallway. "Why would Diana Moore want to talk to *me*?"

As she approached the phone and saw the

receiver resting on the little table by the foot of the stairs, Jessie slowed and then hesitated for a moment. She had never in a million years expected Doctor Moore to call, and she was surprised that the older woman even remembered her. Reaching for the receiver, she still couldn't quite figure out what she was going to say, and at the back of her mind she was worried that perhaps she might have inadvertently caused offense.

Hearing whispers, she turned and saw her parents peering at her from the kitchen. She waved for them to go away; they ducked out of view, but as she raised the receiver to her ear and lips she had no doubt that they were still listening.

"Uh, hello?" she said cautiously. "Is this -"

"What you said last night," Doctor Moore replied on the other end of the line, interrupting her, "about wishing you could get some practical experience. Did you mean it?"

"Well, I -"

"Yes or no, young woman?"

"Yes. I guess."

"You guess?" Doctor Moore sighed. "Please don't say stupid things like that. You want experience, do you not?"

"Sure. I mean, yes. Absolutely. But -"

"I'm afraid that I have rather hit the wall of reality," Doctor Moore said, interrupting her again. "Stubbornness can only get me so far, and I have to acknowledge that I am a seventy-year-old woman confined to a wheelchair. As much as I hate to rely on anyone, I have limitations. As such, if I am to return to the field for one final hurrah, I am going to need assistance. Now, the last thing I want in any situation is company, so I have been doing some thinking and I have come to the conclusion that one assistant will suffice. Would you consider yourself to be a reasonably strong girl?"

"I don't know," Jessie replied. "I mean, yes. I guess."

"There's that awful phrase again. Why do young people always say that they're *guessing* about things? I'm offering you an opportunity to blow off the dust of papers and books, and to get out there into the real world. Are you interested in seizing the day, or are you just another lazy fool seeking a nice comfortable chair?"

"I don't quite get what you mean," Jessie said. "What exactly are you asking me to do?"

"I would have thought that should be painfully obvious by now," Doctor Moore said with a sigh. "Young lady, I am asking you to accompany me on my final research trip. I am asking you to assist me, to facilitate the work that I absolutely must complete. I've decided that the time has come, after forty years, to finally go back to Hardlocke House!"

CHAPTER EIGHT

IN THE COLD LIGHT of day, the fly was resting on the mirror's wooden frame. Having spent all night searching in vain for food, the fly was now conserving energy by resting. It hadn't moved in almost six hours.

Suddenly the wooden frame shuddered, and the fly took off again as the mirror cracked and an anguished, dead scream rang out.

CHAPTER NINE

"YOU?" DOM SAID, sitting in a state of some shock in the front room. He paused, his mind racing with the possibilities, and then he looked at Jessie again. "*You?*"

"I know it's come out of the blue," Jessie replied, "but apparently she thinks I'd be the least irritating person to have around."

"She's barely met you!" Dom pointed out. "Wait, that didn't come out quite right. What I mean is that she's notoriously picky about who she works with. Your mother and I have been trying to get her to collaborate on various projects for years, and she's barely even been willing to make eye contact with us. You almost need to have a Nobel prize in order to get into her office, and even then there's no guarantee. And now suddenly she meets you once at a party and decides you should join her team?"

He stared at her for a moment longer.

"You?" he added again, incredulously.

"It's not going to be a team," Jessie said, looking at her mother. "It's going to be just us."

"Just the two of you?" Karen asked.

Jessie nodded.

"That's completely out of the question," Karen continued. "You're only seventeen, you can't go off hundreds of miles away with someone you barely know, to spend time at a rundown, abandoned old house."

"I'm almost eighteen," Jessie reminded her.

"That's not the point! The point is that you're not going!"

"Let's just take a moment here," Dom said. "Jessie, this is quite a surprise. I know people who have spent years of their lives trying to get to work with Diana Moore. I know people who I would consider to be geniuses who have prostrated themselves at that woman's feet and *begged* just to shadow her, just to watch her work, and they got absolutely nowhere. The son of a university donor even offered a five million pound grant in exchange for spending one day with her in her office, and he got the door slammed in his face. And now suddenly she turns around and invites..."

His voice trailed off for a moment as he stared at his daughter.

"You?" he added finally.

"I'm not claiming to entirely understand her reasoning," Jessie replied. "Honestly, I'm as shocked as you are, but I really want to take this opportunity. You know I've been struggling to figure out what to do after I finish school, right? Well, these three nights could change my life. This could be the start of something for me."

"Three nights?" Karen said, raising a skeptical eyebrow.

"Friday night to Monday morning."

"At this old house?"

"It used to be an orphanage, but... yeah."

"You don't even like camping," Dom pointed out. "You have a phobia of earwigs. Are you *sure* you want to go and do this?"

"Doctor Moore has it all figured out," she told him. "We'll get driven right to the house and dropped off. Then the driver will leave, and it'll just be the two of us for the three nights. I can handle sleeping on the floor or whatever it takes."

"Even if there are earwigs?"

"Even if there are earwigs. I know I'm basically going to be nothing more than a dogsbody, but I'm willing to do that if it means that I can watch Doctor Moore working up close. If nothing else, this could be massive for my prospects when I apply somewhere. And it's not like it's dangerous. I mean, we all know that it's *just* an old house."

"Not dangerous?" Karen replied. "It could be structurally unsafe. There could be hobos living there. Satanists might use it for rituals."

"Those things are all pretty unlikely," Dom said. "Jessie, would you mind leaving your mum and I alone for a few minutes? We really need to talk this over."

***

Once she was out in the kitchen, Jessie lingered in the doorway and tried to hear what her parents were saying. She wasn't having much luck so far, but at the same time she didn't want to risk getting caught, so finally she turned and headed over to the breakfast bar. Taking out her phone, she brought up a video of Doctor Moore that she'd not finished watching earlier, and she tapped to play.

"Belief in ghosts," a younger version of the doctor was saying, "is basically a childish response to the unknown, to the unknowable even, that in some unfortunate cases gets dragged into adulthood. It's a weakness."

"You make it sound almost like a kind of mental illness," the unseen interviewer said.

"And it might well be one, yes," Doctor Moore replied. "There's definitely some work that needs to be undertaken to determine whether this kind of delusion might commonly co-exist with other conditions. I wouldn't be at all surprised to learn that this is indeed the case."

"A recent survey showed that almost half of Americans, and more than a third of British people, believe in ghosts. Do you worry that some people might find some of your theories offensive?"

"Why would I worry about something like that?" she asked. "I don't pay any attention to feelings or emotions when I conduct my work. My findings are my findings, full stop. If other people can't deal with reality, then that's their problem, not mine."

"That's rather harsh," the interviewer pointed out.

"Far too many people in this world choose to believe in what they *want* to believe in, rather than in what's real," Doctor Moore explained in the video. "It takes discipline and courage to challenge one's own belief system, but I'm certain that's something we should all be doing, every single day. We should interrogate our own assumptions and try to determine whether we're doing all we can to ask the important questions. That's the key to my work. It's not about finding answers, not really. It's about finding questions. I've always believed that the best answer to one question is -"

Hearing footsteps, Jessie stopped the video and turned to see that her parents had come through. She immediately noticed that her mother looked distinctly ill at ease, which she figured meant that her father might just have managed to be persuasive.

"What did you tell Doctor Moore?" Dom asked cautiously.

"That I'd need to talk it through with you guys first."

"And how did she respond to that?"

"She told me that I shouldn't listen to you." She paused. "I mean, actually she put it a little more rudely than that."

"Huh," Dom replied.

"Not entirely surprising," Karen added.

"But I *will* listen to you," Jessie continued, "and if you really don't think that I should go, then -"

"Relax," Dom said, interrupting her, "we're letting you go."

"You are?"

"Your mother's not happy about it," he explained, "but I've managed to talk her round."

"Barely," Karen said through gritted teeth.

"Doctor Moore might be a lot of things," Dom continued, "but she's a reliable, responsible adult and we have no doubt that you'll be safe with her. You'll also learn a great deal. Just remember to apply common sense to every situation, and don't be afraid to question the great lady's decisions if you really think she might have gone off the deep end."

He paused. "I just don't understand why she wants to go back to that place. She debunked it and moved on. What's so special about Hardlocke House?"

"No idea," Jessie lied. "I guess she's got some new theories she wants to check out."

"And you're taking certain equipment with you," Dom added, stepping past her and heading toward the utility room. "If she really wants to be at Hardlocke House by Friday, then we don't have much time, but I'm not letting you go unless you've got everything you need. Somehow I doubt that the house has all the necessary modcons. I won't have you freezing during the night."

"Thanks for -"

"And I still need to talk to Doctor Moore," he added. "Until I've managed to get her on the phone and find out exactly what she's got planned, we're not giving the final nod on this." He paused. "Besides, if she's taken a liking to you, that might help your mother and I get closer to her."

"Thanks for letting me do this," Jessie said to Karen, as her father left the room. "I know you don't approve, but this is something I really want to do. I can't turn down the chance to see someone like Doctor Moore work up close."

"Oh, for heaven's sake," Karen replied, rolling her eyes, "I have absolutely no problem with you going and spending a few days running around after Diana Moore. I just hoped that you might rebel and insist on going even if your father and I put our feet down. My plan was to deny you permission and then hope that you might have snuck out in the middle of the night and run off to go with her to that rundown old house." She sighed. "I guess I should have realized by now that you're just not very rebellious."

"Sorry."

"Don't apologize for it!" She rolled her eyes again as she turned and headed out of the room. "Can't you get a piercing or a tattoo or something like that? Like a normal teenager? Is that really too much to hope for?"

Smiling, Jessie realized that she didn't have much time to prepare. Doctor Moore was planning to be at Hardlocke House by Friday afternoon, which was only two days away, and that meant that everything would have to be ready by Thursday evening at the latest. She could already think of so many little jobs that would have to be added to her already significant list, and – as she sat alone on the sofa – she was starting to think that she wouldn't get all of them done in time.

CHAPTER TEN

BUT SHE DID, AND two days later she sat in silence in the back of the van that was driving her and Doctor Moore to Hardlocke House.

The driver, a friendly guy named Sutton, had picked her up from home a little after 8am. Her parents had tried to make small-talk with Doctor Moore, who had barely said a word as she remained strapped into place in the van, with sunglasses concealing her eyes. Jessie had said goodbye to her parents and had told them not to worry, and then she'd climbed into the van with her meager bag, and she'd felt strangely pleased with herself as the van had set off along the road. She didn't want to be a bad person, but she'd noticed that her parents had been positively dripping with jealousy.

After a few minutes on the road she'd tried

to engage Diana in conversation, figuring that as part of the team she might have better luck than her parents, but she'd had no luck. After a few more attempts, she'd figured that it would be best to just sit in silence and wait to be spoken to. And so two hours rolled by before the silence was finally broken.

"We should be there in about thirty minutes," Sutton called out from the front of the van. "We've been really lucky with the traffic."

"I noticed," Jessie replied with a faint smile, hoping that it would be okay to answer him. "Yeah... we've been really lucky. Really... great traffic."

She looked over at Diana, whose face betrayed no hint of emotion. In fact, Jessie briefly began to wonder whether the doctor might have fallen asleep, until a moment later Diana turned her head slightly. Now Jessie could just about see that the woman's eyes were open, and she began to realize that there might be another reason for the silence.

Fear.

Was Doctor Moore – the great Diana Moore – scared?

The idea seemed preposterous at first, but then Jessie noticed that Diana's hands were twitching. Exactly forty years had passed since Diana Moore had last been at Hardlocke House, and

Jessie was starting to realize that the place must have been playing on the great woman's mind a great deal. Hardlocke House was the only case that had actually beaten Doctor Moore, and now she was going back for a second try. What if she failed again? What if she discovered something that undermined her entire career?

Looking out the window, Jessie realized that she could understand why Diana might be feeling a little nervous.

***

"Ladies and... Well, ladies... we're here."

As the van came to a halt at the end of a long, overgrown dirt track that had cut through the forest, Jessie leaned down and tried to peer through the back of the front seats. She'd been feeling a tightening knot of anticipation in her chest as the van had made its way through the forest, and she'd been expecting some kind of grand moment when they arrived, but instead she saw only more trees.

She looked around, still hoping to spot the house, but there was nothing. She couldn't help wondering whether there might have been some kind of mistake.

"End of the line," Sutton said as he climbed out of the van and wandered around to open the door next to Jessie. "Strict instructions, I'm afraid.

The last quarter of a mile is to be completed on foot."

"Instructions from who?" Jessie asked, before realizing that there could only be one answer. She turned to Doctor Moore. "Is that right? We have to walk the last part?"

"I warned you that you'd have to carry some equipment," Doctor Moore replied calmly. "It's a little late to start complaining now."

"Oh, I'm not complaining," Jessie replied quickly. "Not at all."

"Good." Doctor Moore hesitated. "Well, young lady?"

"Well?"

"Sutton can't get in to help me with you in the way, can he?"

"Sorry," Jessie muttered, suddenly realizing her mistake. She unfastened her seat belt and grabbed her bag, and then she climbed out of the van and stepped aside.

Sutton cast a smile at her before clambering into the van and starting to loose the straps that had been holding Doctor Moore's wheelchair in place.

Taking a few steps back, with her bag slung over her shoulder, Jessie looked around. A cold breeze was blowing along the dirt track, rustling the autumn leaves, most of which had fallen from the trees and landed on the ground. There was a certain dampness in the air, and Jessie realized after a moment that they really were stuck out in the middle of nowhere. She had no idea where the nearest property stood, but she figured that Hardlocke House must be at least five miles from civilization. Although, as she looked along the road, she realized that she still couldn't see the house itself.

A moment later she heard a whirring sound, and she turned to see that Sutton was helping Doctor Moore descend from the van on a small ramp.

"Do you feel that?" Doctor Moore asked. "There's nothing quite like autumn in England, is there? When I was last here, it was the middle of summer, which as any fool knows is by far the worst season. Autumn seems so much more appropriate, don't you think? After all, we're surrounded by the dead."

"We are?" Jessie asked.

"The leaves, girl," Doctor Moore continued, as Sutton pushed her off the ramp and turned her around. "We're standing on a blanket of death. Well, you are, at least. I roll across it."

"I'll get the bags," Sutton said, heading around to the back of the van.

"I like it out here," Jessie said, hoping to finally get a conversation going. She made a show of savoring a deep breath. "We're so far from anything else."

"No-one to hear all the screams, you mean."

Jessie turned to Doctor Moore.

"Relax," the older woman added. "That was a joke. I hope, anyway."

Jessie smiled, and then she saw Sutton walking over with two large, heavy-looking bags, which he set down on the ground. It was at that moment that Jessie suddenly realized that perhaps it wasn't just the van that they'd be leaving behind for the final part of the journey.

"Are you coming with us?" she asked him.

He shook his head.

"Orders are orders," he told her, before turning to Doctor Moore. "Although I'd be happy to help you ladies get these bags to the doorstep. They're pretty heavy and -"

"There's no need for that," Doctor Moore replied, interrupting him. "Jessica will be more than capable."

"They really *are* quite heavy," he added.

"She'll be fine," Doctor Moore said firmly. "She's young and fit, it'll do her good to perform some manual labor. Children these days are so lazy, they barely know how to break a sweat."

"Totally," Sutton said, looking back over at Jessie. "I think they should all be sent down into a coalmine for a year, to learn what real backbreaking work feels like. That'd toughen them all up and sort out the weak from the strong."

Jessie stared at him, not knowing quite what to say.

"I think," Doctor Moore said after a moment, "that was an attempt at humor."

"It was," Sutton replied, before patting Jessie on the shoulder as he stepped past her. "Well, don't say I didn't try. I guess there's nothing left for me to do other than head off and tell you lucky ladies that I'll see you right back here on Monday morning." He climbed into the driver's seat, and then he turned to them again. "Don't do anything I wouldn't do."

Jessie managed a faint smile.

"He can be irritating," Doctor Moore said, as Sutton pulled the door shut and started the engine, "but he does do what he's told, and that's a rare quality these days. I arranged for us to meet him here at precisely 9am on Monday morning, and I can assure you that he'll be bang on time. He's entirely reliable."

As the van drove away, Jessie felt a flicker of doubt in the pit of her stomach. Up until that moment, the prospect of spending a weekend with Diana Moore at Hardlocke House had seemed exciting, almost too good to be true, but now she was starting to realize that she was well and truly stuck. She watched Sutton driving away, and then – once he was out of sight and the sound of the engine had receded into the distance – she turned back to

Doctor Moore and tried to think of something interesting or useful to say.

"Well?" Doctor Moore asked after a moment, looking down at the bags. "Are you ready?"

"Sure," Jessie replied, quickly starting to gather the bags up. She was surprised to find that they were much heavier than she'd expected, but she was determined not to appear weak so she tried to pretend that she wasn't struggling, even as she hauled the final bag onto her shoulders and felt a twinge of pain in the small of her back. Her knees were on the verge of buckling.

She took a moment to steady herself, and then she tried to focus on the fact that she only had to walk about a quarter of a mile. At the same time, however, she realized that all the extra weight was already pressing her feet down into the mud.

"Ready," she said, forcing a smile.

"Me too," Doctor Moore said.

An awkward pause followed.

"Well?" Doctor Moore continued. "This wheelchair isn't electric, my dear, and I'm a seventy-year-old woman. I can't be expected to push myself, can I?"

"Right," Jessie said, struggling under the weight of the bags as she stepped around behind the chair and took hold of the handles. "Sorry."

She tried to start pushing, only to find that

the wheelchair was somewhat bogged down in all the mud and dead leaves. For a moment she worried that she might not be able to get it moving at all, but then she summoned a little extra strength and lifted the chair slightly first, and finally she was able to start pushing Doctor Moore along the road.

"You're being very bumpy with me," the doctor complained. "Please, try to be a little more gentle."

"Sorry," Jessie gasped breathlessly, already starting to wonder whether she could manage a whole quarter of a mile without collapsing. "I'll do my best."

CHAPTER ELEVEN

"I SEE IT," SHE said half an hour later, after making slowly but steady progress. Up ahead, one corner of a large, gray stone house had just come into view as the road began to curve around a bend. "That *is* it, isn't it?"

"It is," Doctor Moore replied. "That's Hardlocke House."

Still struggling to keep the wheelchair going, Jessie reminded herself that they were now almost at their destination. So far, she'd managed to keep from huffing and puffing too much, and she hoped that she hadn't let Doctor Moore realize just how difficult the journey had been.

Ahead, the entire house was now visible, and Jessie saw the huge, imposing facade with scores of dark windows. She'd come across plenty of pictures of Hardlocke House, of course, as well as videos of the place, but there was still something strangely intimidating about actually seeing it in person. In fact, she found that she was unable to take her eyes off the building, and soon she started looking at each of the windows in turn. She couldn't see anything other than the reflected sky, but she was so mesmerized by the sight of the house that at first she didn't even realize that Doctor Moore was saying something.

"Stop," the doctor told her. "Stop right now."

She looked at another of the windows, one that was darker than the rest. Even from a distance, she began to think that perhaps she could just about make out -

"Stop!" Doctor Moore screamed.

Suddenly coming to an abrupt halt, Jessie almost toppled over as the weight of all the bags shifted. She steadied herself against the wheelchair's handles, and then she looked down at the top of Doctor Moore's head.

"Are you deaf, girl?" the doctor snapped angrily.

"Sorry, I -"

"Just wait a moment, will you? There's no rush. We still have several hours of daylight."

"Sorry," Jessie said again, as she realized that Doctor Moore seemed quite agitated. Again, she figured that the sight of Hardlocke House must be dredging up a lot of memories, so after a moment she took a step back. She was tempted to set the bags down and get a moment of relief, but she figured she'd probably get criticized for that so she decided to keep them on her shoulders. As she waited for the command to set off again, however, she began to worry that Doctor Moore seemed almost to be in some kind of trance as she continued to stare at the house.

And then she realized that she could hear a faint whispering sound.

Doctor Moore was quietly talking to herself. Jessie didn't dare to make it obvious that she was listening, but – as the trees creaked in a gentle wind and as the leaves on the ground rustled slightly – she leaned forward just a little and tried to make out some of the words that were coming from the doctor's lips.

"I always knew I'd be back," she managed to hear, among some other words that were less clear. "Here I am. I told you."

Jessie waited, not daring to interrupt, but after a few more seconds the whispering stopped.

All around the road, the wind was picking up now, and some of the leaves on the ground were starting to blow toward the house. At the same time, the trees were groaning as they began to lean slightly.

"Well?" Doctor Moore barked suddenly. "What are we waiting for? You've had enough of a rest. Let's move!"

Jessie gripped the handles and began to push again. The pain in her back was getting stronger, but she figured it was nothing too serious so she forced herself to keep going and after a couple of minutes they reached the point at which the road gave way to a large open clearing at the front of the house. Now that she was closer, Jessie saw that the estate was more substantial than she'd expected, with several smaller outbuildings dotted around near the house itself. For a moment, she found herself wondering why anyone would build a house so far away from the rest of the world, but then she remembered all the stories about Sarah Clarke and about the establishment of the orphanage. Hardlocke House certainly seemed like an ideal place to hide.

"Over to the bottom of the steps," Doctor Moore said, sounding a little tense now. "That's right, all the way."

Reaching the foot of the steps, Jessie let go of the wheelchair and finally began to set the bags down. She felt a sharp pain in her back, and she involuntarily let out a gasp as she lowered the last of the bags to the ground. Turning to Doctor Moore, she immediately saw that her discomfort had been noted.

"Are you in any pain?" the doctor asked, before removing the sunglasses that she'd been wearing all day.

"I'm fine."

"Are you sure? Don't be brave."

"Honestly, I'm fine."

"Well, that's impressive." She paused, before reaching into her pocket and pulling out a large, old key. "Given the practicalities involved, I suppose it would be appropriate for you to be the one who goes up there and unlocks the front door."

Jessie hesitated for a moment, before reaching out and taking the key.

"It's not going to bite you," Doctor Moore added, rolling her eyes. "The house has been empty and abandoned for almost four decades. It's owned now by an investment firm that never quite got around to doing any investing. As far as I've been able to ascertain, the place hasn't been touched. Fortunately, I remain on good terms with some of those involved, so I was able to borrow the key for a few days. Now, if you wouldn't mind, shall we proceed?"

"Sure," Jessie said, before looking up toward the large, black front door.

"Any time now would be good."

Realizing that there was no need to be nervous, Jessie made her way up the steps. The key felt cold in the palm of her hand, and a little rusty too, but it slipped easily enough into the hole. When she tried to turn it, however, she was surprised to find that it was sticking somehow. She tried jiggling it around, and she was already worried that at any moment Doctor Moore would start questioning the delay.

"Is this the first time you've ever unlocked a door?" the doctor asked after a few more seconds.

"It's just a little stiff," Jessie replied, and now she was starting to feel flustered. "Like you said, it probably hasn't been used for a few years so I guess it -"

Before she could finish, she felt the key click a little deeper into the lock, and the door immediately jolted and began to open, almost as if it was suddenly being pulled from inside. Still holding the key, Jessie felt a blast of icy air against her hand and wrist as she took an involuntary step forward, and then she found herself staring into the dark interior of Hardlocke House.

She waited, as she felt freezing cold air curling out of the darkness and starting to chill her face. After blinking a couple of times, however, she was just about able to make out the house's large hallway, as well as the staircase that rose up in the center toward the upper floor. Her gaze was drawn to the top of the stairs, and for a moment she couldn't help but imagine a figure standing up there, staring back down.

"Ahem!" Doctor Moore said, and Jessie turned to look back at her. "Would you mind?"

"Sorry, Doctor Moore," she replied, hurrying down the steps.

"You don't need to apologize so much," the doctor replied as Jessie took hold of the wheelchair's handles again. "And please, for the sake of my sanity, call me Diana."

"Okay."

Jessie paused as she tried to figure out how exactly she was going to get Doctor Moore – Diana – up the steps, but she quickly realized that she'd simply have to bump her up backwards, one step at a time.

"Sorry," she said as she maneuvered the wheelchair into position, ready to start. "This might feel pretty rough."

"I'm not some pathetic, fragile thing," Diana replied. "Believe it or not, I can handle a little tough treatment."

After taking a deep breath, Jessie began to drag the wheelchair up the steps. With each bump, she had to fight the urge to apologize, but she was starting to make quick progress and soon she was halfway. She hesitated and adjusted her grip slightly, and then she resumed her work, finally managing to get the chair all the way to the top, at which point she carefully turned it around and wheeled it over the threshold and into the hallway.

"My word, it's cold in here!" Diana gasped, rubbing her hands together. "I knew it would be, but this is extreme!"

"I guess there's no heating, huh?" Jessie said.

"There are wood-burning stoves in some of the rooms," Diana replied, "and you might be lucky if you check the woodshed. I seem to recall that there's one around the side of the house. It's a little hut-like building. Would you mind going and taking a look?"

"Sure," Jessie said, before hesitating for a moment. "You mean... now?"

"I don't know about you, but I do rather like being warm," Diana said. "Or at least, not freezing to death."

"Should I just leave you here?"

"I shall be just fine," Diana replied. "Besides, you'll be quick, won't you? I'm sure you'll only leave me alone in here for a minute or two."

CHAPTER TWELVE

AFTER FUMBLING FOR A moment with a wooden bar, Jessie finally managed to pull open the door of the little white-walled hut, and she saw that a few logs had indeed been left inside.

"Great," she said to herself as she ducked down and clambered inside, once again feeling cold air all around.

She immediately felt cobwebs brushing against her face. She tried to pull away, but there were too many to avoid and a moment later she spotted a large, spindly spider scurrying away from the light and disappearing behind some of the logs. Not being a big fan of spiders, Jessie resolved to start from the other end of the pile, although she was fairly sure that this too would have its fair share. Still, she had no choice, so she began to pull out a few large logs.

Sure enough, several more spiders immediately crawled away.

"At least you're not earwigs," she muttered.

Some of the logs contained nails, so she had to be careful as she gathered a few and threw them out through the door. She quickly found that some of the logs were rotten and teeming with insects, so she left those particular specimens behind as she searched for drier specimens. A few more spiders hurried out of the way as Jessie leaned over and -

Suddenly her left foot slipped on one of the lower logs. She fell forward and landed hard, feeling an immediate pain in both her forearms. Letting out a gasp, she began to haul herself up, only to freeze as soon as she spotted a particularly large nail poking out several inches from a log a little further down. A shiver ran through her bones as she realized that if she'd fallen at a slightly different angle, she would have taken that nail straight in her abdomen.

Focusing on being a lot more careful, she set about trying to find some more logs.

***

"And that," Diana said as she closed the stove's heavy metal door, "is how one starts a fire. Can't you feel the difference it's making already?"

"I can, actually," Jessie replied, holding her hands out for a little welcome warmth. "So will this heat the whole house?"

"Mostly just in here," Diana said, "although whichever room the pipe passes through upstairs should feel some benefit as well." She managed to wheel herself back a little and look around. "This was the old study, you know," she continued. "I remember being in here forty years ago, back when the Malones had the place. Of course, when the house was an orphanage, this was used by Sarah Clarke as an office."

Jessie turned and looked around the large, high-ceilinged room. Several paintings had been left hanging on the walls, showing moments from history as well as few biblical scenes. Red wallpaper gave the room a slightly warmer feel than the entrance hall, and Jessie was actually surprised to see that the house wasn't in too bad a state after all. Considering that it had been left empty and untouched for almost four decades, the place looked almost habitable.

Spotting a large oak desk over by one of the windows, Jessie stepped over and ran a hand across its dusty surface. The wood was cold to the touch.

"That belonged to Sarah Clarke," Diana said.

Startled, Jessie immediately stepped back.

"It's just a desk," Diana added with a smile.

"A lot of Ms. Clarke's items remain in the house. I suppose it was simply never economical to remove them, and you could argue that they give the place some of its character. Hardlocke House has been empty for long periods during its history, and nobody who moved in ever really seemed to settle. Not even the detestable Malones."

She wheeled herself over to join Jessie, and for a moment they both stared at the desk.

"You can tell a lot about a person by examining the things they left behind," Diana added. "I imagine Sarah Clarke used to sit at this desk whenever she was welcoming a new boy to the orphanage, or when she was disciplining one. She probably spent a great deal of time working right here."

"And that chair," Jessie said, looking at the large chair behind the desk, "was that..."

Her voice trailed off.

"That would have belonged to her as well," Diana said. "Go on, sit in it."

Jessie turned to her.

"There's no reason not to," Diana continued, with a slightly mischievous grin. "You're not worried about things that go bump in the night, are you? Please, don't tell me that you're suddenly going to start fretting about that sort of thing."

"No," Jessie replied, as she began to realize that she was being tested. She didn't particularly want to sit in the chair, but she stepped around the desk nonetheless and forced herself to take a seat. The old chair creaked and groaned beneath her, but it felt remarkably sturdy.

"It suits you," Diana said.

"Is that her?" Jessie asked, suddenly noticing – for the first time – the large painting of a woman on the far wall.

Diana turned to take a look.

"It is indeed," she said. "Whatever else you might think of her, Ms. Clarke certainly possessed a commanding presence, don't you think?"

The painting showed a thin, middle-aged woman with her dark hair pulled back into an austere bun. Wearing all black, and with an expression of stark calm, Sarah Clarke certainly looked the part of a ruthless orphanage administrator. In fact, there was nothing remotely cheerful about the image at all, and Jessie could only assume that it had been painted specifically so that it would drive fear into the hearts of all the children who once lived at Hardlocke House.

"I doubt she was much fun at parties," Diana observed. "Then again, I doubt she even knew what a party was. By all accounts, she was very strict. I don't know if she even knew how to smile! According to contemporary accounts, few people enjoyed interacting with her. And the cold hard truth is that I doubt she cared that much."

She glanced around for a moment.

"I suppose she had everything she wanted right here. The house, the children... and absolutely no oversight. She could do whatever she wanted, and there was no-one to stop her."

"And she was murdered right here in the house?" Jessie asked, before looking through the open doorway toward the hall.

"Hardlocke House has twenty-eight rooms," Diana replied, "including two separate classrooms, an assembly room and various other facilities. One must admit that it's a rather grand place, although it was never remotely full. Ms. Clarke never managed to attract as many students as she'd hoped. The most she ever had at one time, I believe, was seventeen, and by the time of her death that number had dwindled to twelve. Even in the harsh times of the eighteenth century, condemning a child to this place must have been considered a cruelty too far. A few unfortunate souls ended up here, however. The truly wretched."

"So are we going to check out every room," Jessie asked, "or are we just going to focus on the main parts, like... in here?"

"*I* am going to explore the lower floor," Diana explained, "at least for the first night. Obviously the chair makes going up and down rather laborious, so I have planned to divide my time quite carefully. This evening and during the night, I shall mostly be in this very room."

"And where do you want me to be?" Jessie replied.

"What do you mean?"

"Am I going to be in here with you," she continued, worrying slightly that she might be sent off alone to some other part of the house, "or do you want me to..."

Again, her voice trailed off.

"I mean, I don't mind," she added, trying to seem brave. "You just tell me where you want me, and I'll do whatever you want."

"Well, you won't be here at all," Diana said matter-of-factly.

"I'm sorry?"

"You won't be in the house," Diana continued. "Why would you ever think that you would be?"

"I don't understand," Jessie said cautiously.

"I don't need an assistant scurrying around the place and bothering me when I'm doing my actual work. No, that would slow me down terribly, and you might have noticed that I have a slight tendency to become irritable whenever I am crossed. You would contribute nothing by being here at night, and you would most likely get in my way. In fact, apart from perhaps helping me up and down the stairs a few times, this room is pretty much your limit. You absolutely will not be going to the rest of the building."

"Then..."

Jessie hesitated for a moment, as she felt the heat of the stove against one side of her face.

"I still don't quite understand," she said finally. "If I'm not going to be here in Hardlocke House with you overnight, then... where *am* I going to be?"

CHAPTER THIRTEEN

"VOILA!" DIANA SAID AS she wheeled herself through the doorway and into the little chapel that stood about a hundred feet from the main house. "Your accommodation for the weekend!"

She stopped next to the back row of pews and turned her chair around.

"Well?" she continued, with a grin. "You're speechless, aren't you? Have you never stayed in a chapel before?"

"I..."

Stepping forward, Jessie looked around and felt a heavy sense of dread in her chest. The chapel wasn't exactly large, with just six rows of pews leading toward a small altar up at the front. A modest crucifix hung on the far wall, between two grubby stained glass windows, while an open door at the side led through into what appeared to be a small office. Glancing up, she saw thick timbers criss-crossing the high ceiling, and she realized after a moment that the chapel was – impossibly – actually colder than the main house.

"Is there a stove in here?" she asked, turning to Diana.

"In the chapel?" She furrowed her brow. "No, I don't think so. Why would there be? You'll be fine in here, though. You've got a sleeping bag, haven't you?"

"I do."

She held up her bag, and then she set it down on the cold stone floor.

"So just snuggle into that," Diana said. "Trust me, you'll be absolutely fine."

"Are you sure you don't want me to be in the main house with you?" Jessie asked. "I can be almost invisible, I swear. I won't bug you or ask any questions, you can just give me an area to stick to and I'll stay right there and -"

Before she could finish, Diana started laughing.

"What?" Jessie continued. "Are you... Was this a joke? Were you just pretending that I'm going to be sleeping in here?"

"Absolutely not," Diana replied. "This is where you'll be staying. I can't have you in the house, and there's really nowhere else suitable." She wheeled herself a little closer. "You have to understand, young lady, that my work is essentially solitary by nature. I can't be doing with any distractions, and I need to know that anything I see or hear in that house is not some kind of trick created by... noise in the dark. And having someone in there would add noise."

Jessie opened her mouth to try another angle, but she was starting to realize that there wasn't anything she could do to change Diana's mind. She'd been nervous about spending the night in Hardlocke House, but suddenly that prospect – or anything, really – seemed entirely preferable to the chapel.

"Go on, take a look around," Diana said.

Reluctantly, Jessie stepped past her and began to make her way along the aisle. The rows of empty pews were creepy enough, and then she reached the foot of the altar and she looked up to see the crucifix hanging high above. Having never been religious, Jessie had spent very little time in churches, and she was surprised to see that the figure of Jesus on the crucifix had been damaged. Its entire face had been broken away, and Jessie noted that there were other signs of damage all over the body.

"Sarah Clarke used to lead the services in here, of course," Diana explained. "I doubt she'd have been able to get anyone else to do it, but I also imagine that she considered it to be one of the perks of her role. Twice each day, she'd have the poor little orphans file in here and then she'd tell them all about how wicked and vile they were, and how they should pray for forgiveness. Apparently she could get quite lively, screaming at the children and telling them that Satan was going to claim their souls."

Jessie looked down and saw that the altar's wooden top was also marked with cuts and scratches, as if it had been repeatedly bashed by something.

"Can you imagine being one of those poor little things?" Diana asked.

Jessie turned to her.

"The children who were brought here had all lost their parents at a very young age," Diana continued. "The records show that the youngest was just five years old and the oldest was eleven. Hardlocke House was never the first choice for any of the children, in most cases it wasn't even the tenth choice. If a child could be homed somewhere else, anywhere else, then that happened. The ones who came here were truly unwanted, it was either here or death. To be honest, from the stories I've uncovered, I think death might have been preferable."

"She can't have been *that* bad," Jessie replied.

She waited for an answer.

"Can she?" she added.

"Are you suggesting," Diana said after a moment, "that Ms. Clarke was perhaps unfairly maligned? That, as a woman with money and ambition in eighteenth century England, she inevitably attracted critics who sought to cast her in a bad light? That certain negative characteristics were either exaggerated or invented, in order to besmirch the good name of a woman who merely wanted to help the poor and underprivileged in her society?"

"That has to be a possibility," Jessie pointed out.

"Of course, and I looked into it." Diana paused. "The truth is, if anything, the stories about Sarah Clarke *underplayed* the extent of her evil. There seem to have been things she did that nobody even wanted to acknowledge. Today, over two hundred years later, we still don't know exactly what happened here, or what led to her death. We can speculate, but the truth – whatever it might have been – was apparently so awful, so hideous, that nobody wanted to talk about it. You would think there would have been plenty of men lining up to gleefully spread those tales, but no such thing happened. Everything was kept vague. What, young lady, do you think Sarah Clarke could possibly have been doing here, for history to have swallowed the facts?"

"What about the children?" she asked. "How many of them died?"

"There is no record of any child dying here at Hardlocke House. Apart from those who disappeared, I suppose. They might well have died. Nobody knows."

"What about injuries or suspicious incidents?"

"Doctors who visited are said to have found no evidence of any harm coming to the children."

"Then what -"

"Nevertheless," Diana continued, "on the morning of November the 11th, 1788, the body of Sarah Clarke was found with twelve stab wounds. One for each child."

"There's a lot in this story that doesn't quite add up," Jessie pointed out.

"Believe me, I know."

"And the Malones thought that they saw Sarah's ghost in the house?" Jessie asked. "I know they weren't the only ones, but their account of things is the most heavily documented."

"They claimed to have encountered Sarah's ghost in almost every room of Hardlocke House. They say they heard screams in the night, and the sound of sobbing, and Lizzy Malone claimed to have seen Sarah's face in the mirror several times, standing right behind her. By all accounts, Sarah was absolutely terrorizing that poor couple."

"Why?" Jessie asked.

"That's a very good question," Diana replied. "Are we to assume that ghosts become unhinged and irrational once they're dead? That they are content merely to scare the living? After all, if I became a ghost and I was haunting a house, and I wanted something, I rather think that I would simply sit down with the new owners and explain the situation to them in a calm and rational manner. I certainly wouldn't spend my time hollering and wailing and generally being a drama queen." She paused again. "Of course," she added, "we know that ghosts aren't real, and we can recognize the Malones' claims in particular from every bad horror film that we've ever seen."

Jessie looked around at the chapel again, and for a moment she imagined twelve little boys sitting on the pews, listening to another miserable sermon from their tormentor.

"I should leave you to settle in," Diana said, wheeling herself toward the door. "Shall we have dinner around five o'clock? I can't offer the finest cuisine, I'm afraid, but there'll be enough to keep you full. I shall see you then."

"Sure," Jessie murmured.

Heading over to her bag, she crouched down and began to pull out the sleeping bag. She hated the idea of sleeping in the chapel, but she figured she had no other options. She wasn't going to sleep outside, and the spider-infested little wood shed was definitely not appealing. As she straightened out the sleeping bag and laid it on the floor, she told herself that three nights in the chapel wouldn't be *that* bad. A little discomfort was no price to pay, really, for the chance to be around the great Doctor Diana Moore.

"Oh, Jessie?" Diana called out from the yard.

"Yes?" Jessie replied.

"Be a dear and bring in some more fire wood when you get a chance! As much as you can find! I don't want to be cold all night!"

"Okay!" Jessie shouted, before sighing as she felt herself shivering slightly in the icy chapel. "No worries," she murmured under her breath, "I can do that."

CHAPTER FOURTEEN

"RICE IS SO UNDERRATED," Diana said a couple of hours later, as she and Jessie sat in front of the stove, which at least was keeping the room warm. "I don't understand people who say that it has no taste. I can taste it just fine. Can't you?"

"I can," Jessie replied, as she spooned some more plain rice into her mouth. She'd decided to be diplomatic with some of her answers.

"I can't be doing with all those flavors that people add to it, either," Diana continued. "I have quite a sensitive stomach, so I'm not having strange spices. You like your rice, don't you?"

Jessie nodded, although she was finding it difficult to summon much enthusiasm for a meal that consisted solely of plain boiled race that had been cooked up on a camp stove outside. She sat in silence, shoveling her way through the meal, but after a moment she realized that there were still a few things that she wanted to know about her involvement in the weekend's activity. She hesitated, worried about asking too many questions – or about asking the wrong type of questions – but finally she couldn't help herself.

"Why me?"

"What do you mean?" Diana replied, with her mouth full of rice.

"I mean, why *me*? There must have been hundreds of people who would have jumped at the chance to come out here with you, and I'm sure all of them would be way more qualified. I'm nobody, I've got no experience that might be useful, I haven't studied this type of thing, so I was just wondering why you chose me for this project?"

"You ask the right questions," Diana told her.

"I just really don't get it."

"I chose you precisely *because* you have no experience," Diana replied. "It's very easy for experience to blind a person. They start to expect certain things, and then they subconsciously look for anything that will validate those expectations. Even the sharpest minds on the planet can be guilty of that. I certainly have been, from time to time. That's why I wanted someone completely unsullied by the corrupting influence of the academic world. I wanted someone like you."

"Thanks," Jessie said cautiously. "I think."

She looked up at the portrait of Sarah Clarke, and then she turned to look at the door that led into the hallway. Having expected to spend the weekend getting to know Hardlocke House intimately, she was now somewhat disappointed to think that she wouldn't have a chance to explore at all. She wanted to see all the dusty old classrooms, and the dormitory upstairs where the orphans would once have slept. More than anything, she wanted to know how the house felt in the dead of night. She figured that she not believing in ghosts was no barrier to enjoying the thrill of a haunted house.

Looking at the windows, she saw that darkness had fallen. After a moment she saw her own reflection in the glass, and the reflection of Sarah Clarke's portrait behind her.

Turning back to look at Diana, she saw that the older woman seemed lost in thought.

"Are you nervous?"

After a moment, Diana glanced at her.

"Sorry," Jessie continued, "I didn't mean that, I just meant... Have you been to the room where it happened yet?"

"Where *what* happened?"

"The book that flew off the shelf. It wasn't in here, was it?"

"No."

"Where was it?"

"It was in another room."

"But -"

"And I'm not nervous, because I fully intend to prove – to myself, and to everyone else – that there really wasn't anything out of the ordinary here. That sensation that I felt, of a kind of anger floating through the air, was most likely just something that was cooked up by my overactive imagination. I had, after all, spent quite some time around that ridiculous Malone couple. You can't even begin to imagine how much they had a tendency to prattle on."

"So how are you going to make sure something like that doesn't happen again?"

"I've had forty years to prepare myself. I feel that I am finally at the stage that lets me ignore any foolish notions." She paused again. "I can't explain it all to you, but I'm confident that I have everything under control. I wouldn't be back here if I wasn't fully confident that I can fix any... personal irregularities that marred my work last time." She set her bowl aside. "In fact, I would feel sure that I could complete the work in a single night, were it not for the fact that the Malones always insisted on the three night rule. I suppose I should humor them."

"What's the three night rule?"

"They insisted that when a new person

entered the house, the ghost of Sarah Clarke would retreat somewhat. They believed that on the first night she would hide herself and merely observe, and that on the second night she would begin to become a little braver. Only on the third night would she be willing to reveal herself. That was their absurd theory, and of course I had to indulge them. They're long dead, but I find myself *still* indulging them. If you ask me, they were simply hoping to trap paying guests here in their little B&B for a little longer. Not that they ever got around to setting it up, of course."

"So you're not expecting anything to happen tonight?"

"I'm not expecting anything to happen on *any* of the nights," she replied. "Now, I hope you brought some good reading material and a flashlight, because it's soon going to be time for me to have the house to myself."

"Are you really sure that you don't want me to stay?" Jessie asked. "I can be as quiet as... well, as a ghost."

"I shall see you in the morning," Diana said, with a faint smile. "Sunrise, out on the steps. Don't be late. And I am quite certain that I shall have absolutely nothing of interest to tell you. No reports of bumps and creaking sounds, no sensation of being watched, no more books flying through the air and no wailing and sobbing coming from empty rooms. Oh, and -"

She reached into her bag and pulled out a long, thin white candle.

"I feel a little bad for you being out there in the chapel with no heating," she added, handing the candle to Jessie, "so please, take this. It might help a little. Consider it a gift."

***

A short while later, having finished eating, and having made her final last-ditch plea to be allowed to stay in the house, Jessie pulled the house's front door shut and turned to look out across the clearing. The temperature had dropped considerably, and she wasn't entirely convinced that she'd be able to get warm in her sleeping bag, but she figured she had to at least try. She glanced back toward the nearby window and saw the glow of Diana's stove; she felt a shivering flicker of envy, and then she shoved her hands into her pockets and made her way down the steps.

Her feet crunched against the dead leaves as she began to walk around the side of the house. She had nowhere else to go, so she was heading back to the chapel, although after a moment she slowed as she found herself next to a row of windows that ran along the south-facing side of the house. Despite the darkness all around, she stepped over to the nearest window and cupped her hands around her eyes, trying to see through into the room. If she couldn't explore Hardlocke House from the inside, she figured that this would be the next best thing.

She squinted, but she could see absolutely nothing. The darkness of the house stared back at her as she felt the cold glass against her hands, and she soon realized that she had no hope of actually seeing whatever was on the other side of the window.

Still, she tried the next window, and the next, until she reached the one at the far end and saw to her surprise that one of the panes of glass was cracked. She reached out and pressed gently, and she managed to very carefully slide one of the cracked sections out. After setting the piece of glass on the sill, she peered through the hole, only to once again see only darkness.

Reaching into one of her other pockets, she pulled out her flashlight and switched it on. For a moment, she worried that by shining a light into the room she might interfere with Diana's work, but then she told herself that she'd be quick. Besides, she knew that Diana was in a room on the other side of the house, so she held the flashlight up and shone its beam into the room.

She had to adjust the light's position a little, but finally she saw that the room contained several small desks and chairs, which had clearly once been used by the children. Her heart sank a little as she thought of the orphans sitting in their chairs and listening to Sarah Clarke's no-doubt harsh lessons. Although she knew fairly little about what life must have been like at Hardlocke House, she'd heard enough to be sure that the children must have lived miserable lives filled with fear and punishment.

Tilting the flashlight, she was just about able to see along to the room's far wall, which was bare and cracked. Was that where Sarah Clarke had stood while she was teaching the children? Jessie was already shivering in the cold night air, but she felt another shiver pass through her chest as she imagined the dead woman shouting at the children. She felt certain that nobody deserved such awful treatment, and she couldn't shake the feeling that some of that sadness and loneliness was somehow still present in and around the house. After a moment, however, she told herself to stop thinking that way.

"Are you stupid?" she imagined Diana snapping at her, if she ever dared suggest that the house's past was in some way lingering. "Are you a complete moron?"

Realizing that she wasn't going to be able to see anything else, Jessie carefully slid the broken piece of glass back into place before turning and heading back over toward the chapel.

CHAPTER FIFTEEN

"NO, IT'S ABSOLUTELY FINE," she said as she sat on the cold stone steps that led up to the altar, wrapped in a blanket and with the glow from the candle flickering against one side of her face. "I'm having a very interesting time."

"How does Doctor Moore seem?" Karen asked over the phone. "Has she mentioned us?"

"Mentioned *you*?"

"I was just wondering. If she gets to know you better, she might be willing to listen to our ideas for some joint papers."

"No, Mum," Jessie said, rolling her eyes, "she hasn't mentioned you. Or Dad."

"Well, there's still time." Karen cleared her throat. "So how's Doctor Moore treating you? Have you eaten?"

"I've eaten."

"And what are your sleeping arrangements like?"

Jessie looked out across the dark chapel for a moment. She'd switched her flashlight off to conserve its battery, and the light from the candle was only strong enough to cast a very faint glow across the room. She looked at the empty pews, and then she looked back down at her phone.

"Everything's fine, Mum," she said, determined to keep her mother from worrying. The last thing she wanted was to mention the fact that she was camping in an old chapel.

"Are you warm enough?"

"We got a stove running in the house," she explained, which was technically true. She just wasn't going to explain that she was nowhere near the stove. She hadn't admitted that she wasn't allowed to spend much time inside Hardlocke House itself. "I found some wood for the fire," she continued, "and Diana got it going, so -"

"Are you on first-name terms with her now?"

"I guess so," she replied. "I really just called to let you know that I'm fine. I don't want to use up too much of my phone's battery, because I only have that one extra power-bank. Think about it, Mum. The more we talk now, the more we risk being out of contact completely by Sunday."

"That's a terrifying thought," Karen admitted. "As long as you're comfortable, that's the main thing. I'll let you go, but remember to call if anything..."

Jessie waited, but her mother's voice had trailed off.

"If anything scary happens?" she asked. "Like... if I see a ghost?"

"You know what I mean. I'm your mother and I'm allowed to worry. Just remember to look after yourself." She paused. "Admit it, Jessie. The place is *slightly* creepy, isn't it? It has to be."

"It's an old, abandoned house. Aren't they always slightly creepy?"

"But do you feel anything when you're in there?"

"Careful, Mum. If Diana heard you saying something like that, she'd be furious."

"I'm not Diana, so you can be honest with me. Do you sense anything, sweetheart? I know you're a very sensitive girl, so it wouldn't surprise me."

Jessie thought about that question for a moment. She thought of the room with the stove, and she thought of the desk and the portrait of Sarah Clarke, and she realized that she *had* picked up on a kind of strange, indefinable tension when she'd been in there. At the same time, she also remembered everything Diana had told her, and she felt certain that she'd simply allowed the house's reputation to burrow its way into her thoughts. She knew that she had to remain on her guard in case she felt tempted to believe in anything supernatural.

"There's nothing, Mum," she said finally. "It's just a big old empty house. We're here so that Diana can carry out a proper investigation, not to run around like rejects from an episode of Scooby Doo."

"Well, I'm very proud of you," Karen replied. "I'm sure you're really helping the old battle-ax out. Just don't be afraid to answer her back if she gets too tough on you."

"I'll remember that, Mum," she replied. "Goodnight. Say hi to Dad for me."

"Sleep well, darling. Oh, and don't forget to put in a good word for us! If the opportunity comes up, I mean."

Once the call was over, Jessie switched her phone off so that the battery wouldn't be drained. Setting the phone up on the altar, she got to her feet and – still wrapped in the blanket – she picked up the candle and began to make her way over to the little door in the corner.

Stepping into the chapel's only other room, she looked around and saw a small office with shelves covering one of the walls. The shelves were empty now, but Jessie imagined that they'd once been used to store hymn books and other items for the chapel. She wandered over to a desk in the corner and reached down to touch its side, and she ran her fingertips against various cuts and other marks that had been left in the wood over the years. Lowering the candle slightly, she saw that the surface had been covered in several very long scratches that ran almost from one end of the table to the other, almost as if -

Suddenly she heard a loud, firm knocking sound coming from out in the main part of the chapel. Three distinct knocks ran out in total, and by the time she got back into the doorway Jessie already knew that someone had to be at the front door. No other explanation was possible.

She waited, her heart racing, but now silence had fallen again. Although she wanted to tell herself that the sound had been caused by the wind, she knew that was extremely unlikely, so she carried the candle past the front row of pews and began to cautiously make her way along the aisle.

"Doctor Moore?" she called out. "I mean... Diana? Is everything okay?"

She knew that Diana wouldn't have been able to get her wheelchair down the steps at the front of the house, although she realized that there might be some other, easier way out, perhaps at the rear of the building. Then again, would Diana have then been able to get her wheelchair across the bumpy, muddy, leaf-strewn ground that separated the house from the chapel? As she reached the door and stopped again to listen, she checked her watch and saw that it was almost 8pm, which meant that a couple of hours had passed since she'd left Diana alone in the house.

"Hello?" she said cautiously, leaning a little closer to the door. "Is anyone -"

She let out a shocked gasp and stepped back as three more short, sharp knocks hit the other side of the door. This time, she could tell that the knocks had come from a little lower down, around the handle, although silence had fallen once again and Jessie couldn't help but note that she'd not heard any footsteps outside. The ground all around the chapel – all around the house, too – was covered in dead leaves, and she felt sure that she should have heard anyone either approaching or leaving.

Finally she turned the handle and pulled the door open, only to find that there was no sign of anybody outside.

Still holding the candle, she leaned out and looked around. A slight breeze had picked up, a little stronger than earlier, and now she heard the leaves rustling slightly, but this only confirmed her belief that she'd have heard if anyone was nearby.

"Diana?" she said, still wondering whether the doctor had somehow made her way out. She was a little worried that she was being tested. "Is something wrong?"

The candle flickered but continued to burn.

Still hearing no answer, Jessie forced herself to step out into the clearing. She looked toward the house and saw that it was standing in complete darkness, although that wasn't surprising since the old office – with the stove – was all the way around on the house's other side. She looked at the dark windows for a moment, and then she stepped over to one corner of the chapel and took a look back the other way, just to make sure that there was nobody hiding.

"No?" she continued, starting to think that perhaps the wind had been responsible for the sound after all. "Nothing?"

She waited a moment longer, but she was already starting to realize that there was nobody around. She wandered back over to the door, only to find that it had shut. She was sure that she'd left it open, but this at least she felt she *could* ascribe to the wind with a little certainty. She reached out to push the door open and found that it was stuck, and she had to push with her shoulder before she managed to force her way back into the chapel.

She turned and looked back out at the clearing, and she listened to the sound of the wind blowing through the trees and disturbing the leaves on the ground.

Suddenly something blew against her candle, extinguishing the light. Startled, she stepped back, but she told herself that a freak gust of wind must have been responsible. After all, if the wind could blow multiple objects against the door with enough force to make a knocking sound, it should certainly be able to blow out a candle. She hesitated for a moment, and then she carefully swung the door shut.

She waited.

Still holding the handle, she was ready in case the knocking sound returned. She'd be able to whip the door open in an instant, less than a second after hearing anything, but this time there was no sign of anyone on the other side. She stayed in position for a few more minutes, shivering in the darkness, before finally turning and shuffling back along the aisle. She was starting to feel exhausted, and she figured it was time to relight the candle and then see whether there was any chance whatsoever of getting some sleep.

CHAPTER SIXTEEN

A SCREAM FILLED THE AIR, followed by the sound of footsteps racing across one of the rooms upstairs. Turning, the little boy looked toward the open doorway for a moment, and he stood frozen by fear as he listened to the footsteps rushing down the stairs. Finally, almost too late, he turned and scampered into the office and ducked down behind Ms. Clarke's desk.

Holding his breath, he listened as the footsteps slowed and reached the door.

"Thomas?" Ms. Clarke's voice called out. "Thomas, it's me. Are you in here?"

Shaking with fear, Thomas began to pray. All he wanted was for Ms. Clarke to not catch up to him, but he knew the odds were slim. He'd been living at Hardlocke House for a little over a year, since just before his ninth birthday, and in that time he'd learned one lesson that seemed more true than any other in the whole world.

Ms. Clarke could not be fooled.

He'd only wanted to take some cheese from the pantry. He'd been hungry all day, since one of the other boys had stolen his pudding at lunch, so he'd decided to take the risk of creeping out of the classroom. After all, he knew that Ms. Clarke would never have given him any extra food, so he'd decided to take matters into his own hands. Now he wished with all his heart that he hadn't been so stupid.

"Thomas, there's no need to be frightened," Ms. Clarke continued, still in the doorway. "Why don't you come out? Why don't you come with me? Everyone else is waiting in the classroom. You don't want to *keep* them waiting, do you?"

He tried to hug himself into a tighter shape, hoping to minimize the chances of being spotted, but as he did so Thomas pressed slightly against the side of the desk. One of the drawers jolted slightly, and Thomas froze as he realized that he'd made a fatal mistake.

"Oh, Thomas," Ms. Clarke said, as footsteps made their way over to the desk and then stopped again, "whatever is the matter with you? Why are you hiding from me?"

Shaking with fear now, Thomas stared down

at the floor and hoped that somehow some miracle might yet save him. He knew that strict punishment awaited anyone who disobeyed the rules, and he'd seen the after-effects of what had happened to some of the other boys; he'd tried so very hard to be good, but the hunger had been eating away at his gut and finally – when Ms. Clarke had stepped out for a few minutes – he'd given in to temptation. Then, hearing that Ms. Clarke had returned to the classroom before him, he'd panicked and run.

He heard another couple of footsteps coming around the desk, and then he saw a shadow fall across the floor.

"Thomas," Ms. Clarke continued, "this silliness has to stop now. You're only adding to the problem here. Why don't you come with me? You should have told me that you were hungry. I also saw you carving your name into the desk while you were supposed to be working on your numbers. You know not to do that, Thomas, don't you? There's no excuse for that sort of behavior. We don't condone vandalism here at Hardlocke House."

He slowly began to turn and look up at her. As soon as he saw her outstretched hand, with thin, bony fingers, he immediately turned to look the other way.

"Thomas, can you not even face me?" she asked. "Am I so frightfully terrifying? Please, just try, and I promise you everything will be alright."

He swallowed hard, but he knew he had no choice so he slowly turned again. This time he forced himself to look up, and he saw Ms. Clarke smiling at him. Her hand was still reaching out, and after a moment she leaned a little closer.

"Get to your feet, Thomas," she said calmly. "Come on, things won't seem so bad soon. Or are you going to stay here, curled up into a ball and shaking with fear, forever? Is that your plan?"

She leaned closer still.

"Come on," she added. "I know you can do it."

Realizing that he had no choice, Thomas somehow forced himself to stand. He didn't want to take her hand, but again he knew that his options were limited. Reaching out, he flinched as soon as he felt her cold fingers, but she quickly closed them around his hand and began to lead him around the desk.

"It's okay," she purred softly. "You're being very good."

She managed to get him out into the hall, and then along the corridor that led back to the classroom. As soon as they reached the door, Thomas saw the other eleven boys sitting at their desks, but he was surprised when Ms. Clarke prompted him to keep walking.

"Aren't we... going in there?" he asked her.

"Not quite yet, Thomas," she replied,

tightening her grip on his hand. "Silly thing, you've hurt your knee. Hadn't you noticed? We need to get it cleaned up."

Looking down, Thomas realized that she was right. At some point, probably when he'd first dropped behind the desk, he'd grazed his knee rather badly. The skin had been torn away, and a trickle of dark blood was running down toward the top of his socks.

"We can't leave it like that," Ms. Clarke said as she led him toward the little medical room at the end of the corridor. "Come on, this won't take a minute."

As they walked, Thomas glanced into the classroom again. All the other boys were staring back at him, and he was instantly struck by the fear on their faces. It was as if they all knew what was going to happen to him next.

***

Sitting on a simple wooden chair, one that was too tall for him, Thomas looked down at his bare knees as he heard Ms. Clarke humming to herself. She was gathering a few items from the cupboard, and Thomas could only watch as a bead of blood glistened in the center of his wound.

"Do you know the song I was just humming now?" Ms. Clarke asked as she walked over and set a bowl of water on a nearby table. "It's an old piece of music that comes from the colonies. It's used to invoke a sense of the Lord's strength in times of great suffering. I find that it helps to use music in this way. Don't you ever think about that, Thomas? Don't you ever think that all the beauty of the world can be summed up, in one way or another, by music?"

She knelt before him.

"Look at me," she added.

Thomas did as he was told. As soon as he saw Ms. Clarke's eyes, he was shocked by the kindness they betrayed. He'd heard so many stories about her since his arrival at Hardlocke House, and he'd seen flashes of her temper, but otherwise he was starting to wonder whether perhaps the stories had been wrong. Although she could certainly be rigid and disciplined, and some of her sermons were a little on the long side, Thomas couldn't ignore a kind of tenderness that seemed to be part of the woman's soul. For the first time, he began to wonder whether some of the stories might have been a little exaggerated.

"You know," she said softly, "sometimes I think of Hardlocke House as a big tree."

Thomas furrowed his brow.

"That probably seems strange to you," she continued, "but I *do* see it as a tree, and everyone here is a leaf on that tree. Do you know something funny about leaves, Thomas?"

He thought about the question for a moment, and then he shook his head.

"Leaves can't stay on a tree forever. Eventually they fall away and die, but that doesn't mean that they're gone. They can still be beautiful in death, and eventually they rot down and nourish the tree that once nourished them. Even if they fall a little further away from the roots than they'd like. We're all leaves on the tree of Hardlocke House, including me, and we won't be here forever. But while we *are* here, it's important for us to behave ourselves and not cause too much trouble. Do you understand?"

He paused again.

"I think so," he said, although he really wasn't sure.

"Can I clean your knee now, Thomas?" she asked. "Would you mind terribly?"

He paused, and then he nodded.

"Thank you," she added with a courteous smile, before taking a piece of cloth and dipping it into the bowl of water. "This might sting a little, but it's preferable to leaving it uncleaned. Does that make sense?"

He nodded again.

"What's wrong?" she asked. "Has the cat got your tongue?"

"No," he said, his voice shaking with fear.

"I'm sorry, Ms. Clarke. I didn't mean to be bad."

"It's okay," she said calmly, with a soothing tone to her voice. "Just remember what I said, okay? There might be some pain."

She pressed the cloth against the wound and began to give it a good clean. Although he felt a little soreness, Thomas couldn't help but note that it didn't really hurt at all. Ms. Clarke's touch was so soft, and after a few seconds he realized that he was actually starting to feel less scared.

"You're being very brave," she told him, as she turned and took another cloth from the table. Looking back at him, she smiled. "Why, Thomas Kinkade, I think you might be the bravest boy in this whole house."

"I'm not brave," he whispered.

"Don't talk yourself down," she replied, turning to the the table again. "You *are* brave, whether you know it or not, and I feel confident that one day you shall grow up to be a fine young man. That's all I want from my boys here. You've all had such unfortunate starts in life, but that doesn't mean that you can't have wonderful futures. With the Lord's help, I -"

She stopped speaking suddenly. Her head was still turned away from Thomas as her hand rested on the table, but she seemed to have fallen still for a moment. And then, just as Thomas began to wonder whether anything was wrong, he realized he could hear her letting out a faint rasping sound.

He waited.

"Oh Thomas," Ms. Clarke said, slowly turning back to face him, revealing a pair of black eyes. She suddenly seemed much paler than before. "The Lord can't save you now!"

Suddenly she lunged at him, opening her mouth to reveal two rows of razor-sharp teeth.

CHAPTER SEVENTEEN

"NO!" JESSIE GASPED, sitting up as she woke suddenly from the nightmare. Trembling with fear, sweating profusely as the top of the sleeping bag slipped down, she struggled for a moment to remember where she was.

Looking up, she saw the altar towering above her, and the crucifix on the wall, and in that moment she realized that she'd eventually settled her sleeping bag on the raised platform next to the altar's steps. It had seemed like the best place to sleep, and somehow she'd managed to nod off after a few hours of struggling to get warm. The windows were beginning to lighten as the sun rose outside.

And then she'd had that awful nightmare...

The details were already fading, but she knew she'd been dreaming about Hardlocke House.

There had been a boy, his name had been Thomas, and he'd been terrified of Sarah Clarke. Eventually she'd taken him into a small room to tend to a cut on his knee, and everything had been fine at first, until...

She thought back to that final moment, in which Sarah's face had twisted and become filled with evil.

Although she hadn't been part of what was happening in the dream, Jessie still felt a shudder as she remembered the way that Sarah's face had suddenly seemed to transform. In the very last moment, right as she'd begun to wake up, she'd heard Thomas let out a cry of shock, but she quickly reminded herself that Thomas had just been a figment of her imagination. No such boy had ever existed.

Rubbing her face, she tried to tell herself that it had been *just* a nightmare. She knew there was absolutely no point mentioning the matter to Diana, and she figured that she'd simply allowed the stories of Hardlocke House to get to her a little. A moment later, she looked up at one of the stained glass windows and admired its beauty in the early light of dawn, but then she remembered what Diana had said to her.

"I shall see you in the morning. Sunrise, out on the steps. Don't be late."

"Damn it!" Jessie blurted out, stumbling to

her feet as she realized that she was probably keeping the doctor waiting.

***

Hurrying around the corner, across the dead leaves that littered the clearing, Jessie saw to her surprise that there was no sign of Diana at the top of the steps. She'd expected to find her waiting, perhaps a little annoyed, but the house's front door was shut and as she reached the foot of the steps Jessie realized that there was no sign of a warm glow inside coming from the stove.

Morning sunlight was streaming through the trees, catching beads of dew that shivered on the grass.

For a moment, Jessie wasn't quite sure what to do. She was pretty sure that she wasn't supposed to go marching into the house uninvited, but at the same time she wasn't sure that simply loitering and waiting was the right approach. She turned and looked out toward the forest, and she found herself wondering whether she was really late at all. When Diana had mentioned sunrise, had she meant the moment when the sun first began to brighten the night, or had she meant some vague time when the sun was actually fully up?

Checking her watch, Jessie saw that the time was a little after 6am.

She looked up at the house's cold, dark windows again, and she realized that Diana might simply be asleep. The last thing she wanted was to intrude, so she decided finally to simply sit on the steps and wait. Settling down, she looked once again toward the forest, and she realized that there was no hint of birdsong. She looked up at the tops of the trees and saw them swaying in a gentle wind, and she wondered why no birds seemed to be coming anywhere near the house.

Taking her phone from her pocket, she switched it on and waited to get some signal. She'd not planned to call home again until the evening, but now she found herself missing her parents a little so she figured she could sneak in one more quick call while she waited. She also had a few friends she wanted to speak to, and some apps to check, but as she unlocked the phone she saw to her disappointment that she had no bars at all.

She waved the phone in the air, hoping for better luck, but still there was nothing. She'd managed to get signal in the chapel, so she figured she'd just have to stick to her original plan and wait until evening.

Suddenly hearing a clicking sound, she got to her feet just as the front door creaked open, and she felt hugely relieved to see Diana wheeling herself into the doorway.

"Ah," Diana said, "there you are, bang on

time. I always place great value on punctuality, so you've passed your first test with flying colors. I suppose you'd better come inside."

Jessie opened her mouth to ask how the night had gone, but Diana was already wheeling herself back inside. Figuring that this wasn't the time for small-talk, Jessie turned her phone off and put it back in her pocket, and then she made her way up the steps and into the house's entrance hall, which she noticed was once again very cold. She walked through to the office and realized that the stove must have been cold for a while, and she watched as Diana stopped to look at some papers on the desk.

It was the same desk, in every aspect, that Thomas had hidden behind in the nightmare. Still, Jessie figured it wasn't so strange that the house had managed to influence her dreams.

"Do you know the names of the boys who were here when Sarah Clarke died?" she asked suddenly, before she could really stop herself.

"Not off the top of my head," Diana said. "Why?"

"I just wondered," she continued, thinking back to the boy in her nightmare. "It doesn't matter. Did you get any sleep?"

"Hmm?" Diana replied, clearly far more interested in her papers, some of which showed images of rooms in the house. "Oh, some. A couple of hours. When you're my age, I'm afraid sleep isn't so very important anymore. Of course, that's something of a blessing when you have so much work to get done. It's almost as if the body starts to realize that time is pressing."

Jessie waited, but now Diana seemed totally engrossed in whatever she was doing.

"I got a couple of hours," she said finally. "It wasn't so bad in the chapel."

Again she waited, but she received no answer. After a moment, Jessie realized that Diana didn't seem remotely interested. She briefly considered mentioning the nightmare, and the strange knocks on the door, but she figured that she didn't want to say anything that might cause Diana to doubt her suitability for the project. After all, the nightmare had been just a dream, and the knock could have been caused by anything, so she kept her mouth shut as she wandered over to the desk and looked down at various old newspaper cuttings that Diana had laid out.

"So nothing at all happened during the night?" she asked.

"Did you think it would?" Diana replied, glancing up at her. "Remember, according to the Malones, the ghost of Sarah Clarke always retreats on the first night that someone new is here. Then on the second night she begins to observe more closely, and on the third night she makes her presence known. Even if you believe in all that nonsense, Ms. Clarke's lack of an appearance last night should be no surprise. It's tomorrow night, in theory, that she should become apparent. Although the Malones *did* say that she could be detected on the second night."

She took a moment to look through some more of the cuttings.

"It's all rubbish, of course," she added. "There's nothing here, and Andy and Lizzy Malone were a pair of witless morons. Did the candle keep you warm at all last night?"

"Uh, sure," Jessie lied. "Thank you."

"I must admit, I rather envied you," Diana said. "Tucked up in your sleeping bag, you probably had a much better time than I did. I spent most of my time in here, reading and pondering certain matters. The house creaked a few times, but we all know that's simply what old houses do during cold nights. I'm sure a lesser mind would have read more into those noises, though. If one wanted to fool oneself into believing that one was being haunted, this would be the place to do it."

"Sure," Jessie muttered.

"Today I want to carry out some research regarding Ms. Clarke's time here," Diana continued. "Regardless of the ludicrous ghost stories, this is a site of historical interest. Again, I shan't be letting you have the run of the place, but I will require your assistance in one very specific regard. I hope you're feeling strong."

"Strong?"

Diana turned to her, this time with a bigger smile than before.

"Well," she continued, "it's a nice bright Saturday morning, and I think I would like to take a look at the accommodation quarters. And I'm afraid, young lady, that this means I must get upstairs."

CHAPTER EIGHTEEN

"NEARLY THERE!" DIANA ANNOUNCED cheerily, as Jessie finally got close to the top of the stairs, carrying the older lady in her arms. "Just a few more steps! You can do it!"

Although she'd tried not to show it, Jessie had struggled quite a lot with the weight of Diana, so she felt immensely relieved as she reached the landing and set her down on the floor. She was careful to be gentle, not wanting to cause any discomfort, and her arms were aching as she took a step back.

"Perfect," Diana said, turning herself around and leaning against the wall. "There, that wasn't too arduous, was it?"

"I'm fine," Jessie gasped as she tried to get her breath back.

"You're stronger than you look, you know. I was a little worried that your arms might snap off, but you managed just fine. Although I must admit, you're starting to look a little pale. If you need to sit down for a while, by all means do so."

Looking around, Jessie saw that several corridors led off from the landing, and she could just about make out doors in the distance. The house's upper floor seemed so still and dead, even more so than downstairs, and Jessie couldn't help looking at some of the nearby doors and thinking of all the empty rooms.

"Well?" Diana continued.

Jessie turned to her, and it took a moment before she realized what she had to do next.

"Right. Sorry."

She started making her way back down to the hall, where the empty wheelchair was waiting. She couldn't help noticing that Diana had seemed very cheery so far, especially while she was being carried up the stairs, but then – as she reached down and picked the wheelchair up – she realized she could hear a faint whispering sound. Looking back up the stairs, she was unable to see Diana but she could just about make out the voice as it continued to murmur softly.

"Are you okay?" she called out.

She waited, but Diana failed to respond.

Figuring that she shouldn't show too much

concern, Jessie began to carry the wheelchair up to the landing. She was more and more convinced that the whispering voice was coming from Diana herself, and sure enough the voice stopped just as Jessie reached the top. Diana was still sitting on the floor, still leaning against the wall, and she seemed dazed for a moment before finally offering Jessie a broad smile.

"Well done, young lady. Now, if you'll just help me back up into my chariot, I can get on with my work and you can... I suppose you can have a few hours to yourself. Come back at midday, and we can think about something to eat. Did you have breakfast, by the way?"

"I've got some protein bars in my bag," Jessie said as she began to get ready to pick Diana up again. She wanted to ask about the whispering, but she wasn't quite sure how to bring the matter up. "They'll keep me going."

She hauled Diana into the chair, and then she stepped back and watched her getting settled.

"Are you sure there's nothing more useful I could be doing this morning?" Jessie asked. "I mean, I came all the way out here, I figure there might be some kind of job you have for me."

"That's very thoughtful of you," Diana replied, already wheeling herself around and setting off along one of the corridors, "but your main role for the next few hours is to keep out of my way. I'd like you to stay out of the house, so just go and read a book or something and then come back around midday. Is that clear?"

"Totally," Jessie said, although she couldn't hide the sense of disappointment in her voice. She still felt as if she could be more useful.

She watched as Diana headed off along the corridor, and then she turned and made her way back down the stairs. Despite her frustrations, she told herself that it would be a big mistake to go against Diana's orders, so she resolved to simply sit around and hope that eventually she might be given some better tasks. As she got down to the main hall, however, she glanced to her right and then stopped as soon as she saw the corridor that led past a few old classrooms.

She'd seen the exact same corridor in her nightmare.

Although she knew that this meant nothing, that she'd most likely noticed the corridor during the previous evening, she felt drawn to take a closer look. She glanced up the stairs again, but Diana was long gone and she realized that there was no harm in making her way over to investigate. Confident that she'd soon find that any similarities were only superficial, she walked over to the start of the corridor and saw the windows of several classrooms, but to her surprise she realized that this was the *exact* corridor that little Thomas had walked along in the nightmare.

She looked over her shoulder, but she knew that there was no way Diana could get downstairs, so she began to make her way along the corridor.

After a few steps, she saw the classroom where the other eleven boys had been sitting. She remembered their fearful faces in the nightmare as they'd watched Thomas being led past. So far, everything was exactly the same as she'd imagined.

A moment later she reached an open doorway at the end of the corridor, and she felt a flicker of dread in her chest as she look through and saw the medical room where Thomas had sat to have his knee cleaned. The same wooden chair was in the corner, and he also recognized the table that was set over by the far wall. Stepping into the room, she realized that it was exactly as she remembered from the nightmare, even though she was certain that she'd never seen so much as a photo of that part of the house before.

She looked at the spot where Sarah Clarke had sat in the dream, and she once again thought back to the sight of the woman's black-eyed face.

"It's just a coincidence," she whispered to herself, hoping to cast her fears aside. "I just..."

Her voice trailed off, and after a moment she realized what must have happened. She must have seen a photo of the room at some point; she'd forgotten the photo, but somehow it had lodged in the back of her mind and burst back out during the nightmare. Although that chain of events was somewhat difficult to believe, it made more sense than anything else.

Heading out of the room, feeling a little better, she carefully closed the door before making her way back along the corridor. As she passed the classroom, however, she slowed and stopped at the door. She could see the rows of desks, and already one line from her nightmare was ringing in her ears.

"I also saw you carving your name into the desk while you were supposed to be working on your numbers."

She looked through to the hall, just to make sure that she was still alone, and then she walked into the classroom and began to examine the desks. She wasn't even sure where she was supposed to be looking, but she told herself that she'd be able to put her mind at rest if she could just prove that there was no name carved anywhere. Eventually she even dropped to her knees so that she could look at the undersides.

Suddenly hearing a bumping sound coming from upstairs, she sat up quickly, only to bang her head against the side of one of the desks.

"Piece of -"

Letting out a gasp of pain, she rubbed the sore spot and got to her feet. She was worried that she might have alerted Diana to her presence, and after a moment she realized that she'd spent enough time chasing after whispers and phantoms that had existed purely in the nightmare. She'd found no evidence of a name carved into any of the desks, so – still rubbing the top of her head – she headed out of the room and made her way to the hall.

Once she was outside, she grabbed her book from the chapel and then she took up a spot on the steps. She had several hours to kill, but she hoped that reading for a while might help to calm her racing thoughts, and she was quite looking forward to the chance to catch up on some of the books she'd bought over the previous year but not managed to read yet. She felt that she'd allowed the nightmare to get under her skin, and that was the last thing she needed while she was dealing with someone as clear-headed and rational as Doctor Diana Moore.

Back in the abandoned classroom, tucked away in the corner, the name Thomas had indeed – long ago – been carved into one of the desks.

CHAPTER NINETEEN

"I TRIED TO TRACE the twelve orphans, of course," Diana said at lunchtime, as she sat in her wheelchair at the top of the steps with a sandwich in her hands. "The task proved quite impossible, I'm afraid. Records from those days are really not very complete."

"That's not too surprising," Jessie replied, emptying the last crumbs from her bag of crisps into the palm of her hand.

"I *would* like to know what happened to them," Diana continued. "Regardless of all the nonsense that's been claimed about this house, something interesting certainly happened here and it would be utterly fascinating to hear an account of it all from the point of view of those poor little children. I imagine, however, that they were simply taken away to other places, where they were raised and then put to work. I doubt that any of them lived remarkable lives."

"And what about Sarah Clarke herself?" Jessie asked. "Where was she buried?"

"In an unmarked grave, apparently."

"In a cemetery?"

"On the grounds of the house," Diana said with a faint smile. "Why, does that give you pause for thought?"

Jessie looked around, and she realized that Sarah's body could be anywhere.

"I believe the Malones attempted to locate the corpse," Diana continued. "They tried dowsing for it, and various other completely unscientific methods. Unfortunately for them, the estate covers several acres and they found it impossible to pin down the location, so they really had no chance of striking gold. Not that there's any need to find the body, of course. It would just be a nifty little curiosity."

"So did you find anything interesting?" Jessie asked, turning back to her.

"What do you mean?"

"Upstairs."

She waited, but Diana merely furrowed her brow.

"When you were looking in the old accommodation quarters," Jessie reminded her.

"That's what you were doing up there, isn't it?"

"Of course," Diana said, rolling her eyes. "Silly me, I'm afraid I got distracted for a moment there. I didn't find very much, as it happens, but I didn't really expect to. I looked around the entire house forty years ago. Really, there's a certain degree of killing time to our work today, since we simply need to make sure that we're here for the third night. That's when..."

Her voice trailed off.

"Well," she added finally, "that's when absolutely nothing will happen, and we shall be able to say with confidence that there is nothing untoward here at Hardlock House. You know, now that I'm back here, I can't understand why I was so foolish. I shouldn't have waited forty years to prove to myself that I was mistaken."

"It's only human to have doubts," Jessie pointed out.

"I'm going to spend the afternoon upstairs again," Diana replied, "so I'm afraid you'll have to carry me up there. And then, you'll be pleased to learn, I actually have a little job for you to do."

***

"I've got a little job for you," Jessie muttered under her breath as she carried the shovel out through the forest, heading to the spot that Diana had specified.

"You're going to love it."

Finally reaching the edge of the line of trees, she discovered a small clearing that was exactly as Diana had described.

"There's a dip in the ground next to a large gnarly old oak tree," the older woman had explained, "and based on my research, I have a suspicion that this might be where the body of Sarah Clarke was deposited. To be honest, I wasn't going to waste much time hunting for it, but seeing as you were asking, and as you seem a little disappointed that I'm not using you very much, I think it would be a splendid idea for you to go out there and see what you can dig up. Literally."

Stopping at the foot of the dip, Jessie looked around and tried to figure out what – exactly – had made Diana get so interested in this particular part of the forest. She'd asked, of course, only to be given vague answers about papers and books and conversations that were apparently too complicated to explain. After a while, Jessie had begun to feel that she was simply being sent out of the way, although that didn't really seem like Diana's style. If anything, Diana had seemed to enjoy making Jessie sit around all morning, so she couldn't help but wonder whether she was really expected to find anything.

Still, figuring that she couldn't slack off, she started digging in a random spot.

"You only have to go down a few feet," she'd been told. "I really don't think the body would have been buried too deep."

"Wouldn't that make it more likely that animals got to it?" she'd asked.

"In theory, yes. In practice, I'm not so sure that would have happened. After all, do you see much wildlife in the vicinity?"

After asking a few more questions, and receiving suitably vague answers that didn't really help, Jessie had simply accepted her lot and had gone to fetch the shovel that Diana claimed she'd probably find in one of the sheds. The walk out into the forest had taken about an hour, and now as she continued to dig she couldn't help but wonder whether Diana was using the opportunity to talk to herself in relative peace. She still hadn't really worked out what Diana had been saying whenever she started muttering away to herself, although she wasn't too worried. Based on everything her parents had told her, Diana was known to be pretty eccentric.

Suddenly hearing footsteps racing across the leaves, Jessie dropped her shovel and turned to look over her shoulder. The footsteps continued, rushing between the trees, and after a moment she realized that there seemed to be two distinct sets.

And then three.

Turning to look the other way, she listened

as more footsteps hurried through the forest. She told herself not to worry, that the sound was most likely caused by some kind of wildlife, but a few seconds later she heard the sound of someone giggling.

Children.

She looked the other way, and now the sound seemed to be coming from all around. For a moment, the whole forest seemed to be filled with the strange noise, until the footsteps stopped as abruptly as they'd begun.

Jessie looked all around. Her mind was racing as she tried to figure out what had happened, and then she turned the other way as she heard another faint giggle.

She opened her mouth to call out, but at the last moment she stopped herself.

As silence returned, save for the sound of treetops rustling high above, Jessie told herself that she had to stay calm. She knew that the human mind could play tricks, so she tried to focus on the fact that most likely it *had* just been wildlife that had caused the noises. Sure, she hadn't seen so much as a bird since arriving at Hardlocke House, but that didn't mean there were no creatures in the forest at all. And she'd seen some spiders in one of the sheds, which meant that there was definitely life around somewhere.

Grabbing the shovel again, she resumed

digging, only to stop almost immediately as she saw that she'd cracked open something white and hard that lay half-buried in the dirt.

Reaching down, she brushed some of the soil away, before lifting up what appeared to be a piece of bone. She told herself that she couldn't possibly have found a body so quickly, but she set the shovel down and used her fingers to excavate a little further. Sure enough, she soon found the front of a skull, and as she lifted it up she found herself staring at two hollow eye sockets.

"You've got to be kidding me," she whispered, before looking down and spotting part of a jawbone.

She pulled the jawbone out, and her hands were starting to tremble with nerves as she saw a row of discolored teeth. And then, just as she was actually starting to allow herself to believe that she might have discovered the remains of Sarah Clarke, she saw another jawbone piece buried deep in the soil. She pulled that out, and then she dug a little deeper, and finally she pulled out part of another skull.

"What the..."

She dug again, and in less than a minute she'd found a third skull. This one was more intact that the other two, and as she held it up she began to realize that what she'd discovered might not be Sarah Clarke after all.

Suddenly another giggle rang out, seemingly coming from directly in front of her. Jessie looked up. She saw nobody, but she was starting to realize exactly what she'd found. In which case, she had a horrible feeling that if she dug a little deeper she'd find nine more skulls.

CHAPTER TWENTY

"REMARKABLE," DIANA SAID, SITTING in the old office of Hardlocke House and staring at the twelve skulls – some fairly intact, some badly broken – that stood arranged in a row on the desk. "I never dreamed that we might make a discovery such as this."

"But it's them, right?" Jessie asked, still struggling to get her head around the find. "It's the orphans. I mean, it has to be."

"It doesn't *have* to be," Diana replied. "You must avoid believing in absolutes unless you have actual evidence. But, yes, that is by far the most likely explanation. I suppose I was wrong when I assumed that they'd been taken to other homes following the death of Sarah Clarke. The next question is who killed them, and why? And how?

And how did those two idiots, the Malones, not find them?"

"It's horrible," Jessie said. "They were just children."

"They were, but you must take the emotion out of our work here. These are valuable specimens. And you said that you discovered the rest of their bodies as well?"

"I found some ribs, a pelvis, a few other parts. I couldn't excavate them all, but I grabbed a bag and brought the heads so that... I guess I was worried that you wouldn't believe me if I didn't show you some proof."

"Of course I would have believed you," Diana replied. "You're not a known liar, are you?"

Jessie shook her head.

"And what of Sarah Clarke herself? Did you not discover any of her remains?"

"She might be deeper."

"Or she might not be there at all." Diana paused for a moment, before wheeling herself back across the room. "I hadn't anticipated the need to preserve any specimens," she continued. "Still, it's Saturday already and we only have to keep them safe until Monday. That should be well within our capabilities. Then we shall deliver the bones to some colleagues of mine and we shall have to wait to see whether they can tell us more about what happened. There certainly appears to have been significant damage to the skulls, so hopefully we can learn exactly how these poor unfortunate children were killed."

She began to wheel herself over to the doorway.

"How did you know they'd be there?" Jessie asked.

Diana stopped and turned to look back at her.

"You sent me right there," Jessie continued. "That can't have just been a guess."

"My dear, I have spent forty years obsessing over this case," Diana replied. "Please, allow me to have made a small amount of progress. And it *was* a guess, albeit an educated one. I identified that area as the most likely place where any body would have been disposed of."

"Based on what?"

"I don't have time to go into that now."

"But -"

"I don't have time!" Diana said again, more firmly this time. "I thought that you *might* find Sarah Clarke's body. I certainly didn't anticipate those twelve little skulls that you have so neatly lined up in a row. This discovery changes a great deal, although I must admit that I'm still at a loss to understand what happened to the children. The eighteenth century might have been a brutal time, but the slaughter of an entire school's worth of young men is simply ghastly." She looked over at the skulls for a moment. "The sad truth is, we might never know exactly why this tragedy occurred."

She turned to leave the room.

"I heard something in the forest," Jessie said suddenly, before she had time to stop herself. She'd sworn to keep quiet about anything even vaguely suggestive of ghosts, and she immediately regretted her admission.

Diana looked at her again.

"What do you mean?" she asked, with a clipped tone that instantly indicated disapproval.

"It's nothing," Jessie replied quickly. "Sorry. Forget I said anything."

"I shall do no such thing," Diana continued. "When you say that you heard something in the forest, precisely what did you mean?"

"I really think it was nothing. It's just that, for a moment, I thought I heard... children."

Diana furrowed her brow.

"Like I said," Jessie added, "it was probably just the wind."

"Probably?"

"Definitely! It was definitely just the wind. It sounded like footsteps, but I'm sure that was just wind blowing against the leaves. And the laughter was probably just -"

"Laughter?"

"No! I mean..."

Her voice trailed off as she realized that she'd already dug herself in pretty deep.

"I thought that *maybe* I heard laughter out there," she said finally, picking her words with great care, "and although I know that obviously I didn't, I can still see how someone else might have thought that."

She waited for an answer.

Diana merely stared at her.

"So that's a good lesson, right?" Jessie continued. "In how easy it is to let your mind play tricks on you, I mean. It's like you said, we can't be absolutely sure that our own minds don't ever do that, so we have to recognize those moments and make sure that we don't let them influence our work."

Again, she waited.

Again, Diana gave no response.

"I don't think that there were ghost children out there," Jessie said, hoping to defuse the situation. "Genuinely, I don't. And as for the knocks on the door in the night, I..."

Realizing that she'd done it again, she swallowed hard.

"I'm absolutely certain that there's a logical explanation," she continued. "Just because I don't know what it is, that doesn't mean there isn't one. That's something I've learned from you, Diana, and -"

"Don't suck up," Diana replied, interrupting her. "You've recognized your own lamentable weakness, and that's a good thing. Now you have to make sure that it doesn't happen again."

"Of course. I understand."

"I'm going to go and get on with my work. I shall need your assistance in getting up the stairs again, and then you will leave the house for the rest of the day."

"Sure, and -"

"And I think you should call me Doctor Moore from now on," she added. "It wouldn't do for us to be overly familiar with one another."

"Okay."

She watched as Doctor Moore wheeled herself out into the hall. She knew she had to go after her, but for a moment she hung back, trying to calm her frayed nerves. Since arriving at Hardlocke House, she'd managed to make some good progress with the doctor, to the extent that they'd been getting on pretty well. Now, in a few minutes' worth of inopportune honesty, she seemed to have set all that work back to the beginning, and she figured that she'd probably made herself look like a complete idiot in the doctor's eyes. She only hoped that somehow, eventually, she might find a way to undo the damage.

"Are you coming?" Doctor Moore called out.

"Sorry!"

She hurried through and prepared to gently lift the doctor out of the wheelchair.

"Okay," she said, "I -"

Suddenly she felt Doctor Moore grab her left hand, and in an instant the index finger was twisted back so far that Jessie was convinced it might break.

"Listen to me very carefully," Doctor Moore sneered angrily, pulling the finger back even further. "You will never, under any circumstances, mention any more foolish ideas to me. Is that understood?"

"Yes!" Jessie gasped, as the pain in her finger increased. "Please, you're hurting me..."

"I'm fully aware of what I'm doing!" Doctor Moore snapped. "I'm here at Hardlocke House to conduct serious scientific work, and I will not have that put in danger by the superstitious raving of an immature brat who lacks the ability to distinguish between fiction and reality. Is that, also, understood?"

"Yes! Please, stop!"

She waited, but the anger in Doctor Moore's eyes was only growing and she was twisting the finger back even further, as if she genuinely intended to cause serious harm.

And then, suddenly, the doctor let go of her hand and pushed her away. Jessie immediately began to check her finger, which fortunately –

despite a lingering pain – seemed not to be damaged.

"Now get me up the stairs," Doctor Moore said firmly, "and then I don't want to see hide nor hair of you until this evening. You are to keep out of my way!"

"Yes, Diana. I mean, Doctor Moore."

Struggling to hold back tears, Jessie began to lift the doctor out of the wheelchair. Whereas earlier they'd chatted during the process, now Doctor Moore remained resolutely silent and Jessie felt that she too should probably stay quiet. She lifted the doctor up into her arms, and then she turned and slowly began to carry her up toward the landing.

Back in the old office, the twelve skulls remained in place on the desk. Although she had not done so intentionally, Jessie had laid them out so that their eyeless sockets were all looking straight toward the portrait of Sarah Clarke on the far wall.

CHAPTER TWENTY-ONE

"I OWE YOU AN APOLOGY."

Looking up from her bowl of rice, Jessie assumed at first that she must have misheard. Ever since the discussion earlier in the day, Doctor Moore had barely said a word, and even dinner had so far been eaten in complete silence. Jessie had resigned herself to the cold shoulder for the rest of the evening, and she'd figured that – at best – things might begin to get better the following morning.

Even that had seemed like a forlorn hope.

"I was rather too harsh with you earlier," Doctor Moore continued, sitting in her wheelchair at the top of the steps at the front of the house. "You must understand that I have waited forty years to come back to Hardlocke House, and a great deal is resting upon the results that I get here. One might even say that my entire career is in the balance."

"It's okay," Jessie replied. "I'm sorry I said those stupid things."

"No, they weren't stupid." Doctor Moore paused. "If you heard something that sounded like footsteps, then you heard something that sounded like footsteps. And if you heard something that sounded like something knocking on the door to the chapel, then... again, that's what you heard."

"I'm not saying that there was anyone there," Jessie said cautiously.

"And that is the correct way to approach these matters. I should have been clearer about that this afternoon. Instead, I fell into the kind of behavior that I abhor in others. I allowed myself to become emotional when there was no need, and for that I am genuinely sorry. I pride myself on having a much greater sense of self-control."

"It's really fine," Jessie said. "You must be pretty stressed."

"Stressed would be an understatement," Doctor Moore replied. "Tonight is our second night here, which is when – according to the stories told by the Malones and other people who lived here over the years – the ghost of Sarah Clarke begins to become more confident. In the extremely unlikely event that there *is* a ghost here, then it is reasonable to assume that tonight I might begin to notice her presence."

Jessie waited for her to continue, but after a moment she realized that the doctor seemed to be much more nervous than before.

"If you want, I can stay in the house tonight," she suggested.

Again she waited.

"I'm sorry," Doctor Moore replied, as if she was emerging from a daze, "what did you say?"

"Just that I don't mind staying in the house with you," Jessie told her. "I know you didn't want me to before, but doesn't it make sense to have two people in there, so that you have someone who can verify anything that happens? I don't mind acting as a second opinion. Or a witness."

"Nice try," Doctor Moore said with a faint smile, "but no." She took a deep breath as she turned and looked back through into the hall. "I'm afraid I must face this alone. I know that there is nothing here, not really, but ghost stories would not have endured for so long if they were not capable of seducing our minds."

"Have you been into the library yet?"

"The library?"

"That's where you felt something forty years ago, isn't it?" Jessie asked. "You said that a book flew off a shelf, and that then you felt a kind of presence."

"Indeed. And I *have* been in there, last night as it happens. I felt nothing, but I suppose tonight and especially tomorrow will be the real tests. I just think that..."

Her voice trailed off for a moment. She seemed drawn back into the past, as if she could only remain in the present for a moment at a time before her mind drifted back to her previous visit. When she finally blinked and looked around, she seemed a little dazed.

"What was it really like?" Jessie asked. "The presence you felt forty years ago, I mean. You described it, but I didn't quite understand."

"It was like..."

Again, Doctor Moore's voice trailed off.

"It was as if an immense form of evil and anger and malignancy had temporarily entered my body," she explained finally. "It's so hard to describe, but it felt as if I was briefly filled with all the rage that one might imagine inhabited the mind and body of Sarah Clarke. I felt her soul entering me and then expanding, spreading out as if it was trying to take control of me. I felt her arms filling my arms, her legs entering my legs as if putting on a pair of boots, and I felt her eyes opening behind my eyes, eyelashes and all. And then I heard, or rather I *felt*, the gasp of some other mind. A few seconds later, the sensation simply faded away to nothing."

"That must have been pretty intense," Jessie suggested.

"Intense?"

Doctor Moore chuckled.

"Intense is one way to describe it. What really struck me, though, was how specific it was. This was no vague idea, it was a real belief that the woman was inside me. It was certainly unlike anything else I have ever experienced in my life, which is why it was so difficult to ignore. But ignore it I did, and I left it out of my report entirely. To my eternal shame, I was confronted with something that I didn't understand, and I chose to turn away and pretend that it hadn't happened."

"Were you scared?"

"I -"

She hesitated.

"I suppose that I was," she continued, "yes. I hadn't allowed myself to think of it in that way, but yes, I *was* scared. I was scared and I ran away, and now forty years later I'm finally returning. Better late than never, I suppose." She looked down at her legs. "Not running this time, though. Look at me, decrepit and old. I can't even climb a set of stairs without assistance. Wretched arthritis."

"I don't mind helping," Jessie said. "Honestly."

"You're very kind to a mad old woman."

"It's okay, Doctor Moore. I'm still just very grateful that you let me come at all."

"I wouldn't really get very far by myself, would I?" Doctor Moore pointed out, and then she hesitated for a moment. "You said that you heard a knocking sound on the door during the night. Exactly what happened?"

"That's pretty much it. I heard it twice, though, and I'm not certain that it could have been caused by the wind. There's no chance that anyone else might be in the area, is there?"

"That would be very unlikely. The nearest town is many miles away, and I can't imagine that the local children stray this far. And the house shows no sign of having been vandalized in any way."

"It really *did* sound like laughter in the forest, though," Jessie added. "Right before I uncovered the skulls, I mean."

"Well, I suppose it's possible that some children were nearby," Doctor Moore admitted. "I certainly hope not. I'd hate to have our work interrupted by the local riff raff. As far as I'm aware, people have generally stayed away from Hardlocke House over the years. It's just been left to rot." She looked up at the higher windows. "Foolish superstitions can be so terribly difficult to dislodge."

"I..."

Jessie hesitated for a moment. She knew it was a bad idea to mention the dream, but she felt that Doctor Moore seemed to be in a much more approachable mood, and she wanted to be completely honest.

"I also had a dream," she said finally. "It was about Sarah Clarke, and about a little boy named Thomas. Sarah was trying to clean a wound on his knee, I can't remember exactly what had happened but he'd hurt himself somehow, and then she seemed to change in an instant. It was like she was sweet and caring one moment, and the next she was filled with this almost inhuman anger. I know it was *just* a dream, I have no doubts there, but it was pretty creepy. I think maybe it shows that I've let this place get into my head a little."

"And you met Sarah Clarke in this dream?" Doctor Moore asked.

"It was more like I was observing. Just as she changed, I woke up. It was almost like one of those stereotypical nightmares in films, to be honest. It stopped just when I got to the interesting bit." She paused. "Sorry," she added, "I shouldn't be wasting your time talking about stuff like this."

"It's not a waste of time," Doctor Moore replied. "I always like new information, and the fact that you've begun to dream about the house is definitely new information. It shows that you're paying attention, and your attitude to the dream shows that you're not getting caught up in foolish ideas." She paused again. "In fact, what you just told me sounds rather similar to something that I heard forty years ago, when I first came here. Lizzy

Malone in particular claimed to have been plagued by recurring nightmares about the house. She described them to me in great detail."

"But they weren't similar to mine, right?" Jessie asked.

She waited for a response, but Doctor Moore once again seemed lost in thought.

"Allow me to explain something," the older woman said finally. "Andy and Lizzy Malone were fraudsters, but I believe that at times they genuinely thought they were experiencing something at the house. Lizzy, in particular, struck me as someone who had begun to lose track of what was real and what was not. She, and to some extent her husband, were consumed by their own lies. Indeed, there were times when I thought Lizzy might be on the verge of a nervous breakdown..."

CHAPTER TWENTY-TWO

"YOU DON'T BELIEVE ME," Lizzy Malone said forty years earlier, with a hint of desperation in her voice, as she sat on a sofa in Hardlocke House's front room and put her head in her hands. "You think I'm a liar."

"I didn't say that," Diana replied, watching her from an armchair by the window.

"You didn't have to," Lizzy sighed. "I saw that look in your eyes. It's the same look I see in everyone's eyes when I talk about what's been happening here. Even Andy's sometimes." She appeared for a moment to be holding back tears. "Can you imagine what that's like?"

"Let's move on to -"

"Can you just imagine it for one second?" Lizzy snapped, betraying a growing sense of anger.

"Have you ever been ridiculed for knowing something that everyone else thinks isn't true?"

"I've posited theories that I've struggled to explain properly to people."

"But you managed, right?"

"In most cases. In one or two, I determined that it was I who had made the mistake."

"Now imagine how you'd feel if you know you were right, but you thought you could never make anyone else realize that. Imagine you'd seen these things with your own eyes, you'd heard them, you'd even felt something touching you in the night. Imagine you'd had dreams that allowed you to see what happened here at Hardlocke House all those years ago. Imagine the dead were reaching out to you. The little boys..."

Her voice trailed off for a moment.

"Imagine all of that," she added finally, "and still, you can't make anyone believe a damn word you're saying."

"Such a situation simply could not come to pass," Diana replied firmly. "If you're right about something, you'll always find a way to prove it. That's how the world works. And if you can't prove your claims, then it stands to reason that those claims must be false. If you're making extraordinary claims, Mrs. Malone, the burden is on you to produce the necessary proof."

Instead of answering her, Lizzy began to

look around the room. She seemed apprehensive, almost as if she expected to spot something at any moment, and her eyes – slightly reddened, and with dark rings – twitched slightly. Exhaustion had left her in a wired, frantic state.

"When did you last sleep?" Diana asked.

Lizzy turned back to her.

"When did you last sleep?" Diana asked again.

"I think it's been about three days now," Lizzy replied. "No, wait. Four. Four days. Every time I try, I just..." She paused, before leaning forward. "I hear things!"

***

"She's obviously suffering from some kind of delusion," Diana said a short while later, as she stood in the corridor with James, one of the documentary's producers. "The lack of sleep can't be helping, either. She might well be experiencing hallucinations by now. She's really not very intelligent, which -"

"Hey!" he hissed, grabbing her arm and pulling her a little further along the corridor, toward the main hall.

"What are you doing?" she replied, slipping free. "Unhand me!"

"I just didn't want her to overhear."

"Why not?"

"Because you were just calling her..." He paused, before shaking his head. "Never mind that. I get it, you don't have a very high opinion of them."

"Andy Malone has the confidence of a fool," Diana replied, "whereas Lizzy at least seems to have moments of doubt."

"She seems way more into it that her husband," he pointed out. "When he talks about the ghosts here, sometimes I can tell that he doesn't believe a word he's saying. With Lizzy it's different. I can see it in her eyes, I think she thinks she's telling the truth."

"That doesn't absolve her of responsibility," Diana pointed out. "She has allowed herself to reach this low state, and for that I pity her. The road to madness requires one to take many steps. It's only when those steps are added together that one starts to see the seriousness of what one has allowed to transpire."

"Your final comments in this documentary aren't going to be very favorable, are they?"

"These people are scum," she replied. "They're parasites, seeking to make money by scamming fools. If you ask me, what they're doing should be illegal, but I accept that they're being very careful to avoid doing anything that might be actionable. Worse than all that, however, is the fact that they're wasting our time here. They're wasting *my* time!"

"Can I ask you a favor?"

"You can ask me anything. I reserve the right to refuse."

"Can you try to be a little less harsh with her?" he continued. "When we're filming the final part of the documentary, I mean. I don't mind if you try to tear down her husband, the guy's an idiot, but I'm worried that our viewers might not like it so much if you're too mean to Lizzy. They might start to side with her."

"Nobody with even an ounce of intellect would side with that stupid girl."

"Nevertheless, let's just try to rein it in a little. We're here to investigate the claims these people are making, not to batter than into psychological submission and leave them completely wrecked. Believe me, there's only so much clever editing my team can pull off to hide your attacks on them."

"If the truth leaves them completely wrecked, as you so delicately put it," she replied, "then they should think long and hard about why that is the case." She paused for a moment to clear her throat. "Now, if you'll excuse me, I've had enough of that woman's pathetic claims for now. I'm going to go and take one last look at some of the other rooms in the house. And who knows? I might spot something spooky that completely changes my mind!"

Rolling her eyes, she turned and walked away. James hesitated, before hearing a faint sobbing sound coming from the front room. He made his way over to the door and looked through, and he saw that Lizzy was in tears.

"Sorry," she muttered, wiping her eyes, "I didn't mean to cause a scene."

"Don't worry about it," he replied, leaning against the jamb. "I guess Doctor Moore can be a little harsh at times, huh?"

"She thinks Andy and I are lying."

"I warned you that she's skeptical, but if you want your claims to be taken seriously, she's the kind of person you're going to have to convince. She's an expert in this field, and her validation would be a serious boost for your business."

"The problem is, she's right."

James furrowed his brow, and for a moment he wasn't sure whether or not he'd misheard.

"I'm sorry?"

"About Andy, I mean," she continued. "Andy doesn't believe me either, he always looks for a way to make money out of these things. He takes what I tell him and he exaggerates, so it's no wonder that people think we're a couple of con artists. Every time I try to tell him that I'm telling the truth, he just gets this look in his eyes, like he thinks we're about to make a fortune. I just wish we could drop the plans for this house, sell it, and move on with our lives."

"I thought the idea was to turn it into a little hotel where ghost-hunting couples could come and stay for a spooky weekend. That's what you're doing, isn't it?"

"I just want out," she told him, as she sniffed back more tears. "I don't ever want to hear the name Hardlocke House again."

"I think it's a little late for that now," he replied with a smile, as he checked his watch. "We have one more little interview to film, and then we'll be out of your hair. The documentary should air before the end of the year, and I'm sure you'll get a lot of business. That must take the edge off living in a haunted house, right?"

"You don't believe me either," she said bitterly.

"I'm just here to make a documentary," he said, holding his hands up in mock surrender. "I'm staying completely impartial in all of this. My job is to present the unvarnished truth to the great viewing public, and let them make up their own minds. And for what it's worth, I think you're gonna come out of this really well. You look good on TV, Lizzy, and that counts for a lot these days." He checked his watch again. "Now, if you'll excuse me, I have to go and make sure everything's set up for filming. We want your lighting to be just right, don't we?"

He winked at her, before hurrying out of the room, leaving her sitting alone.

"I don't want to do this!" she whispered, once again putting her head in her hands, and this time also starting to rock back and forth on the sofa. "I just want to get out of this house and never come back!"

CHAPTER TWENTY-THREE

"THERE'S NO GHOST HERE at Hardlocke House," Diana said a short while later, standing in the old office as the cameras rolled. She looked down scornfully for a moment at Andy and Lizzy as they sat beneath the portrait of Sarah Clarke. "It's nothing more than an old house with a lot of history."

"But I've seen her," Lizzy replied, clutching a tissue that she'd been using frequently to dab at her eyes. "I've seen something on the stairs, and in here too, and -"

"You've seen nothing," Diana said, interrupting her. "Shadows, at most, and your mind filled the rest in."

"That's not possible," Lizzy stammered. "Just because you haven't seen any of those things, that doesn't mean that *I* didn't. There are lots of reasons why she might not have appeared to you. For some reason she seems to be fixated on me. I don't know why."

"And did you ever see the face of this supposed ghost?" Diana asked, clearly unimpressed.

"No. I mean, once, but that was -"

"It was all in your mind," Diana said firmly. "The sooner you accept that and begin to look for a way to fix your damaged thought process, the better."

"It's okay," Andy said, putting an arm around his wife and pulling her close. "Don't let her get to you."

"You asked me to come here and give you my honest opinion," Diana continued, "and that is exactly what I have done. I have applied my usual principles to this situation and I've come up with what I consider to be a very clear-headed account of what's happening here. If you expected to pull the wool over my eyes, you have very much failed."

"You can't expect to come in here for three days and understand this place," Andy replied, clearly angry as his wife began to sob uncontrollably. "You think you're so special with your theories and your science, but that's no substitute for the experience we've been living every day since we moved into Hardlocke House. I'm sorry, Doctor Moore, but you're wrong. I just wish you could open your eyes and see the truth."

Diana turned and smiled at the camera for a moment, and then she looked at James as he waited a little further back.

"We're done with this particular investigation," she told him, as Lizzy continued to cry. "Shall we wrap things up and get out of here?"

***

"I have to include Doctor Moore's closing comments," James said as he sat with the Malones once filming was over. "The documentary wouldn't be complete without them, and people would totally be asking questions about why they weren't included. But you don't have to look at this as the end. There are plenty of people out there who'll still really want to come and see Hardlocke House for themselves."

"What if we refuse?" Andy asked.

"I don't know what you -"

"What if we don't let you broadcast your little so-called documentary?"

"You can't stop us."

"We can withdraw our permission."

"Not according to the contracts you signed," James pointed out. "Not unless you're willing to pay the fee that the contract specifies."

"And how much is that fee?" Andy snapped.

"One million pounds. To cover the full cost of our time here."

"How the hell could you possibly have spent a million pounds on this thing?"

"It's all in the contract."

"You people are jackals," Andy replied, before letting go of Lizzy and moving across the sofa until he was directly opposite James. "I know how this works," he continued, lowering his voice. "What's it going to take for you to focus on the more favorable footage when you put this documentary together? What'll it take for you to cut that bitch out completely, or at least for most of the run-time?" He leaned closer. "I can offer you one hundred pounds, cash, if you help us out. Do you get where I'm coming from here?"

"Mr. Malone..."

"This isn't bloody *Panorama*! It's not life or death!"

"The documentary will go out before the end of the year," James said, choosing his words with care, "and all I can promise you is that we'll take a fair look at both sides of the argument. Personally, I think you're underestimating the British public's appetite for ghost stories. Even the slightest hint of something at Hardlocke House should get them flocking here. Remember, all publicity is good publicity. Or something like that."

"Maybe we should just forget about it,"

Lizzy whimpered.

"Do you see what you've done?" Andy asked, glaring at James. "You've broken my wife's spirit! You've broken her heart!"

"I should leave you two to talk," James replied, turning and heading to the door. He took a cigarette from his pocket as he went.

"You're crushing our dreams!" Andy hissed.

"Dreams of turning a rundown old house into some kind of theme park?" James asked, stopping and looking back at him. He heard a heavy thud from one of the other rooms, but he paid no attention as he lit his cigarette and took a drag. "I think you two should be happy with what you've already got from this process, and you should relax for a few months until the documentary actually goes out. Then I think you'll probably be pleasantly surprised by how it all shakes out. Trust me on this, I'm a professional and -"

Before he could finish, he heard footsteps hurrying along the corridor, and he turned just in time to see that Diana was heading toward the front door.

"Doctor Moore," he said with a smile, "I was just telling these people that we -"

"It's time to go!" she snapped, clearly flustered as she stormed out of the house. "We've wasted enough time here! I want to leave! Now!"

James opened his mouth to ask her whether

anything was wrong, but he thought better of it at the last moment. He'd learned to avoid anything that Diana Moore might consider to be a dumb question, and he was quite glad to be almost finished with the project. All he had to do was drop her off at the train station and then she'd be out of his hair. Until the next documentary rolled around, at least.

"You heard the lady," he said, turning back to look at the Malones.

Lizzy was still quietly sobbing, while Andy was sitting on the other end of the sofa with his head in his hands.

"We'll show ourselves out," James added, wandering through the open front door and then down the steps.

The TV crew was all packed up and ready to go, and Diana Moore was waiting in the passenger seat of James' car. After exchanging a few words with one of the cameramen, James took a moment to finish his cigarette and then he climbed into the car and fished the keys from his pocket.

"You know the worst thing?" he muttered. "Those two idiots in there are probably gonna clean up with this place. There's never a shortage of people who'll put down cold hard cash for a chance to -"

"Can we please just get out of here?" Diana snapped angrily.

James turned to her.

"Are you okay?" he asked.

"Clearly not! I want to get to the station!"

"You seem -"

"Shut up, man!" she snarled. She looked at the house for a moment, with fear in her eyes, before turning to him again. "Why are you sitting there gormlessly staring at me, when we could be halfway to the station by now? Do I have to walk?"

"No, of course not," he replied, startled by her outburst as he started the engine. "Okay, let's hit the road and leave Hardlocke House in the dust. I bet you won't be in a hurry to ever come back here, huh?"

Diana failed to reply as the car set off. She watched in the rear-view mirror as the house receded into the distance, and she felt a sliver of relief once the place was out of sight. Still, she couldn't shake a heavy sense of dread in her chest as she replayed one particular moment over and over in her mind. She felt as if her very core had been shaken, as if her strongest beliefs had been challenged, although she was determined to hide that fact from anyone. As she tried to work out how she was going to include that final moment in her report, she began to realize that her hands were trembling. All she wanted was to get back to her office and try to find some way of reconciling her experience with the core beliefs that underlined every aspect of her work.

More than anything, she wished that she'd never set foot in Hardlocke House in the first place.

"Hey," James said after a moment, as he noticed a cut on Diana's chin. "Are you okay? You're bleeding."

***

As Lizzy continued to sob in the office, and Andy paced back and forth while explaining to her that everything was going to be alright, the rest of the house stood in calm, stoic silence.

In the library, a single green book lay on the floor.

CHAPTER TWENTY-FOUR

TWELVE HOURS LATER, AS Hardlocke House stood in darkness and silence, and as Andy slept soundly, Lizzy Malone lay next to him and stared up at the ceiling.

Moonlight was casting the shadow of treetops into the room, and a light breeze ensured that those shadows were swaying slightly. Lizzy found the movement somewhat calming, although her mind was still racing and she couldn't help but think back to Doctor Moore's withering speech. When the documentary crew had first arrived, Lizzy had been convinced that they would help, that they'd find proof of what she'd been claiming for so long. Now that the crew had left, she felt helpless and hopeless, and she was beginning to worry that even Andy failed to understand the true nature of whatever they were facing in the house.

Suddenly, hearing a distant creaking sound coming from somewhere downstairs, Lizzy sat up and looked over at the open door. There was no sign of anyone out on the landing, but after a few seconds she heard the sound again.

"Andy," she whispered, reaching over and nudging him. "I heard something downstairs. Wake up!"

"Go back to sleep," he murmured, before rolling over to face the other way.

"I heard something!" she hissed, but she knew she was never going to get his attention. She'd learned that Andy saw Hardlocke House as very much a nine to five kind of job. When he was off the clock, he had no interest.

She sat for a few more minutes, and then she began to climb out of bed. She knew she should just try to get to sleep, but at the same time she realized there was no chance of rest. Her mind was alert and she felt that she just had to go and make sure that there was no sign of anything untoward in the house. Even as she crept barefoot across the cold bedroom, she was starting to feel a knot of fear in her belly, and that knot only tightened as she stepped out onto the landing and saw the grand old staircase descending to the house's lower floor. She made her way to the top of the stairs and looked down to the hall, and then she glanced over her shoulder to make sure that there was nothing nearby.

All around her, the silence of the house seemed to be waiting for something to happen. It was as if the house knew a secret.

A moment later Lizzy heard a scuffing sound, and she instantly turned and looked down at the front door. Something was out there, rubbing against the door's other side, and Lizzy immediately knew that she'd have to go down and take a look. Andy would never get out of bed for something so vague, and she couldn't possibly just ignore what she'd heard. She hated the fact that she always felt drawn to see what was causing any particular noise, but sure enough she began to make her way slowly down the stairs as the sound continued.

It's just the wind, she told herself.

As she reached the bottom of the stairs, the sound stopped, but she knew that couldn't be the end of it. The house had never left her alone so easily before.

Stepping over to the door, she reached out and touched the handle. She told herself that there would be nothing on the other side, but she still worried that the house had another surprise in store. One thing she'd never told Andy – or anyone, including the documentary team – was that sometimes she felt as if the house was teasing her, as if it possessed some malevolent spirit that was targeting her and her alone. No matter how hard she tried to ignore that sense, over the previous few months she'd become more and more sure that something within Hardlocke House was toying with her. How else to explain the fact that Andy still saw the whole project as a business opportunity rather than a genuine nightmare? And how else to explain the fact that the presence within the house had failed to show itself to Doctor Diana Moore?

Opening the door slowly, Lizzy couldn't help but feel as if the house was mocking her.

Suddenly a dark shape rushed at her, and she felt something heavy hit her in the chest and push her to the ground. Startled, she let out a brief cry, and then she froze as she saw that a large dog was standing on her chest. For a few seconds she had no idea how to react, and she could only stare as the dog looked around the hallway. And then, as quickly as it had arrived, the dog turned and limped back out of the house.

Sitting up, Lizzy watched as the dog made its way down the steps and across the clearing. One of the animal's hind legs seemed to be lame, and she felt a flicker of sympathy for the poor thing as it made its way toward the forest and finally disappeared between the trees.

"Lizzy?"

Turning, she saw that Andy was standing at the top of the stairs, rubbing his eyes.

"I heard a noise," he muttered, sounding slightly irritated. "What's going on down here?"

***

"We're in way too deep to pull out now," he said as they sat in the office. "We'd never get back the money we paid for the place, and we'd be losing the opportunity of a lifetime. Come on, Lizzy, be serious for a minute. We have to see this through."

"I saw -"

"A dog, sure," he added, interrupting her yet again. "You keep saying that, but I've not seen any evidence of a dog out here tonight. There's no dog poo out there, I haven't heard anything barking, there's just no sign of anything having come to the house at all. Where would one even have come *from*?"

"I don't know," she replied, "but it seemed to be looking for something."

"Looking for something?" he replied incredulously. "And you know that how, exactly? Did it ask you?"

"Andy..."

"Did it get out a magnifying glass and start peering into the cracks between the floorboards?"

"You're not taking me seriously," she muttered, as she took a deep breath and tried to stay calm. "You never take me seriously."

"Not when you start talking about ghost dogs turning up in the middle of the night," he said with a heavy sigh. "I mean, you really have to listen to yourself. Can't you hear your own voice when you're telling me all these things? You sound like someone who's losing their marbles."

"I think maybe I am," she whispered. "This house is driving me crazy."

"You don't really think that."

"Or something *in* the house," she continued. "Some kind of presence. It hates me, Andy. I can feel it, it's all around and it seems to come closer whenever I'm alone."

He let out a heavy sigh, one that was clearly intended to demonstrate the fact that he was tired of the conversation.

"I think it's trying to make me look like a fool," she told him. "I know that sounds nuts, but just listen for a moment. This thing targets me when nobody's around, and then it retreats as soon as anyone else comes along who might see what it's doing. That can't be a coincidence!"

"You make it sound like you actually believe there's a -"

He caught himself just in time.

"Go on," she said firmly.

"Forget it."

"That's the truth, isn't it?" she asked. "You don't believe there's anything here and you never did. Despite everything you said to that film crew over the weekend, at the end of the day you simply don't believe in ghosts."

"You're putting words into my mouth."

"You think this is all going to be fun and games," she replied, "but you're not the one who's being driven out of their mind by the house. I don't think I can stand being here for much longer, Andy." She reached out and took hold of his hand. "I'm begging you. Let's just cut our losses and get away from this place. I know it won't be easy, but we can find a way. As long as we're together and we've got each other, we can do anything!"

"There's no way we're giving up on this house!" he said firmly.

"What if it's the only thing that can save me? Andy, I don't know that I can last much longer here."

She squeezed his hand tighter.

"Please?" she added.

"This might be our last chance," he replied. "To make something of ourselves, I mean. This might be our last chance to become rich."

"I'm begging you," she continued, with tears in her eyes. "Let's just get away from Hardlocke House. Let's leave while we still have the chance."

CHAPTER TWENTY-FIVE

"TO HIS CREDIT," Diana said, "when the documentary went out, James Murphy made sure to emphasize my findings. He showed that the Malones were nothing more than a pair of fraudsters."

"So you think it was all just a cynical ploy from the beginning?" Jessie asked. "They didn't ever believe any of the things they claimed?"

"*She* might have done. Maybe. It's all academic now. They're long gone."

"I just can't believe that they really thought they could turn Hardlocke House into some kind of tourist attraction," Jessie replied, looking up at the front of the house again. "They must have been totally deluded."

"And now," Diana said, "if you don't mind, I think it's time for me to go back inside and prepare for the second night. I have enough wood and I can start the fire myself. Shall we meet on these steps again at sunrise tomorrow?"

"Sure," Jessie said. "And thank you, Doctor Moore. I won't let you down."

"I know you won't," she replied as she wheeled herself back inside. "Oh, and please, call me Diana again."

***

"I'm sorry, Mum, I really can't hear you very well. You're breaking up. Can we try again tomorrow?"

Sitting on the steps at the foot of the altar, in the flickering light of the candle, Jessie listened as her mother's voice crackled from the phone. The signal was pretty atrocious, and she'd barely been able to make out a word, although she was fairly sure that her mother was able to hear her properly. The problem seemed to be strictly one-way.

"I'm going to go now," she continued. "Everything's fine here. I'm going to get some sleep and then tomorrow's our last full day at the house. I miss you, and Dad too. I'll see you both on Monday."

She listened again, but if anything the static was getting worse.

"Okay," she added finally, feeling a little sad that she wasn't going to be able to talk to her mother properly. "I love you. Goodnight."

She waited, just in case the signal improved, and then she cut the call before switching the phone off. Sitting with her sleeping bag draped over her shoulders, she was struggling not to shiver, but she figured that she's survived one night in the cold little chapel so a second shouldn't be too difficult. The hardest part, she assumed, would be getting to sleep in the first place. And then, she realized, she might end up having another of those crazy dreams about the history of the house.

She felt as if the past and present were somehow blurred together at Hardlocke House.

***

"Now, children," Sarah Clarke said, standing in front of the altar and looking out at the twelve boys who were sitting on the various pews in the chapel, "I want to talk to you today about the importance of faith. Do you know what faith is?"

She waited, but the boys all remained silent.

"Faith is an absolute belief in the Lord," she

continued, "based on a conviction that you feel in your heart. It's not something that can be faked, it's something that must be as much a part of you as your very soul. Now, I want you to be honest. Put your hand up, any of you, if you believe that you have faith in the Lord. I'm talking about true faith here. The kind of faith that permits not one scintilla of doubt."

At first, the boys all sat still. They glanced nervously at one another, and then three of them slowly began to raise their hands at once. The other boys quickly followed suit, until twelve shaking hands were raised high – and somewhat unconvincingly – in the chapel.

"That's commendable," Sarah replied, "but it's also what I expected. I can't help wondering whether some of you are merely doing this because you believe it to be the right answer."

She turned to take a book from the altar.

"*My* faith," she continued, "is -"

Stopping suddenly, she stared down at the book with a panicked expression, as if some inner trauma had compelled her to fall silent. Her eyes twitched slightly as a hint of darkness spread like clouds around the pupils. She blinked a couple of times, trying to clear her thoughts, but if anything she could feel herself sinking deeper into a kind of daze.

"My faith," she stammered, barely able to get the words out, "has been with me since... I was a... young..."

Again, her voice trailed off.

The boys began to lower their hands, although they could all tell that something seemed to be wrong. They looked at one another, until finally – having seen something similar happen to their teacher before – they all carefully stood up and tried to creep toward the door. Each boy knew the importance of remaining quiet, and they could also hear the sound of Ms. Clarke's teeth chattering as she remained at the altar.

Just as he got close to the door, Edmund bumped against one of the pews. He instantly froze, gripped by fear.

"And where," Sarah sneered, slowly turning to look at the boys, revealing her jet black eyes, "do you think you're going?"

Eleven of the boys rushed back to their seats, but Edmund – who had been the furthest forward, and who felt pinned to the spot by Ms. Clarke's gaze – found that he couldn't move at all. He was too terrified to join the others on the pews, and all he could do was stare back at his teacher as a broad smile began to spread across her lips.

"Oh, Edmund," she said finally, making her way down the steps and starting to walk along the aisle, "what's wrong? You look absolutely terrified of me."

She reached out to either side and let her fingertips drag along the tops of the pews, tapping each one as she passed the other boys. The sound seemed so loud in the hushed room.

Edmund, meanwhile, finally managed to move, but only to step back until he was standing against the door. He was starting to tremble with fear, and as Ms. Clarke moved closer and closer the boy felt the panic twisting tighter in his chest. A moment later, a wet patch began to spread across the front of his trousers.

"Oh, now that *is* unfortunate," Sarah said, stopping next to the last pew and shaking her head. "Edmund, what are we going to do with you? You can't go on like this, you're always the meekest boy and that's no way to prepare for your adult life. Something simply has to change."

She paused, before stepping closer and reaching out with her right hand. Her skin was paler than before, and the skin on her fingers seemed to have retreated slightly, clinging tight to the bones. Her nails, meanwhile, were long and sharp, and their usual whiteness had changed to become yellow and rotten.

"Edmund," she purred, reaching for the boy's face, "you -"

Suddenly she pulled back and tripped, dropping to her knees, and she quickly put her hands over her face.

"Run!" she gasped.

All the boys remained completely still.

"I told you to run!" she screamed, grabbing one of the pews in a desperate attempt to stay upright. "Get back to the house and wait for me there! Go!"

A couple of the boys got to their feet and hurried past her, taking care to keep well away, and then the rest followed. Once the door was open, they all rushed outside, even Edmund. Thomas was the last to go, and he stopped in the doorway and turned to look back as Ms. Clarke bent down with her hands still covering her face. Black liquid was dribbling from between her fingers and splattering against the floor.

"Go!" she gurgled, lowering her hands and looking straight at Thomas. Black tears were flowing from her eyes now, running freely down her face, and more dark liquid was erupting from her mouth. "Go!" she tried to say again, although she could barely get the word out. "Get away from me!"

Thomas grabbed the door and pulled it shut, and then his footsteps could be heard running away from the chapel.

"You shouldn't have done that," Sarah groaned, leaning down until her forehead bumped against the floor. Her face twisted to become an angry sneer. "That little fool deserved to be punished. How are you ever going to raise these children and prepare them for the world, when you keep being so soft with them? All you need is one, don't you understand? One of them is enough!"

She rolled onto her side and began sobbing uncontrollably.

"Why are you doing this to me?" she gasped, as more black tears ran from her eyes. "I never did anything to you!"

Her face twitched suddenly.

"You came here!" she snarled. "You came to my home!"

She rolled onto her back and looked up toward the ceiling.

"Dear Lord," she said, her voice trembling with fear, "guide me and protect me, and deliver me from the evil that has fallen upon me. If I am not strong enough to shake it off, then I beg you to bind me to you, Lord, and make sure that the children are saved. I do not matter, only the children are important. You must save them and -"

A sudden burst of pain shook her body. Letting out an anguished gasp, she arched her back and dug her fingernails into the floor, and a moment later she fell into an uncontrollable fit of laughter.

"You think you're going to be saved?" she shouted, as more and more black liquid gushed from her mouth, running down the sides of her face. "You clearly haven't been paying attention! You've been abandoned, and now you're going to pay the price, and one of your pathetic little children is finally going to give me what I want!"

***

A few minutes later, the chapel's door creaked open. Sarah Clarke stepped out into the doorway. Her eyes were back to normal, and most of the black liquid had been wiped away, leaving only a few smears on her cheeks.

She smiled as she saw the children loitering in the forest. Having ignored the instruction to go back to the house, they were instead waiting to see whether their teacher's latest bout of madness had passed.

"Hello, children," Sarah said calmly, with a faint smile. "I must apologize for the disruption.

Please, won't you come back inside so that I can finish today's lesson?"

She turned and headed back into the chapel.

The boys looked at one another, and then slowly they began to make their way toward the door.

CHAPTER TWENTY-SIX

"WAIT, STOP!" JESSIE GASPED, suddenly sitting up in the cold, dark chapel. Her mind was racing and her heart was pounding, but the dream was already starting to slip from her mind.

Leaning forward, still wrapped in her sleeping bag, she put her head in her hands and felt that her hair was matted with sweat. This dream had somehow felt more real than the first, and it had seemed longer too. She'd seen Sarah Clarke and the orphans in the chapel in the daytime, and Sarah had momentarily seemed to become possessed by some kind of evil. And then, as she wiped some more sweat from her face, Jessie realized that a noise had woken her from this latest nightmare.

She looked around in the darkness. She could see the empty pews, and for a moment she thought back to the boys sitting in those pews in her dream. They'd looked so terrified, and with good reason; Sarah Clarke had seemingly switched to become some kind of cruel monster. Glancing down at the floor, Jessie remembered the sight of the woman writhing in pain as her eyes turned black. No matter how much she tried to focus on the fact that it had all been just a nightmare, she still couldn't quite shake a sense of unease.

Suddenly she heard a loud bump on the door, as if somebody was knocking again from outside.

Still in darkness, she looked straight ahead. There was just enough light for her to be able to make out the door, and she was trying hard to persuade herself that the knocking sound had been caused by the wind. She already knew that was doubtful, however, so she slowly got to her feet and stepped out of the sleeping bag. Taking her flashlight from the steps, she began to make her way along the aisle, while listening out for any hint that there was someone on the other side of the door.

Stopping once she was past the last pew, she realized she'd been inadvertently holding her breath. She switched the flashlight on, and then she reached out to grab the handle and open the door.

She gasped and stepped back as the knocking returned, and this time she saw that the door was shaking a little in its frame. The knocking seemed firmer than before, although once again it seemed to be coming from fairly low down. As quickly as it had resumed, the sound stopped again, and Jessie immediately regretted having not already opened the door.

She watched the handle and told herself that if the sound returned, she'd be brave and force herself to see what was on the other side. If there was anything there at all, she wouldn't give it time to get away.

She waited.

All she could hear now was the sound of her own breath.

After a moment, she began to wonder whether she might still be dreaming. She was pretty sure that wasn't the case, however, and as her hand hovered next to the door handle she reminded herself that she had to stay calm. She checked her watch and saw that it was almost 3am, and she tried to focus on the fact that she was part of a proper scientific study. There was no -

The knocking sound returned, louder still, an in an instant Jessie pulled the door open.

Startled, she watched as a young boy raced away into the forest.

"Hey!" she yelled, stumbling out of the chapel. "Wait!"

The boy kept running, so Jessie hurried after

him. Her feet were bare, but she tried to ignore the sharp, wet sensation of running across the forest floor. She could just about make out the boy in the distance, and after a moment he stopped to look back at her. Bumping against one of the trees, Jessie also stopped for a moment to get her breath back. The boy, silhouetted against a patch of moonlight up ahead, simply stood and stared at her, and Jessie realized that he could be no more than ten or eleven years old.

"I just want to talk to you!" she called out, as she started walking cautiously toward him, ducking to avoid a few low-hanging branches. "You're not in any trouble, okay? I just..."

Her voice trailed off as she stopped and saw that the boy wasn't alone. Another boy was standing a little further back, and she turned to see several more all around her. They were a fair way off, but as she began to count them she somehow already knew how many there were.

"Twelve," she whispered, and a shiver ran through her bones as she looked back at the first boy, the one who'd knocked on the door.

For a moment, she actually considered the possibility that she was looking at a ghost. She tried to remind herself that there was no such thing, but as she took a couple of steps forward she couldn't help but notice that the boy's features remained lost in the darkness.

"My name's Jessie," she continued. "Jessie Banks. Can I talk to you for a minute? I really just want to know who you are and what you're doing here. I don't know this place too well, but if you do, you might be able to help me out with a few things. If I come closer, do you promise not to run away again?"

She waited for an answer, and then she took a few more steps toward the boy. He was now only about twenty feet away, and when she glanced around she saw that the other boys were roughly the same distance. She turned to look at the first boy again, and she squinted in an attempt to get a better look at his face. With each step forward, she figured she should be able to see him better soon, and finally she was just about able to make out two eyes and a nose and a mouth, although something about the eyes seemed -

Suddenly the boy turned and ran again.

"No!" Jessie shouted.

Hearing a rustling sound, she saw that all the boys were going with him. She set off after them, although she let out a gasp of pain as she felt a sharp twig cutting into her foot. She hobbled on for a few more paces before leaning against a tree and taking a moment to check her foot; as soon as she saw the sole of her right foot, she winced at the sight of part of a twig poking out from a small wound. She reached down and pulled the twig out, and then she started limping forward, desperately hoping to catch up to the boys.

Reaching a small clearing, however, she looked around and realized that there was now no sign of anyone. The boys were gone.

"Hello?" she called out. "Please, can you just listen to me for a moment? I want to ask you some questions. You're not in trouble. I couldn't get you in trouble even if I wanted to, okay? I'm not in charge of anything. I just want to know what's going on out here."

She listened for any hint of a response.

"Did you want something from me?" she asked. "Did you knock on the door for a reason? If you did, you're going to have to tell me what it is, because I can't figure it out."

She waited, but as she looked around there was still no sign of anyone. Taking a couple of steps back, she bumped against a tree and then turned again. She was still hoping to spot one of the boys in the distance, although that hope was starting to fade now.

"My name's Jessie," she continued, "and..."

Her voice trailed off as she realized there was no hope left. As she continued to look all around, she was starting to worry that she didn't actually know how to get back to the house. Stopping, she took a moment to try to figure out which way she'd come. Feeling a little disorientated, she took a few stumbling, limping steps in one direction before stopping again as she realized that something felt very wrong. She looked all around again, before trying another direction and stopping yet again.

"Damn it," she muttered, before turning to go the other way. "What -"

Suddenly she found one of the boys standing right behind her. Shocked, she looked down at his face and saw two dead eyes staring up at her. She instinctively took a step away, at which point she let out a cry as her foot slipped and she tumbled back, crashing down a steep, leaf-covered slope that she hadn't even noticed before. She tried to stop herself, but she was too late; slamming hard into a tree stump at the bottom, she was instantly knocked unconscious.

AMY CROSS

CHAPTER TWENTY-SEVEN

STOPPING AT THE END of the corridor, at the foot of Hardlocke House's main staircase, ten-year-old Nathaniel Edwards realized he could hear a faint sniffling sound coming from one of the nearby rooms. He hesitated, wondering whether he should just go up to his room, but then he made his way around to the other side of the hall and peered through into one of the small side rooms.

He immediately pulled back as he saw Ms. Clarke sitting by the window, dabbing at her face with a handkerchief.

"Who's there?" she asked. "Who is it?"

Nathaniel froze for a moment, before turning and heading back to the staircase.

"Nathaniel."

He froze again, convinced that he was in the

most terrible trouble.

"It's okay, Nathaniel," Ms. Clarke said, stepping up behind him and putting a hand on his shoulder, "I -"

Flinching, he turned and pulled away from her. In that moment, he tripped against the bottom step and fell down. He let out a cry of pain as he bumped against the step, and then he looked up at Ms. Clarke and saw her staring down at him with an expression of bemusement.

"You're scared of me," she said after a moment, shocked by his reaction. "You're truly terrified."

"No," he stammered. "I'm not."

"Your poor boy," she continued, wiping a stray tear from her face before reaching a hand toward him, "you must be so -"

Scrambling away, terrified of her touch, he crawled all the way to the far wall. He kept his eyes on her the whole time, in case she lunged at him.

"Please, Ms. Clarke," he said, "I was only going upstairs to pray. I wasn't doing anything wrong, I promise!"

"I never thought that you might be," she replied, furrowing her brow. "You're one of my better behaved pupils, Nathaniel, aren't you? I promise you that you have nothing to fear from me. You're very good with your studies, and I'm exceedingly pleased with your progress. Please, carry on as you were."

She waited, but the boy seemed too scared to move a muscle.

"Nathaniel," she added. "Honestly. Please. Go."

Nathaniel hesitated, before stumbling to his feet and rushing up the stairs.

"There's no need to run!" Ms. Clarke called out to him, but the boy was already out of sight and a moment later she heard him slamming a door shut. "There's no need to be so loud, either."

Sighing, she turned to go back into the other room, but then she stopped as she heard whispering voices. She made her way along the nearest corridor, and she stopped as she saw that three of the boys – Edmund Bachelor, William Warton and William Merriman – were sitting at a desk in one of the classrooms. As soon as they realized they were being overheard, the boys turned to look at Ms. Clarke, and they fell silent.

"Please," she said, forcing a smile before wiping away another tear, "go on. What are you doing in here, anyway?"

"Nothing," the three boys replied at once.

"You too are so scared of me," she continued, struggling to hold back more tears. "That is so sad. When I set this school up, I never for one second intended to become a figure of such fear."

She waited, but the boys were all staring at

her with terrified expressions.

"Please tell me what you were doing before I came in," she said, heading into the room and approaching the desk. "It would gladden my heart to see you at play."

"We weren't doing anything bad," Edmund told her.

"The thought never crossed my mind. I merely came upon the three of you and noticed that you seemed to be conspiring on some great scheme. Tell me, what frolics are you planning to get up to?"

"Nothing, Ms. Clarke," William Warton said timidly. "We weren't doing anything, we promise. We were just sitting here and, well..."

He tried to think of something.

"We were just talking," he continued, "about... the trees."

"The trees?" she replied.

"And how old they are," he said, "and how tall they grow, and how scary they look sometimes when all their leaves have fallen off. That's what we were talking about!"

"Are you sure?" She paused. "I won't be angry. Unless it's something naughty, but I'm sure it's not that."

"It's not," William Merriman said quickly. "We swear!"

"So you don't want to tell me," she replied. "I understand. I suppose I shall just leave you to it.

You're all old enough by now to determine on your own whether or not you are doing the right thing. I have taught you well enough for that." She turned and walked back out into the corridor, and then she glanced at them again. "Remember, boys," she added, "that even though I might not be in the room, the Lord hears you at all times."

She waited for a response, before walking away. As soon as she'd taken her first step, she heard the boys starting to frantically whisper once again, but she forced herself to keep going. The last thing she wanted was to go against the spirit of her parting words, and she trusted her boys enough to feel certain that they would not do anything bad.

Reaching one of the other rooms, she stopped in front of a mirror and looked at her reflection. She leaned closer and examined her eyes, watching for any trace of darkness. Touching her cheek, she pulled her right eyelid down so that she could carry out a closer inspection. Everything seemed normal, but deep down she knew that at any moment the hellish darkness might return.

***

"We all saw it," William Merriman whispered to the others, as they sat in the classroom following Ms. Clarke's departure. "What happened in the chapel wasn't right."

"Ms. Clarke's our teacher," William Warton replied, close to tears. "She knows everything."

"There's something wrong with her," Merriman said firmly. "Everyone knows it. The chapel wasn't even the first time. Whenever her eyes go black, and her skin goes really white, it's like she's someone else. Someone mean."

"There's nothing we can do about it," Edmund told him. "Ms. Clarke's in charge."

"I don't think anyone else knows what's happening here," Merriman replied. "If they did, they wouldn't leave us in such an awful place."

"You don't know that," Edmund pointed out.

"They wouldn't leave us with someone like her," Merriman continued. "I've never seen anyone else ever change the way that she does. I don't think it's natural."

"What are you saying?" Warton asked. "Do you think she's a witch?"

"Witches are supposed to know what they're doing," Merriman said. "When people talk about witches, they make them seem clever. I don't think Ms. Clarke really knows what's happening to her. Haven't you seen her face when she goes back to normal? She seems shocked."

"If she's not a witch," Warton said, "then what *is* she?"

"I don't know," Merriman told him, "but what matters is that we're stuck here alone with her.

It's almost as if she becomes possessed by something else. Haven't you noticed how no-one ever comes to visit? We get all our water from the well, and our food from the garden and from the traps in the forest. No-one comes unless they're bringing a new boy, and that hasn't happened for a while. I don't think anyone's going to come and save us."

"The Lord will save us," Edmund suggested.

"Do you really believe that?" Merriman asked.

"Yes," Edmund replied, before thinking for a moment. "I think. Ms. Clarke says so, and she wouldn't lie to us, would she?"

He paused.

"*Would* she?" he added cautiously.

"Ms. Clarke might not really know," Merriman said. "She might not be herself. I don't know what I mean by that, but as three of the oldest boys here we have to look after the others. It's our duty."

"I don't want to do anything that might upset Ms. Clarke," Edmund said. "She gets scary when she's angry."

"She gets scary anyway," Merriman pointed out. "She's getting worse, too. Those changes, whatever they are, are happening more often, and I don't think she can control them. Sooner or later she's going to do something really bad. Haven't you noticed that sometimes she talks to herself?"

"I heard it the other day," Warton said. "She was in her office and she was whispering under her breath. She stopped as soon as she knew I was there, but she seemed a bit startled. Like she was worried I might have noticed."

"But she's our teacher," Edmund whined, with tears in his eyes. "She's in charge."

"That's just my point," Merriman replied, "I don't think she is. Not anymore."

"Then who is?" Edmund asked.

"That part I don't know," Merriman continued. "Whatever's *in* her is in charge. Whatever that thing is that comes out sometimes. And that's the thing that we have to get away from."

"What are you suggesting?" Warton asked.

"I've got an idea," Merriman said, "but if it's going to work, I need both of you on my side."

CHAPTER TWENTY-EIGHT

ROLLING ONTO HER BACK, Jessie let out a gasp as she saw the blinding gray-white sky above. The tops of a few trees swayed briefly into her view, and she blinked a couple of times as she began to remember the events of the previous night.

Sitting up, she winced as she felt a sharp pain on the right side of her forehead. She touched the sore spot and immediately winced again, and then she spotted the tree stump that had caused the bump in the first place. Turning, she looked back up the slope, and it was at that moment that she remembered the dead-eyed stare of the little boy who'd suddenly been standing right behind her.

Suddenly, hearing a rustling sound, she turned just in time to see a dog in the distance. The animal stared back at her for a moment, before turning and limping away.

"Hey!" Jessie called out, but the dog was already gone.

Still, at least she knew now that there was *some* life in the forest.

She looked around, but to her relief that was no sign of anyone. The sun was up, and as she got to her feet she realized that she'd have to somehow find her way back to the house. She tried to figure out which way was which, and which way she'd have to go in order to find Hardlocke House, but in truth she had no idea. A moment later, however, she heard a voice in the distance.

"Jessica!" Diana was calling out. "Where are you?"

***

"Oh my word," Diana said, sitting in her wheelchair at the top of the steps and watching as Jessie limped around the corner, "you look absolutely dreadful! What happened to you?"

"Long story," Jessie said, stopping and looking up at her. "I saw a dog in the forest, so there's that. On a scale of one to ten, how bad is the bruise on my forehead?"

"Well..." Diana paused for a moment. "Seven?"

Reaching up, she touched the affected area

again, and again she winced.

"Goddamn tree," she muttered. "I suppose I'm lucky it wasn't worse. I could have completely brained myself on the thing."

"Whatever has been going on?" Diana asked. "You look like you've been dragged backward through several bushes!"

Jessie opened her mouth to explain, but she hesitated for a moment as she realized how crazy the story would sound. She'd already pissed Diana off once with her strange claims, and she really didn't want the same thing to happen again.

"It's okay," Diana said. "Just tell me."

"I went out into the forest at around three in the morning," Jessie explained cautiously, even though she was still worried. "I thought..." She paused as she tried to figure out how she was going to tell the story, and finally she decided that she should just be honest. "I heard another knock on the door during the night," she continued, "and when I opened the door, I saw a little boy. He ran away. He might not really have been there, but that's what I saw."

"Okay," Diana said cautiously. "Go on."

"I followed him, and then I saw more of them. Twelve in total. I tried to talk to them, but they kept running off. Every time I got close, they raced away again. I thought I'd lost them at one point, but then one showed up right behind me. I tripped and fell, and I hit my head and I guess I was unconscious out there for a few hours. I woke up just now and heard you calling my name."

"I see," Diana replied. "That certainly sounds like a rather traumatic experience."

"It wasn't fun," Jessie admitted. "I'm not claiming for one second that I actually saw the ghosts of the twelve orphans from Hardlocke House, but that's... how I perceived what was happening. In reality, I think I just had another nightmare and somehow parts of that were bleeding out into the real world for a few minutes. I was feeling pretty groggy and I guess... I mean, I *suppose* I was in a bit of a state."

"It's perfectly understandable that you might have been affected in this manner," Diana said. "I guard against such things happening to me, precisely because I know how powerful and real they can seem. I have no doubt whatsoever that you genuinely believed you were seeing those boys, even if such a thing is obviously impossible."

"Obviously," Jessie muttered.

"You're not getting tempted, are you?"

"Tempted?"

"To believe in the supernatural."

"No," Jessie said quickly. "Absolutely not, I..."

Her voice trailed off as she thought once more of the children in the forest. She found it difficult to believe that the whole thing had been the product of her fevered imagination, but she knew deep down that there was no other explanation. No other *rational* explanation, at least.

"No," she said again, shaking her head. "I can understand why some people might, but I'm not going to go down that route."

"Excellent," Diana replied. "I rather suspect that you need to get a change of clothes, and then perhaps you should try not to do too much this morning. Then you'll hopefully be feeling better after lunch." She turned and began to wheel herself back inside. "Don't worry about me, I have plenty to get on with this morning."

"How did it go during the night?" Jessie asked, as she followed Diana into the house and through to the office.

Diana stopped and turned back to her.

"In the house, I mean," Jessie continued. "Did anything happen?"

She waited, but Diana seemed a little hesitant to answer.

"I heard something," she said finally. "A little after three in the morning, as it happens."

"You did?" Jessie replied. "What did you hear?"

"A single, brief creaking sound, emanating from the staircase. I'm quite sure that a lesser mind would have immediately assumed that the ghostly vision of Sarah Clarke was about to appear, and might even have hallucinated such a thing. I, of course, simply wheeled myself through to investigate."

"And it was nothing, right?"

"I gave any ghostly figures plenty of opportunity to make their presence known," Diana said with a faint smile. "I looked up the stairs, and I waited, and I'm afraid that was the end of the excitement. I gave Ms. Clarke plenty of time to show herself, but either she was too shy or she was never there at all. I even went through to a few of the other rooms and took a look around. I called out to her, just to be sure, but the rest of the night passed without incident. For me, at least. I'm afraid I had no idea that you were out there having such an adventure. Not that I would have been able to do anything to help you, of course."

"Do you know the names of the boys who were here when she died?" Jessie asked.

"The names? Why?"

"I was just wondering," Jessie said, thinking back to the nightmare in which Edmund and the two Williams had been plotting something. She knew that if she could find a list of the names, she could prove to herself that the children in the dream had just been figments of her imagination.

"I think I have some of them somewhere," Diana explained. "I already tried tracking them down, though; I told you already, the historical record is far too patchy. Little orphan boys were nobody's priority back then. Or today, if we're honest."

"Do you remember whether any of them were called Edmund or William?"

"I have no idea," Diana replied. "Perhaps you could ask the skulls. You never know, they might have something to say about the matter. Sorry, just a little joke."

Jessie turned and looked at the skulls again.

"Even I have to admit," Diana said, "that during the night, caught in the moonlight, those poor little things brought a certain atmosphere to the house. If ever some ghostly figures *were* going to appear, I feel sure that would have been the moment, but again... nothing. They really *are* just empty little cradles of bone that once housed the brains of twelve poor children who are long gone."

"I'll go and get changed," Jessie replied, turning and limping out of the room. "I'll be back soon."

By the time she got back into the chapel, Jessie was starting to feel exhausted. Her foot was hurting from the encounter with the twig during the night, but when she reached the door she stopped for a moment and looked out at the forest. She looked for any sign of the boys, and then she turned and made her way into the chapel. She limped between the pews, and then she stopped and looked down at the spot where – in one of her nightmares – Sarah Clarke had fallen down with black tears streaming from her face.

Not that anything like that could actually have happened, of course. Still, for a moment she couldn't help but think about the awful sight of Sarah writhing in agony. The woman had seemed to be possessed, as if some kind of evil had filled her mind. Although she tried to remind herself that the nightmare had been *just* a nightmare, Jessie couldn't help but wonder what has really happened all those years ago, and why Sarah Clarke had ended up dead with twelve stab wounds in her body. Could the children really have murdered her?

CHAPTER TWENTY-NINE

KNEELING ON THE FLOOR in the office, Jessie peered at each of the skulls in turn. She thought back to the boys from her nightmare, and she couldn't help but wonder whether any of those faces had once belonged to the fragments of bone that were now arranged before her in a neat row.

"William?" she whispered. "The other William?"

She looked at another skull.

"Edmund?"

And another.

"Nathaniel?"

She felt foolish, but at the same time she reached out and gently touched one of the skulls. She thought of the dead-eyed child who'd been staring straight up at her during the night, and she wondered again whether she'd really invented the whole thing.

"Hey guys," she whispered, keeping her voice low so that she couldn't possibly be overheard by Diana, "it wasn't you that I saw last night, was it? I know I shouldn't be asking this, I'm probably not helping things at all, but I just wanted to check."

She waited.

Silence.

Suddenly hearing a creaking sound, she got to her feet and turned around just as Diana wheeled herself though from the hallway.

"There you are, young lady," Diana said with a big smile. "I trust that you're suitably rested."

"I am, thank you," Jessie replied, even though she was still feeling a little flustered. "I'm sorry again for being late this morning."

"We have plenty of time for everything we need to get done," Diana told her, parking herself in front of the portrait of Sarah Clarke and looking up at the painting. "We have made it through two nights here at Hardlocke House, and now we have one left. And that remaining night, I am sure I don't have to remind you, is the one during which Ms. Clarke is said to finally reveal herself."

"So what are you expecting?" Jessie asked.

She waited, but Diana continued to look at the painting.

"What are you expecting tonight?" Jessie

continued.

Again, no answer.

Realizing that perhaps she shouldn't intrude, Jessie turned to go back over to the desk.

"Have you had any more dreams?" Diana asked suddenly.

Jessie stopped and looked back at her. She was surprised that the great Doctor Diana Moore, debunker of anything unscientific, might have even a shred of interest in her dreams. Deep down, she couldn't help worrying that she was being mocked.

"Yeah," she admitted. "A couple."

"About Sarah Clarke?"

"And the children."

"I thought as much. When you were asking me about their names, I thought there must be a reason." She held up a single sheet of paper. "Here. A photocopy of a page listing the names of all twelve boys who had been placed under Ms. Clarke's care at the time of her death."

Jessie hesitated, before making her way over and taking the sheet. She told herself that she wouldn't recognize the names, and then she felt a flicker of fear in her chest as she immediately spotted a few in the list that were familiar:

Thomas Kinkaid
Edmund Bachelor
William Warton

Edward Carver
Charles Richards
James Smith
William Merriman
William Lloyd
John Cooper
John Roberts
Nathaniel Edwards
Michael Harmer

"In some cases," Diana explained, "the real surnames were not known, so usually the surname of whoever brought them to the house was used. I imagine that in a few of the more pitiful cases, even the first name might have had to be invented here. But those are the names by which the boys were known during their time at Hardlocke House. Do any of them leap out at you?"

"Well..."

Jessie stared at the list for a moment, before realizing that she must have seen it before. That was the only explanation for the fact that four of those names – Edmund, Nathaniel and two of the Williams – had been mentioned in her dreams. After a moment she looked over at the skulls.

"You seem a little troubled, my dear," Diana continued. "Almost as if you've seen a ghost."

Jessie turned to her.

"That was a little joke," Diana added, taking

the sheet back from her. "All the names on this list were fairly common at the time. If you were to set about inventing some names for children of the period, you wouldn't go far wrong with this little list. Several of them had regal connotations, to start with. What I'm trying to impress upon you is the fact that if some children in your dreams shared these first names, that's no reason to believe in the supernatural. It's merely reason to marvel at the power of the human mind."

"Sure," Jessie replied, although she held back from explaining that she'd also heard some of those surnames mentioned in her dreams too. "I know you're right."

"And that concludes the lesson for this morning," Diana added, setting the piece of paper down. "I can tell that you're still a little out of sorts from your adventure during the night, and I want you to be fully rested by this evening. I might not have mentioned it before, but I expect you to stay awake all night tonight."

"You do?"

"We both need to be alert. After all, the ghostly figure of Sarah Clarke might appear before us, trailing spectral vapors in her wake and screaming at us that she demands vengeance!" She chuckled. "Or some doors might bang and some floorboards might creak. Or, and bear with me on this, but possibly – just possibly – absolutely nothing will happen. I know which option I consider to be the most likely."

"Sure," Jessie said. "Totally."

"I shall need you to be clear-headed and ready to assist me at a moment's notice."

"Does that mean I'm going to be inside the house?"

"Absolutely not. I must face this matter alone. You will be in the chapel, or you can be outside in the clearing if you prefer, but you will not enter the house under any circumstances. Not without my explicit instructions to do so. Is that clear?"

"It's very clear," Jessie replied. "What if I hear sounds that worry me?"

"You mean an errant scream in the middle of the night? The sound of chains clanking? My desperate cry for help?"

"Well... kind of."

"That simply won't happen," Diana said with a grin. "Calm your fears, young lady. This isn't a ghost hunt, after all. Not really. It's a scientific study designed to deal with an aberration in the data from forty years ago. And this time tomorrow, I guarantee you that the so-called haunting of Hardlocke House will finally be consigned to dustbin of history. Which is where it's belonged all along."

***

As she made her way back to the chapel, having been ordered to rest, Jessie slowed as she realized she could hear voices up ahead. She stopped at the side of the building, and she listened as the voices whispered frantically just around the corner, near the chapel's door.

"She's in there," one of the voices said. "She has to be."

"We don't know that for sure," another voice replied.

"Then where is she?" another voice asked. "You don't think she's in the house, do you?"

Jessie edged a little closer, determined to sneak a peek of the figures in broad daylight but also keen to make sure that she wouldn't be spotted. After a moment, however, her feet crunched against the leaves.

"Did you hear that?" one of the voices asked. "Do you think it was her?"

"It can't be," a voice replied a little hesitantly. "Can it?"

She waited, but now Jessie was unable to hear any voices. She didn't want to disturb the children – whoever they might turn out to be – but finally she realized that she had to see what was happening. She stepped around the corner, and she felt a hint of disappointment as she saw that there was nobody at the door. She was sure that she'd have heard footsteps if anyone had run away, but at the same time she was starting to think that she might have imagined the whole thing.

Suddenly she heard a cracking sound over her shoulder, and she turned to see a pale little face peering at her from the chapel's far corner. As soon as it realized it had been spotted, the face pulled out of sight, and Jessie immediately heard the sound of several sets of footsteps racing away through the forest. She hurried around to the other side of the chapel, arriving at the corner just in time to see several figures rushing away between the trees.

"Wait!" she called out, but the figures were already gone.

Sighing, she turned to go back to the chapel's front door, and then she froze as she saw that one little boy was standing nearby, staring at her.

CHAPTER THIRTY

"HI," JESSIE SAID, LOOKING at the boy as she tried to remind herself that he couldn't possibly be a ghost. "Don't be scared, I just want to talk to you."

The boy, who was dressed in dirty, old-fashioned clothing, glanced around as if he was searching for his friends. He shifted slightly on his feet, as if he was poised to run away. When he looked back at Jessie, she couldn't help but notice that he seemed very pale.

"My name's Jessie," she continued. "Jessica Banks, but you can call me Jessie. I'm just visiting here for a few days. So where do *you* come from? Are you from one of the nearby villages?"

She waited, but the boy took a step backward and a moment later a voice called out from somewhere far off in the forest.

"John! Where are you?"

"Is that your name?" Jessie asked. "Are you John?"

The boy looked absolutely terrified as he stared at her.

Figuring that she needed to try to get on his good side a little, Jessie knelt down on the cold, damp forest floor. She was trying to think back to the list that she'd seen in the house, and she was fairly sure she'd spotted at least one John.

"You were here last night, weren't you?" she said. "It's okay, I saw you all. I tried to come after you, but then I fell down and hit my head and -"

"We made sure you were alright!" the boy blurted out.

"You did?"

"We didn't just leave you," he continued. "We checked you weren't dead, and that you seemed to be fine, before we left."

"Thank you," she said. "And what were you doing out in the forest so late, anyway? Didn't your parents wonder where you were?"

"We don't..." He paused for a moment. "We don't have parents."

Jessie swallowed hard. She still couldn't bring herself to believe that she was talking to one of the twelve boys who'd disappeared several hundred years earlier, but she couldn't deny that John seemed pretty strange.

"John!" another voice shouted. "Come quickly!"

"Are you looking for someone?" she asked. "I think I heard you and your friends talking just now. I wasn't eavesdropping. I guess I was just trying to overhear you, so I could kinda figure out what you were saying."

"You talk strangely," John replied. "And you wear clothes that I have never seen before."

"Yeah, you kinda do too," she told him. "So were you looking for *me*, is that it?"

With tears in his eyes, John shook his head.

"Then who *were* you looking for when you came to the chapel?" she asked. "You've been there two nights in a row, I know that. Who -"

"We haven't seen her for so long," he said, interrupting her. "Do you know where we can find Ms. Clarke?"

Jessie instantly felt a burst of fear in her chest, but she quickly told herself to stay calm.

"Do you mean Sarah Clarke," she said, "the woman who used to run this place a few hundred years ago?"

"Years ago?" John replied uncertainly. "I don't know how long it's been. We've been looking for her for a long time, though, but we just can't find her. We're worried that she might be angry with us for... Well, for what we did."

"You know your history, huh?"

"What do you mean? Miss, please, we're just looking for Ms. Clarke. If you know where we can find her, you have to tell us!"

"Have you tried..." Jessie paused, fearful of adding fuel to the fire of what she was starting to think must be a hallucination. Still, she couldn't just stay silent. "Have you tried the house?" she asked finally. "It's right over there."

"She's not in there," he replied. "That's the one thing we know for sure."

"How do you know that?"

"Because she *can't* be in there," he continued. "Not after..."

His voice trailed off.

"John!" another boy shouted in the distance, followed by another. "John, hurry!"

"I have to go," he murmured, and he turned to walk away.

"No, wait!" Jessie said, and he stopped. "Listen, I can't pretend to understand exactly what's happening here right now, but I want to help. If you're looking for someone, I might be able to find them, but you're going to have to give me a little more information. Where did you last see this Ms. Clarke woman?"

"It's been an awfully long time."

"But *where*?"

"What happened was horrible," John replied, sniffing back more tears. "We only did it because we thought it was the right thing to do. We were told, you see? We thought we were helping."

"Helping who? Ms. Clarke?"

"Please just help us find her!" he insisted, becoming noticeably more agitated as more voices called his name in the distance. "I'm sorry, I shouldn't have spoken to you. The others will be so angry if they find out, but I just thought that after all this time someone might be able to help us. I'm so sorry."

"Don't be sorry," Jessie replied, "I just -"

Before she could finish, John turned and hurried out of sight around the corner. Jessie rushed after him, but he was already gone. In the distance, more voices called out his name for a few seconds, and then they too fell silent. Jessie looked around, convinced that John couldn't possibly have managed to get away so quickly, but there was no sign of him anywhere.

"John!" she called out, cupping her hands around her mouth, hoping that she might be able to lure him back. "I want to help, but you have to talk to me!"

She waited, but deep down she knew there was no hope of him returning, at least not yet. She considered going out into the forest and trying to track down the other boys, but so far they seemed only to get close when they wanted something. She was still clinging to the hope that they were just a bunch of weird kids from a local town or village, but at the same time she was also contemplating the possibility that the strange atmosphere at the house had caused her to start imagining things. Those were the only two options, because the third – that she'd actually just talked to a ghost – felt too dangerous to contemplate.

Reaching into her pocket, she took out her phone and switched it on. She desperately wanted to experience a moment of normality, and she hoped that she might have better signal than the previous day. When she finally tried to call home, however, she found that this time her phone couldn't even connect to the network. She tried waving it around above her head, but she still had no luck. Somehow, the signal had seemed fine on Friday but had steadily deteriorated ever since, to the point that now she was unable to get any bars at all.

"Come on," she muttered, before realizing that the situation was hopeless. She switched her phone off, to conserve the battery, and then she turned and made her way into the chapel.

A moment later, as she reached the end of the aisle, she stopped as she saw that her bag had been pulled open, and that all the contents had been left strewn across the floor.

"What the hell?" she whispered, crouching down and starting to gather everything up. "Damn kids."

To her considerable irritation, she quickly found that her food had been particularly targeted, with the biscuits and other items having been ripped from their packets. Her books had been damaged too, torn down their spines and pulled apart into several different sections. While her first assumption had been that someone had simply been looking for something to steal, she now felt as if she'd been targeted by someone who just wanted to cause trouble.

"Not cool, guys!" she called out, turning and looking back at the door. There was no sign of anyone, but she couldn't help wondering whether one of the children might still be loitering out there. "Leave my stuff alone, okay?" she continued. "Little rat bags!"

The damage at least made her feel more confident that the children were just some trouble-making kids from the area. After all, she found it hard to believe that a bunch of little ghosts would go to all the bother of messing with her things. As she gathered everything together and began to assess what could be saved and what would have to be dumped, she began to realize that she was really looking forward to getting home.

One more night, that was all, and then she and Diana would be leaving Hardlocke House behind forever.

CHAPTER THIRTY-ONE

"AND SO WE APPROACH the moment of truth," Diana said as she once again sat in her wheelchair at the top of the steps, watching the forest as the sun continued to dip in the sky. "Nightfall approaches, and we must wonder whether the ghost of Sarah Clarke is preparing to reveal herself."

She looked down at Jessie, who seemed lost in her own thoughts, and she furrowed her brow as she waited for a response.

"Is she practicing her scary expressions in a mirror?" Diana continued. "Is she trying to choose a particularly frightening dress to wear? Is she looking forward to banging a few doors shut?"

"What?" Jessie said suddenly, turning to her.

"You're in a world of your own this evening," Diana pointed out. "I hope you're not worried about anything. Apart from the obvious, that is."

"Definitely not," Jessie replied. She'd made a deliberate decision to not mention her encounter with the boy, because she'd worried that she might seem completely insane. After all, who in their right mind would ever believe that such a thing had happened? Even her own friends back at home would laugh at her, and she couldn't help thinking that Diana might order her to leave. Still, she couldn't get the image of John out of her mind.

"If something is troubling you," Diana said, "you must tell me."

"There's nothing."

"Don't worry about how I might react. I'm sorry I was harsh with you for a while yesterday, but -"

"I said I'm fine!" Jessie snapped, before taking a deep breath. "Sorry, I didn't mean that to come out the way that it did. I think I'm just..."

For a moment, she once again thought back to the sight of John's face. The more she thought about him, the more she felt that he'd seemed extremely pale, with darker patches around his eyes.

"I think I'm just feeling a bit..." She tried to think of an excuse. "Homesick," she added finally. "I'm just missing my parents, that's all. I haven't been able to call them, so I'm just wondering how they're doing."

"Ah," Diana said, nodding sagely. "I see. That's quite understandable."

Jessie managed a faint smile. She hated the fact that she'd just lied, and she doubly hated the particular lie that she'd used, since she felt that she'd made herself seem immature. Still, she was desperate to avoid any situation in which she might blurt out the truth about what had happened during the day, and she quickly told herself that she only had to stay strong for one more day.

"I'm nervous," Diana said suddenly.

Jessie looked up at her, convinced that she must have misheard.

"There," Diana continued, "I admitted it. It started this afternoon, and it's been getting worse ever since." She turned and looked back into the house. "I suppose I shouldn't be surprised. After forty years, I'm about to do one of two things. I'm either going to discover that there was a ghostly presence here all along, in which case my entire career is going to be upended. Or I'm going to discover that I've spent four decades – forty bloody years – getting my knickers in a twist over absolutely nothing. Over a brief, strange feeling that only lasted for a few seconds. Over something that was probably just a hot flash."

"I know I've said this a lot of times," Jessie replied, "but I really would like to be in the house with you tonight."

"I would like you to be in the house as well," Diana said, "but it simply can't be allowed. I have to face this alone. You understand, don't you?"

"Sure. But what about tomorrow? Before we leave, I mean. Once the study's over, can I go in and take a look around?"

Diana hesitated for a moment.

"Well, I suppose so," she said finally. "Yes, I don't see why not. There would be no harm in allowing you to indulge your natural curiosity, once all the serious work is out of the way."

"I'd feel pretty foolish coming all this way and then not even getting to poke around," Jessie pointed out.

"There's one thing I need you to promise me in return," Diana replied.

"Shoot."

"Earlier, when discussing tonight, I might have given the impression that under certain circumstances you are permitted to enter the house," Diana said cautiously. "That is not the case. I am quite sure that the night will pass without incident, but I want you to make me a solemn promise. Whatever happens, whatever you might hear, you will not enter Hardlocke House until sunrise tomorrow morning."

"Okay."

"I need you to really mean it."

"I really mean it."

"Even if... I don't know, but for the sake of argument, even if you are absolutely convinced that something dreadful is happening, that my life is in danger, you must not enter."

"I promise."

"And you will keep that promise? Can you fight any urge you might have to change your mind and burst in? Remember, I am not some damsel in distress who needs saving. I can look after myself, so you must not enter the house for any reason, not until sunrise at the very earliest. Am I clear?"

"Very," Jessie said, although she was surprised by just how vehemently Diana was pressing her point. "I won't enter until sunrise."

"I trust you will keep your word," Diana replied. "And remember to stay awake. In the unlikely event that anything *does* happen, we must both be ready."

***

"What about these?" Jessie asked later, as she stood in the office and looked down at the row of twelve skulls. "Do you want me to pack them away, ready for tomorrow?"

"No, you can leave them out," Diana said. "If nothing else, they should contribute greatly to the atmosphere."

Turning, Jessie saw that Diana was warming

her hands next to the stove. She opened her mouth to ask if there was anything else she could do to help, since she was feeling pretty useless, but then her gaze was drawn once again to the portrait of Sarah Clarke on the opposite wall. Stepping over to take a closer look, she was struck by the woman's indomitable gaze, and she contemplated for a moment how much sheer hard work it must have taken for her to have Hardlocke House built and then to run the place alone. Regardless of anything else, she felt a sense of admiration.

A moment later, however, she realized that she could once again hear Diana muttering to herself.

She turned to look, and she saw that Diana was sitting slumped in her wheelchair. Light from the stove was catching the side of her face, showing that her eyes were open, but the older woman's lips were moving and she was saying something that Jessie couldn't quite catch.

Although she didn't want to intrude, Jessie couldn't help but take a couple of steps closer. She'd noticed Diana behaving the same was several times before, and she wanted to know *exactly* what she was saying.

"I always promised I'd come back," she heard Diana whispering. "I never wavered. I took my time because I had to, I couldn't rush, but I kept my promise. You should have known that I would.

And I brought -"

Suddenly she let out a gasp and leaned back in her chair.

Not wanting to get caught listening, Jessie turned and looked back up at the painting. After a few seconds, she heard the telltale sound of Diana's wheelchair turning around.

"I'm so sorry," Diana said, "I actually forgot for a moment that you were still here."

"I was just looking at the painting," Jessie replied, forcing what she hoped would seem to be an innocent smile. "I was thinking about Sarah Clarke, and about what it must have been like for her to start this orphanage."

"You should go now," Diana told her. "It's late, it's almost seven o'clock, I shouldn't have let you stay this late. Really, you should have been out of here by the time the sun went down."

"Sure," Jessie replied, figuring that if she was ever going to ask Diana about the strange comments she'd just heard, she should at least wait until the following day. "If there's nothing else you need, then I'll be off."

"I can't help thinking about Lizzy Malone," Diana said.

"What about her?"

"There's something I've never told anyone. I've barely even admitted it to myself. The truth is, a few years after I came to Hardlocke House, Lizzy

Malone tracked me down in London. It's an encounter I prefer not to think about, but tonight of all nights it keeps coming back into my mind."

"What did she want?" Jessie asked.

"She wanted..." Diana hesitated, as if she once again was thinking back to that awful night. "She wanted what we all want, I suppose. She wanted to be believed. And she told me something that I've never quite been able to forget."

CHAPTER THIRTY-TWO

"IT'S LATE!" DIANA SNAPPED angrily, on a cold and rainy night thirty-eight years earlier, as she opened the front door of her flat. "Why do you keep knocking when it's obvious that I don't want to be disturbed?"

Seeing a woman shivering in a heavy raincoat, she waited for an answer.

"Well?" she continued.

"Doctor Moore," the woman replied, struggling to speak as her teeth chattered. "I'm sorry to disturb you, but I couldn't wait any longer."

"What's this all about?" Diana asked. "Who are you?"

The woman hesitated, before pulling her hood back to reveal a gaunt, ill-looking face. Her eyes were bloodshot and her lips were horribly chapped.

"I don't know who you are," Diana continued, stepping back and starting to shut the door, "but I don't give money to beggars and I don't buy things on my doorstep, so kindly -"

"It's me!"

Diana hesitated, but still she didn't recognize the woman.

"It's me," the woman said again. "Lizzy. Lizzy Malone."

"What are you..." For a moment, Diana still couldn't see the resemblance, but after a moment she began to realize that maybe – just maybe – there was a slight similarity.

"Please," Lizzy continued, "I know I shouldn't be here, but this is my last chance. I *have* to talk to you about Hardlocke House."

***

"It's spread pretty much everywhere now," Lizzy said as she stood dripping on a patch of newspaper that Diana had laid down in the living room. "It's even in my spine. The doctors think I have three months left at most."

"I'm very sorry to hear that," Diana replied, "but I'm not that kind of doctor. I don't see how I can help you."

"Andy died. My husband. You remember

him, don't you?"

"I'm sorry to hear that too."

"He got involved in a scheme to make money selling old white goods," Lizzy explained, "but it turned out that the stock was all stolen. Andy was left as the fall guy and... Well, he couldn't face it. I found him..."

Her voice trailed off for a moment.

"He hung himself," she added, and now her voice was shaking with emotion. "He put up a noose in our garage and he put it around his neck and he used it to end his life. I think he felt pretty humiliated, and maybe he didn't have the strength to find yet another way of making money, so he took the easy way out. He left a note saying that it wasn't my fault, but I can't help thinking I should have noticed something was wrong. When I found him, I thought he was just playing some kind of -"

"That's quite enough, thank you," Diana said, interrupting her. "I don't need to know all the gruesome details."

"We sold Hardlocke House not long after your visit," Lizzy continued. "Andy wanted to make a go of it, but once the documentary went out and we still didn't get any calls, I managed to persuade him that the situation was hopeless. We lost a lot of money and we moved to London. Peckham, actually. Things were never quite the same again, though. I think losing the house really broke Andy."

She tapped the side of her head. "Up here, I mean."

"That's very unfortunate," Diana replied cautiously, "but I really don't know what I can do to help you."

"The new owners were going to knock the house down," Lizzy said, "but something went wrong and I think they haven't managed to do it. I don't know if they ever will. It's empty at the moment."

"That's a shame. It's a perfectly nice house, albeit one that's rather out of the way. I'm sure somebody could make a go of it."

"I wasn't lying, you know."

"Mrs. Malone, I -"

"I know you think I was, but I wasn't," she said firmly. "Everyone thinks I was, but the truth is, there really *is* something there."

"If you've come here to try to persuade me of some cockamamie theory," Diana replied, "then you've had a wasted journey. My resolve has not changed over the intervening years." She sat on the arm of the sofa, wincing in the process. "Arthritis," she added. "Early onset."

"The day we left," Lizzy replied, "I remember looking up at that house and trying to clear my mind. I thought that maybe, in the end, I might see things clearly once everything was over. I could still feel it, though. That *thing* that lives in there, I mean, and I don't think -"

Diana let out a loud sigh.

"I don't think it's Sarah Clarke," Lizzy added.

"I beg your pardon?"

"I think there's something else in there. Sarah Clarke might be around somewhere, but the thing in Hardlocke House is different somehow. After you visited, it changed its approach and I swear I felt it entering me a few times, like it briefly filled me up and became a part of me. Only for a few seconds at a time, but it's almost like it was probing me. Like it was testing me, trying me out to see if it could use me in some way."

"That sounds rather dramatic."

"I think eventually it decided that Andy and I were surplus to requirements. I think it wanted us to move on, so that someone else could come along, someone it might like better."

"I fail to see how you could possibly have come to such a conclusion."

"It's just a hunch, Doctor Moore. You get hunches, don't you?"

"I develop theories, which I then put to the test. I certainly don't entertain spurious notions based on nothing more than a desire to encounter something ghostly. I have far too much self-respect for that." She sighed again. "Young lady, you're dripping on my carpet."

Lizzy looked down, and then she shuffled

back on the newspaper.

"Sorry," she muttered, before looking at Diana again. "I'm just saying that -"

"No, young lady, I think you need to listen, not speak." Diana took a deep breath. "When I first met you and your husband a few years ago, I recognized immediately that you were a pair of cretins. That might be harsh, but it's true. However, whereas I despised your husband, I actually felt a degree of sympathy for you. It was quite obvious to me that you genuinely believed all that nonsense about ghosts, and that the experience at Hardlocke House was having a detrimental impact on your mental and physical well-being. I couldn't help snap you out of any of that, of course, but I certainly recognized the nature of your predicament. And I'm sorry that you have been unable to break out of it over the intervening years, but that is your own problem."

"Will you please just listen to me?" Lizzy asked, still dripping rainwater onto the newspaper. "If I can just explain it to you again, I'm certain that you'll understand."

"There's nothing you can say that will possibly change my mind."

"But can you just listen to me? Please? No-one else will."

"I think you should leave," Diana said firmly. "Go home and stop thinking about

Hardlocke House. If you really only have a short time left in this world, then make the most of it and stop fixating on all this childish rubbish." She waited, but Lizzy simply stared at her. "My advice is genuine, and heartfelt," she added. "I can't make you take it, though."

"You're not going to listen, are you?"

"No, I'm afraid not."

"Your mind's made up."

"I recognize the truth. I shan't deviate from that."

"I should have known," Lizzy muttered, furrowing her brow as she reached into her pocket. "I tried to stay positive, but I should have realized that I wouldn't be able to get through to you. You were my last hope. I had to try. The thing is, after that presence was inside me in the house, I can still feel it now. Just little echoes, tremors here and there, but it's like it's somehow still attached to me even from all this distance. It might even have caused my cancer. It might have made Andy do what he did. And I can't handle it, not even for three more months. I feel like it's never going to let me go."

"Please," Diana said, as she saw that Lizzy was holding a knife, "young lady, I am ordering you to -"

Before she could finish, Lizzy slashed the knife across her own throat. Letting out a gasp of pain, she stumbled back, bumping against the wall. She reached up and felt the wound, but she hadn't yet cut deep enough; after taking a deep breath, she cut again, this time much more firmly, and she finally succeeded in slicing a gash from ear to ear.

"No!" Diana gasped, as blood began to spray from Lizzy's throat.

Dropping to her knees on the newspaper, Lizzy let go of the knife. Blood was arcing from her wound, splattering against the low ceiling, and for a moment she seemed froze in place. Finally, however, she toppled forward and landed face-down against the carpet as the last life drained from her body, and as a pool of blood spread far beyond the confines of the newspaper.

CHAPTER THIRTY-THREE

"YES, MYRTLE," DIANA SAID a few hours later as she stopped in the doorway and turned to her friend, "I shall be quite alright. Thank you again for letting me stay with you tonight, it's just that the police are still all over my flat and I just needed to get out of there."

"It must have been so horrible," Myrtle replied, with tears in her eyes. "Diana, are you sure you wouldn't like another brandy?"

"One was more than enough," Diana said calmly. "And now, if you don't mind, I think I shall try to get some sleep. This evening has been somewhat trying, and I'm afraid tomorrow might well be rather full as well. If nothing else, I shall have to start looking for a new carpet."

After exchanging a few more pleasantries

with her friend, Diana gently bumped the door shut and then turned to look across the room. Two single beds had been immaculately made up, and Diana's little overnight bag was resting on the dressing table. She'd tried to keep a stiff upper lip while the police had been in her flat, and during their incessant questioning, but in truth she'd been feeling increasingly shaken by what had happened. Lizzy Malone's suicide had felt like the most awful intrusion into her routine.

Still, she knew she was strong enough to withstand such a shock, so she headed to her bag and began to search for her nightgown. As she did so, however, she glanced at her own reflection in the mirror, and for a moment she froze.

"After that presence was inside me in the house," she heard Lizzy's voice whimpering in the back of her thoughts, "I can still feel it now."

"What a load of rubbish," she muttered, as she started going through her bag again, although Lizzy's words soon burst back into her mind.

"Just little echoes, tremors here and there, but it's like it's somehow still attached to me even from all this distance."

"Stupid woman," Diana muttered, even as she felt a flicker of pain in her right hip. Stress, she assumed, was the reason her arthritis was acting up again.

"I can't handle it," she remembered Lizzy

complaining, "not even for three more months. I feel like it's never going to let me go."

"Shut up!" Diana hissed, turning and looking back across the room.

She immediately felt a sense of shock as she realized that she'd reacted in such a way to a simple memory. Lizzy's voice had felt so real and so close, as if some part of the dead woman was lingering. For a moment Diana looked around at the darker corners of the room, worried that she might spot Lizzy, but then she put such thoughts out of her mind and returned her attention to her bag.

Diana Moore was not the type of woman to let herself get spooked by an unsettling incident.

***

"Are you sure you're up for going home today?" Myrtle asked over breakfast, as she reached for the marmalade. "You're welcome to stay here for as long as you like, you know."

"Thank you, but I have to go back some time," Diana pointed out. "Please, don't make a big thing of it."

"I can come with you, if you like."

"Again, that's not necessary. I had a good night's sleep and I feel very much refreshed. Admittedly the flat might be in a bit of a state, but that certainly won't get any better if I delay. You know me, Myrtle, I prefer to grab the bull by the horns and get on with things."

"I suppose so," Myrtle muttered.

"I only hope that the police aren't going to pepper me with foolish questions," Diana continued, before looking over at her friend. "There's nothing more than I can -"

Stopping suddenly, she saw to her horror that Lizzy Malone was standing at the far end of the kitchen, directly behind Myrtle. Diana looked into the dead woman's eyes for a moment, before seeing that a thick, jagged tear was indeed visible running straight across her throat.

"It must have been a terrible shock," Myrtle mused as she finished getting her toast ready. "I don't know how I'd have managed if I'd seen something so awful."

Unable to reply, Diana simply stared at Lizzy. She blinked a couple of times, hoping to make the awful image go away, but Lizzy seemed determined to merely stand and observe. There was a certain cool, icy calm in her expression, something that had certainly been lacking the night before. Diana wanted to ask Myrtle to look, to get her friend to confirm that there was nothing there, but at the same time she was scared that the opposite might happen, that Myrtle might indeed see the horrific apparition.

"Are you alright?" Myrtle asked. "You look

a little pale."

"I'm waiting for you," Lizzy said suddenly. "You know where to find me."

"I beg your pardon?" Diana stammered.

"You just look a little pale, that's all," Myrtle replied. "I really do think that perhaps you're underestimating the shock of this whole ordeal."

"There's no point delaying," Lizzy continued, as black blood began to run from her eyes, and from the corners of her mouth too. "I already let you know what I want. You felt it when you were at the house two years ago. You can delay for as long as you want, but we both know that eventually you're going to come back for me."

"No," Diana whispered, tense with fear. "You're not real."

"I'm sorry?" Myrtle replied, furrowing her brow. "What did you just say?"

"That house is empty," Diana continued, "and that's how it should stay. There's nothing there but a bad history, and if you ask me the whole place should be razed to the ground."

"Suits me," Lizzy said with a faint smile, as the black liquid began to dribble down the front of her shirt. "The house isn't really what's important. You understand that, don't you? Please, Diana, tell me you know what's going on here. I would be so disappointed in you if it turned out that you were deceiving yourself."

"I -"

"You felt me once," Lizzy continued. "You know how strong I am. How long are you going to wait before you come and feel that same way again?"

Before Diana could reply, Lizzy tilted her head and one side of her skull began to crack open. Blood poured from a thick wound that quickly split her face, and a moment later a dark hand began to reach out from inside the woman's head. Diana could only watch with a growing sense of horror as some other force seemed to be trying to climb out from inside Lizzy's body, and a moment later she heard the sound of the woman's ribs being ripped open.

"Why delay the inevitable?" a voice snarled, as another mouth appeared behind Lizzy's crumbling jaw. "You're a smart woman, Diana, aren't you? You know that if something's going to happen anyway, you might as well get on with it!"

"No!" Diana gasped, and in an instant the world darkened around her and seemed to spin.

Suddenly she sat up, and it took a few seconds before she realized that she was in one of the beds in Myrtle's spare room. She looked around, but she understood now that she'd been suffering a nightmare. Reaching up, she found that her face was drenched in sweat, and then she checked her watch and saw that it was almost five in the morning. She laid back down, but her heart was pounding and she couldn't help but think back to the sight of Lizzy's body splitting open and something trying to force its way out.

"Why delay the inevitable?" she heard Lizzy asking, her voice echoing in the silence of the bedroom. "You might as well get on with it!"

***

"Would you like some company this morning?" Myrtle asked breezily as she scraped the last of the marmalade onto her toast at the breakfast table. "I need to pick up a few things anyway."

"I shall be quite alright, thank you," Diana replied, although she couldn't help keeping her eyes fixed on the far end of the kitchen, watching the spot where – in her nightmare – Lizzy Malone had appeared.

"Well, if you're sure," Myrtle muttered. "My spare room's always available, though. You know that. If you need it again tonight, you only have to let me know."

"You're very kind," Diana said, still watching the empty space as she felt her nerves begin to calm a little. "I should get back to normal as quickly as I can, however. After all, I have so much work to get done, and that's all that really matters to me. The work."

CHAPTER THIRTY-FOUR

"I THOUGHT YOU SAID Lizzy Malone died of cancer," Jessie reminded Diana, as she tried to make sense of the story she'd just heard.

"You must forgive me," Diana replied. "I suppose I didn't want to open that particular can of worms. The truth is, the poor dying woman committed suicide in my flat. Right in front of me, as it happens."

"That must have been so awful," Jessie said. "I can't imagine what it must be like to have something like that happen."

"One simply gets on with things. And purchases a new carpet."

"The nightmare you had must have been terrifying."

"I admit that it was unsettling at first,"

Diana told her, "but I quickly learned to put it into perspective. I merely told you that part of the story because I wanted you to realize that even the best of us can't claim to be immune to such things." She checked her watch. "And now, I really think it's time to call it a night. At the very least, we have a tiring few hours ahead of us both."

"Totally," Jessie replied, turning and heading toward the door. She wanted to ask more questions, but she figured she could do that the following morning.

"And remember," Diana called after her suddenly, "you're not to come back inside. Not until sunrise."

"I remember."

"No matter what you hear, or *think* you here."

"I promise," Jessie said, glancing back at her as she reached the doorway. "No matter what I hear."

Once she was outside, Jessie stopped on the top step for a moment. She told herself that there was no reason to be nervous, but as she looked up at the facade of the house she couldn't help worrying about the night to come. And then, realizing that there was nothing else left for her to do, she pulled the front door shut, leaving Diana all alone inside Hardlocke House.

***

A couple of hours later, sitting in her sleeping bag at the foot of the altar, Jessie finished one chunk of her ripped book and set it down, before picking up the next.

Some crumbs from her broken biscuits were on the floor nearby.

Checking her watch, she saw that it was a little after 9pm. She thought for a moment about Diana, all alone in the house, but she quickly reminded herself that this was exactly what Diana had wanted. She just hoped that by the time morning rolled around, Diana would be satisfied with whatever outcome she got. Still, she couldn't help but wonder whether the ghost of Sarah Clarke really *was* lurking in the shadows of the house, waiting to make her presence known.

In her mind's eye, she saw Diana slowly rolling her wheelchair through into the house's hallway and looking up the stairs. She had to admit that she felt Diana was pretty brave to spend three long nights all alone in Hardlocke House. She understood why she wanted to be alone, but that didn't make it any easier for Jessie to accept that she hadn't been allowed to get her sleeves rolled up and take part in the most important part of the visit. Still, she knew she was going to get to take a look around the place in the morning, and she figured that would just have to be enough.

She looked back down at the book, but a moment later she heard a brief, loud knock on the chapel's door.

"Seriously?" she said, glancing along the aisle. Whereas on the first two nights she'd felt fear when she'd heard the knock, now she was a little less concerned. She'd more or less managed to convince herself that the children were tearaways from the local area, so as she put her book aside and got to her feet she was focusing on trying to explain to them that they should just go home.

She watched the door, hoping that there would be no more knocking.

A couple of seconds later, however, the knocking sound returned, clearer and more distinct than before.

"Okay, then," she said, taking the flashlight and using it to find her way between the rows of pews.

Reaching the door, she wasted no time in pulling it open. There was nobody waiting outside, so she leaned out and looked around at the dark, empty forest, just in case some of the boys might be watching from a little further off.

"You should really get out of here!" she called out, convinced that they'd be able to hear her. "Don't you think it's pretty sad that you've got nothing better to do than hang out in a forest at night? Don't you guys have video games to play?"

She waited, half expecting to hear laughter, but the forest seemed completely still and quiet.

"I didn't appreciate that little stunt earlier, by the way," she continued. "You totally shouldn't mess with someone's stuff, okay? If you want to play round here, I can't stop you, but I don't want to be part of it. Please, just leave me alone."

Again she waited, shivering slightly in the cold air, but she was starting to realize that the children were unlikely to apologize. All she could hope was that they'd leave.

"This is private property," she added, sounding increasingly desperate. "If you don't leave right now, I'll..."

What?

She couldn't think of a convincing threat to make.

"Fine," she added with a sigh. "Just don't make me come out here again."

With that, she shut the door.

Instantly, she heard another knock.

She pulled the door open again, shocked that anyone had come close enough already, but once again there was nobody outside. This time she couldn't deny that something was wrong, because she knew full well that no-one could have raced to the door, knocked, and then run out of sight in the blink of an eye. She opened her mouth to call out to them, but after a moment she realized that she just wanted to be left alone. The last thing she needed was to let them see that she was annoyed. She hesitated, and then she began to shut the door again.

At the last second, however, she spotted something hanging on the door's outside handle.

Reaching down, she unhooked a silver necklace. She held it up to get a closer look, and she saw a simple little cross dangling from the chain. She was sure that the necklace hadn't been there a moment earlier, but when she looked out toward the forest again she realized that nobody could have run to the door and then away again so quickly.

The knocking had almost seemed to be a way to make sure that she noticed the necklace.

Stepping back, she shut the door again, and then she examined the necklace more closely as she headed back along the aisle. She was no expert, but she could tell that the necklace was old, and there were cuts and marks all over its surface. The necklace glinted in the flashlight's harsh beam, and as she stopped at the foot of the altar she found herself wondering who could possibly have wanted her to find such a thing.

A moment later, hearing a creaking sound, she turned and saw that the door was slowly opening.

Convinced that she'd shut the damn thing properly, she watched for a moment before heading back over. She took another look outside before closing the door and making sure that this time it was properly secured, and then she walked once more along the aisle. She looked at the necklace again, and then – hearing a bumping sound – she turned and looked back across the chapel.

There was no sign of anyone, but she began to look at the rows of empty pews.

In her mind's eye, she could see the image of the twelve little boys sitting on those pews in her dreams. She tried to focus on something else, but as she stood all alone in front of the altar she couldn't help feeling as if twelve sets of invisible eyes were staring back at her. She took a couple of steps back, and then she felt the necklace fall from her hands. Looking down, she saw it land at her feet. Crouching down, she picked the necklace up, and then out of the corner of her eye she realized she could see a shape moving closer along the aisle.

Gasping, she looked up, but the figure was gone in an instant.

Feeling the hairs starting to stand up on the back of her neck, Jessie slowly got to her feet. She wanted to turn away, but she couldn't quite bring herself to take her eyes off the aisle.

"Hello?" she said cautiously, even though she felt a little foolish. "Hey, I'm not kidding, if anyone's in here right now, you need to leave. It's one thing to mess around outside, but coming in here like this is totally not fair. Do you hear me? I'm armed, and I can defend myself."

That last statement was a total lie, but she figured an intruder wouldn't necessarily know that. Unless, having already gone through her bag earlier, they knew *exactly* what she did and didn't have with her.

She backed up the steps until she bumped against the altar. No matter how hard she tried to tell herself that there was nobody in the room with her, she couldn't shake the feeling that at any moment she was going to spot the figure again. The more she thought about it, the more she began to realize that the figure had seemed much taller than the children.

Finally, realizing that a couple of minutes had now passed since anything untoward had happened, she tried to relax. She turned and looked over her shoulder, only to spot the crucifix hanging on the wall, and for a moment she looked directly at the broken face of the figure up there. Its features had been completely worn away, as if somebody had been trying to scrub off all traces of the face that had once existed. Although she couldn't be sure, Jessie was fairly confident that the face had been complete in her dreams.

"I'm losing my mind," she muttered, turning and looking down at her sleeping bag.

A few biscuit crumbs were still on the floor,

and she realized she should probably gather those up. After all, she'd been taught to always clean up her own mess, so she stepped over to her bag and grabbed some wipes, and then she crouched down and reached out to remove the crumbs.

"No!" a voice screamed in the distance. "Stop!"

Jessie immediately got to her feet, gripped by a sense of fear. That voice had seemed familiar, and deep down she already knew where it must be coming from.

"No!" the voice shouted again. "Please, no!"

"Diana?" Jessie whispered, before rushing along the aisle, heading toward the door. "Diana, I'm coming!"

AMY CROSS

CHAPTER THIRTY-FIVE

RACING AROUND TO THE front of the house, Jessie stopped for a moment and looked up at the front door. She'd heard no more sounds coming from inside since those initial cries about a minute earlier, but she was absolutely certain that Diana was in trouble.

Hurrying up the steps, she reached out to open the door, only to find to her shock that it was locked.

"Seriously?" she muttered, trying again and again before finally banging against the door. "Hey!" she called out. "Diana, it's me! Are you okay in there?"

She waited, but no reply came, and after a moment she remembered what Diana had told her earlier.

"You're not to come back inside. Not until sunrise."

Feeling increasingly panicked, she banged on the door again.

"Diana!" she shouted. "Hey, I heard you yelling at someone. Are you okay in there?"

Again, she waited.

"Can you at least tell me what's going on?" she continued. "If you don't, I'll have to..."

Her voice trailed off, and in that instant she remembered another of Diana's commands.

"Whatever happens, whatever you might hear, you will not enter Hardlocke House until sunrise tomorrow morning. I need you to really mean it. Even if... I don't know, but for the sake of argument, even if you are absolutely convinced that something dreadful is happening, that my life is in danger, you must not enter."

She tried the handle one more time, before stepping back from the door and making her way down the steps. She looked at the house's dark windows, and she realized that there was no longer any light coming from the stove in the office. In fact, there was no obvious sign of life anywhere in the building.

"And you will keep that promise? Can you fight any urge you might have to change your mind and burst in? Remember, I am not some damsel in distress who needs saving. I can look after myself,

so you must not enter the house for any reason, not until sunrise at the very earliest. Am I clear?"

"Diana!" she shouted, before stepping over to one of the windows and standing on tip-toes in an attempt to see inside. She cupped her hands around her eyes and peered through into the office, but all she saw was darkness.

"I trust you will keep your word."

She remembered Diana's words clearly enough, and she knew she'd promised to obey, but at the same time she'd never actually considered the possibility that something might go wrong. Diana had sounded horrified a few minutes earlier, as if she'd genuinely seen something in the house, and Jessie couldn't stand the thought of just leaving her alone to face whatever was happening.

Hurrying to another window, she tried again to see inside, then again, but she still had no luck. And then, in a flash of inspiration, she remembered the damaged window she'd looked through on the very first day.

Rushing around to the other side of the house, she tried to find that window. It took a moment, but finally she spotted the damaged piece of glass, and she pulled it aside before peering through into the room. She had to take the flashlight from her belt and switch it on, and finally she shone the beam through and saw the same bare little room with a few desks and chairs scattered about. In that moment, she realized that the room appeared to be the same one from her nightmare, the same room where Edmund and the two Williams had been working on some sort of plan.

She tilted the flashlight, but she still saw no sign of anyone.

"Hey," she called out finally, hoping that this time Diana would be able to hear her better, "it's me. Diana, I know I promised to stay out, but I heard you shouting and I just want to make sure that nothing's wrong in there."

She waited.

Silence.

"Diana, can you hear me?"

Still desperately trying not to panic, she listened for a moment before turning and looking along the side of the house. Despite all her promises earlier in the day, she was starting to think that she had to take action, which meant only one thing: she was going to have to break the window properly and climb inside. Sure, she'd be risking Diana's fury, but that seemed like a better option than simply sitting around and doing nothing until morning.

Hearing a creaking sound, she looked back into the room. She had to adjust the flashlight, and in that moment she caught a faint glimpse of a shape passing the open doorway. By the time she was able to raise the flashlight, however, the shape was gone.

"Hello?" she said. "Diana, is that you?"

The flashlight's beam was shaking as it danced across the room's far wall, picking out part of the corridor beyond the door.

"Diana," Jessie continued, "is -"

Before she could finish, she heard the creaking sound again, and she realized this time that it sounded familiar. It was the sound of the wheels of Diana's wheelchair, and sure enough a moment later part of that wheelchair backed into view, although it stopped with only the handles visible.

Jessie struggled to aim the flashlight directly at the chair.

"Diana," she said, "I'm so sorry, I know you didn't want me to interfere, but please don't be mad at me. I just heard you shouting and I had to come and check that you were okay. You understand that, don't you? Just let me know that you're fine, and I'll go back to the chapel and stay there until the morning."

She waited.

"Please?"

She waited again, and after a couple of seconds the wheelchair rolled forward, out of sight again. Jessie could hear the creaking sound continuing for a moment, however, until it moved too far along the corridor.

"I guess that's something," she muttered, finally stepping back from the window.

She considered calling out again, but she figured that in some way she'd got her answer. At least she'd seen that Diana was okay in there, and there'd certainly been a chance for her to ask for help. Although she was still worried, and she couldn't quite believe that Diana had actually locked the front door, she realized with a sigh that she wasn't going to get any more of an answer. Short of smashing a window, which now felt like a step too far. She looked up at the higher windows, and then she turned and began to make her way back to the chapel.

"I tried," she reminded herself. "I guess she'll tell me what happened in the morning."

Reaching the chapel, she stepped inside and pushed the door shut. She made her way along the aisle, and then she stopped as she heard a very faint buzzing sound. As she looked around, the sound stopped, and a moment later she spotted movement down on the floor. To her surprise, a fly was perched on one of the larger biscuit crumbs.

"Get out of there!" Jessie said, reaching down and waving the fly away.

Grabbing the wipe again, she finished cleaning up the last of the crumbs, and then she headed through into the chapel's little side office, hoping to find something she could use as a bin. She needed to tidy up a little anyway, but as she shone the flashlight around she realized that she hadn't really explored the side room very much. She spotted a fancy-looking fruit bowl on one end of the large oak desk, and a moment later the fly landed on the bowl.

"Get away," she whispered, before turning to see that there was a large, broken mirror on one of the walls. She wandered over and took a look, and then she reached out and ran a fingertip against one of the broken glass edges.

At that moment, the fly buzzed against her face again, briefly landing on her cheek before she once again waved it off.

"Quit it!" she snapped, surprised that she hadn't noticed the fly during the other days in the chapel. Then again, she figured it had most likely been drawn out by the biscuit crumbs. She could hear the damn thing still buzzing around, but as she backed away toward the door she figured she could just shut the fly in the room.

She stepped outside and pulled the door shut, and then she turned to go back over to the sleeping bag.

"What the -"

Startled, she saw Diana Moore standing right behind her. And then, before she had a chance to react, Diana grabbed her face and slammed her head hard against the wall, knocking her out in an instant.

AMY CROSS

CHAPTER THIRTY-SIX

"NO," WILLIAM MERRIMAN WHISPERED as he sat in Hardlocke House's main dormitory, "you're not listening. We have to do this tonight, or we might never get away."

The other boys were gathered around him, leaving their beds empty at the sides of the room.

"We can't run away," Michael whimpered. "Ms. Clarke will get really angry!"

"It's Ms. Clarke we're running away *from*," Merriman reminded him. "Listen, I'm the oldest here, so I should be the one who gets to make decisions. And we all know that there's something wrong with Ms. Clarke. It's not just that she gets angry. Something else happens to her, something that I don't think is normal. I know you all know what I mean, it's almost as if she gets -"

Before he could finish, all the boys heard a creaking sound from the corridor. They turned and looked at the door, which remained closed.

"It was probably nothing," Merriman said.

"Go and look, then," Edmund suggested.

"Why me?"

"Because you're the oldest," John Cooper said. "You said it just now. You're the oldest, so it seems only fair that you should be the one who does it."

The other boys murmured their agreement.

Merriman hesitated, but he already knew that he had no choice. Unless he wanted to seem like a terrible hypocrite, he was going to have to go and check that there was no sign of Ms. Clarke, so he slowly got to his feet. He wanted to seem big and brave and tough, but the most he could manage in that moment was to step around the bench and gingerly start making his way toward the door.

"What if she overheard us?" Michael asked. "What if -"

"Quiet!" one of the other boys hissed.

Once he reached the door, Merriman took hold of the handle. He'd heard no other sounds coming from the corridor, and he reminded himself that the house was creaky and groany sometimes. Still, he hesitated before very carefully turning the handle, which itself caused a very faint clicking sound. He forced himself to turn the handle all the way, and then he opened the door as slowly as he could manage before leaning out and looking both ways along the corridor.

Nothing.

There was absolutely no-one there.

Breathing a sigh of relief, he carefully shut the door before heading back to the others. In an instant, he felt much braver and much more in control.

"Well?" Edmund asked.

"I told you it was nothing," Merriman said, starting to flex his newfound sense of confidence. "You should learn to listen to me more. Now, I'm telling you that something really bad is going to happen if we stay here. Whatever's wrong with Ms. Clarke, it's getting worse and worse, and I think eventually she's going to hurt one of us. I'm making a decision, and the decision is that we're getting out of here tonight."

"Where will we go?" William Warton asked.

"We'll work that out once we've left," Merriamn said firmly. "Come on, we don't have any time to waste. It's time for us to leave Hardlocke House forever."

***

"Quiet!" Merriman hissed a few minutes later, as he became the first boy to reach the bottom of the stairs. Stopping for a moment, he turned and looked back up at the other eleven, who were at various stages of following him down. "Stop talking!"

"I'm scared!" one of the others said.

"Quiet!" Merriman said again, and this time he held a finger up against his lips.

He waited for a moment, to make sure that this time they were all listening to him, and then he turned and began to creep toward the front door. He had no idea whether Ms. Clarke kept the door locked at night, but he had a couple of back-up plans in mind; they could try another door, or they could get out through one of the house's many windows. As he got to the door, he reached out and took hold of the handle.

"William," Ms. Clarke said suddenly.

Gasping, he spun around and saw a figure sitting in the office, shrouded in darkness.

"Who else have you got there with you?" Ms. Clarke continued, slowly getting to her feet. "I hear several steps upon the stairs. Why, I do believe that you are *all* trying to leave. What a merry little band you are."

Too scared to move a muscle, Merriman could only watch as Ms. Clarke began to make her way closer.

"Is it her?" Edmund whispered. "We're doomed!"

Stopping in the doorway, Ms. Clarke looked

up the stairs and saw the other eleven boys.

"You're attempting to depart as a group, I see," she said after a moment. "Why, that shows some remarkable presence of mind. You must have really worked on a plan for tonight. You must have got together and plotted. I don't recall whether we have covered this subject in your lessons, but plotters have tended to not do very well in the history of our little country. You'll recall the likes of Wat Tyler and Thomas Baker and Guy Fawkes."

She looked back down at Merriman.

"And are you the ringleader, William?"

"I... I..."

He was starting to shake with fear, and he could barely get any words out at all.

"It breaks my heart to see you boys so scared of me," Ms. Clarke continued. "My dear boys, each and every one of you is so special and so close to my heart. I think of you as my own children, and I have done nothing but work tirelessly for your benefit. And now I find you trying to flee in the night. How do you think I would have felt if you had succeeded, and if I had gone up to wake you in the morning, only to find your little beds all empty? Why, I think I would never have recovered."

She paused, before stepping over to the door and pulling it open, allowing the cold night air to blow into the hall.

"Well?" she added. "I am not stopping you. Hardlocke House is not a jail. Any of you who truly wish to leave, may do so. The world is out there. I cannot lie to you, you might very well come to regret leaving this safe haven, but I believe you are all old enough to make your own choices. Just know that if you *do* decide to leave, I will have to be strict and stop you ever returning. Any decision you make today cannot be undone."

The boys – some of whom were still on the stairs – simply stared at her.

"No?" she said with a faint smile, before shutting the door. "That is so very comforting. Is it possible that you do not hate me quite as much as I feared? Or did a few of you perhaps exaggerate your little stories about what I have done?"

She stepped past them and headed back into the office, and then she took a moment to light some candles.

"I think there might have to be some changes around here," she said calmly, as light from the candles began to flicker against the side of her face, revealing her blackened eyes. "I was so worried about being too strict with you, that perhaps I went too far in the opposite direction. Oh, I know you think that I'm wicked and mean, but you really have no idea just how much harsher I could be with you. I have been soft, but now..."

Her voice faded for a moment, as she stared

down at the candles.

The boys waited for her to continue, but she seemed lost in thought.

"What's she doing?" Edmund whispered.

"How angry is she?" Nathaniel asked. "Do you think she's going to punish us?"

Merriman, the only boy who could see through into the office, was watching Ms. Clarke's face carefully and noticed after a moment that the darkness in her eyes was fading a little. He had seen the transformation occur many times before, but something seemed different this time, and he slowly began to realize that the woman's entire body seemed strained somehow, as if she was struggling to keep from shaking.

"Should we go back up?" John Cooper asked. "If we go back up, she might just forget that this ever happened."

"Wait," Merriman replied, as he saw Ms. Clarke's mouth twitching as if she was trying desperately to say something.

Gripping the table now, Ms. Clarke tilted her head slightly as sweat began to pour down her face. She let out a faint gasp, and then finally she began to shake with laughter.

"Poor pathetic things!" she snarled through gritted teeth. "Do you really think you can -"

She stepped back from the table and turned to Merriman, and in that moment her eyes returned to normal as an expression of fear filled her face.

"Run!" she screamed frantically. "Before it's too late! All of you, get away from me!"

CHAPTER THIRTY-SEVEN

HALF THE BOYS RUSHED toward the door, and half tried to run back up the stairs, with the result that they all slammed into one another. Several of them fell down, letting out little cries of pain, and then they all froze again as they turned and saw Ms. Clarke limping, doubled over, toward them.

"Didn't you hear me?" she groaned, clutching her belly as if she was in great pain. She looked at them, and they all saw the darkness that was swirling in her eyes, threatening to take over completely. "I told you to -"

Suddenly she flinched, as if gripped by some other force, and she reached out and steadied herself against the side of the door.

"You don't want to pay any attention, boys," she snarled, "do you hear? You made the right choice by staying, and now there's only the little matter of your punishment. You know you have to be punished, don't you? It's the only way you'll learn."

She pulled a piece of stone from her pocket and help it up so that they could see a fragment of the face from the chapel's crucifix.

"What do you think of my latest work?" she sneered. "I always hated this thing's judgmental expression."

The boys gasped as she dropped the face, letting it smash on the floor.

Lunging forward, Ms. Clarke put a hand on the side of Merriman's face, and then she dropped to her knees in front of him. The darkness was surging in her eyes, but a moment later it began to fade again; Ms. Clarke's features began to soften until tears started running down her cheeks.

"Listen to me," she stammered, her voice breaking with terror, "there's not much time. I can't hold it back for much longer, and I fear that soon it will overcome me completely. You boys must get away from me, but I don't know if there's time. She might make me come after you, so..."

She hesitated, before reaching into a pocket in her dress and pulling out a knife, which she thrust into Merriman's hands.

"I cannot believe that I am saying this to you," she continued, "but it is the only way. You are my strong, brave little men, and I am begging you to have mercy. I have spent hours tonight trying to summon the courage to do this myself, and I have failed, so you are my only chance. You must trust me when I tell you that this is the only way I can be at peace with the Lord, and then you will be able to run. Please, William..."

He stared at her, not quite understanding, and then he looked down at the knife. In that moment, his hand began to tremble.

"This might protect you," she continued, carefully removing her necklace and holding it out toward him. A little silver cross glinted in the low light. When Merriman failed to respond, she tucked it into one of his pockets. "It failed me, but I think I tried it too late. I still have faith, though, and you must too. I do not know why the Lord tests us in this way, but I truly believe that everything will be alright in the end. Keep my cross close to you, and pray that it helps guide you to safety. It is a symbol of my love for you all."

"I don't want to hurt you," Merriman cried, still holding the knife.

"You can share the burden," Ms. Clarke told him. "I know this might seem wicked, and counter to everything I have ever taught you, but this is the Lord's work. He would want this evil to be wiped from the world. I don't know why I was chosen for the burden of such an awful thing, but ever since I arrived here I have felt it increasing its grip on my soul. There is something here, William, something terrible that seeks a vessel, and it is I who have been chosen. Please, you must end this horror and then you must run before it has a chance to enter one of you."

"I don't understand," Merriman sobbed, and now he too was crying.

"Please, just do it."

She tried to move his hand closer, until the blade's tip was pressed against her chest.

"I am too cowardly to do it myself," she added.

Realizing what she wanted, he started shaking his head.

"Bless you, my child," Ms. Clarke continued. "Do not blame yourself for this. I love you." She used a finger to wipe the tears from his cheek, and then she looked up at the others. "All of you."

With that, she put her arms around Merriman and pulled him tight, hugging him with such force that he was unable to keep the knife from slicing straight into her chest. She let out a gasp as she held the boy firmly, and a few seconds later she began to cough up blood.

"Do not ask to be forgiven," she whispered, as she began to weaken and let go of him, "for in the Lord's eyes, and in mine, you have done nothing wrong."

Falling back, she slumped against the floor, leaving Merriman still holding the bloodied knife.

"I didn't mean to do it!" he cried. "She -"

Before he could finish, Ms. Clarke's body shuddered and tensed, and she coughed up more blood as she began laughing uncontrollably. She clutched the wound in her chest and began to dig her fingers deep into the meat, as if she wanted to increase the pain; the deeper her fingers slipped, however, the more her laughter seemed to shake her entire body as more and more blood burst from her mouth.

"Help me!" she gasped suddenly, trying to sit up, reaching out to Merriman with a trembling hand. "For the love of all that's holy, stop this before it takes control again!"

"You're the oldest," John Cooper said, stepping toward Merriman. "You should do it."

"I can't," he whimpered. "It's not right."

"It *is* right," John replied, before taking the knife from him. "You heard what she said. You saw the look in her eyes. We have no choice."

"Please," Ms. Clarke cried, writhing in pain as the evil tried to force its way back into her mind. She let out a pained cry as darkness once again began to fill her eyes. "Lord, forgive me for my weakness. I have failed you, and I have failed the children, and I have -"

Suddenly John pushed the knife into her chest. With tears in his eyes, he pulled it out and then stabbed her again, and again and again until finally – after the twelfth wound had been made – he fell back and let the knife fall to the floor.

Ms. Clarke was gasping on the floor as blood spread across the front of her dress. She was trying desperately to breathe, but after a moment the darkness returned to her eyes and she tilted her head back. Falling still, she let her hands rest on her wounds as she began to grin wildly.

"Oh, you foolish boys," she gurgled, "now you've only made things easier for me. This pathetic woman was never going to help me get away from here, but one of you will be perfect. And I think I know which one I shall try first."

She lunged toward John, but he managed to pull away just in time. Turning, she tried to grab Merriman, then Edgar, before finally she slumped down against the floor with blood pouring from her mouth. She tried to speak, but she was unable to get any words out and after a moment she leaned forward until her forehead slammed against the floor with a heavy, cracking thud. At that moment, the darkness in her eyes began to clear once again, and she blinked a couple of times before opening her mouth and letting out a faint, sorrowful groan.

And then she fell still.

For a moment, the twelve boys watched in

silence. Finally, however, the rest of them began to make their way down the stairs one by one, until they stood in a semi-circle around Ms. Clarke's lifeless body.

"What..."

John Roberts hesitated.

"What happened to her?" he asked cautiously. "Is she..."

"There was something inside her," Merriman replied, unable to stop staring at the teacher's corpse. "I don't know what it was. I don't think *she* knew, either. Whatever it was, though, I think -"

Before he could finish, Ms. Clarke's body jerked and began to sit up. Its eyes were filled now with a darkness that was starting to spread through the veins in her face. Reaching out with one trembling hand, she grabbed John Cooper's arm.

"No!" Merriman gasped, dropping the knife but then taking the silver cross from his pocket and holding it out. "Stop!"

Recoiling from the cross, Ms. Clarke fell down once again. She let out one last laugh, and then her eyes melted away, leaving torrents of dark liquid to spill out from the sockets.

"We have to run!" Merriman shouted, still holding the necklace as he stepped back and turned to the others. "We have to get out of here! Now!"

AMY CROSS

CHAPTER THIRTY-EIGHT

ON A COLD WINTER morning, a carriage pulled up outside the front of Hardlocke House, pulled by two black horses. The coachman immediately jumped down and made his way around to open the door on the carriage's side, at which point Sir Cecil Etheridge climbed out and made a show of taking a deep breath.

"And so we come to this wretched place," he said, looking up at the windows of Hardlocke House. "Still, it is a school of sorts, and a place for orphans. It will have to do."

He turned to look back into the carriage.

"You will be better off here than on the streets, Richard," he added. "Remember that, if you are ever minded to complain of your lot."

He waited, but the boy continued to cower

inside the carriage.

"Richard," Sir Cecil continued, holding a gloved hand out toward him, "remember what I told you before. If you are to be any sort of man at all, you must be brave."

Finally, the boy climbed out of the carriage. No more than five or six years old, he was quaking with fear, and as he took a step forward he looked all around. He saw the chapel over on the far side of the clearing, but even at his young age he was able to pick up on something unnatural about the scene. He turned and looked the other way, and he shuddered at the sight of the cold forest. Already, he was thinking that he would very much like to get back into the carriage and hope for some miraculous reprieve.

Suddenly a crashing sound rang out from inside the house, followed by the sound of glass breaking.

"What is going on here?" Sir Cecil muttered, drawing his sword and hurrying up the steps to the open front door. "Has this place gone to the -"

Stopping in the doorway, he stared in shock at the gruesome sight of a large dog tearing at the arm of a bloodied corpse. For a moment, not knowing how to react, he could only watch as the dog twisted the arm away, pulling the bone from its socket. Thick strings of bloodied meat hung between the limb and the torso as the dog backed away with its prize.

"Get out of here!" Sir Cecil stammered finally, rushing over and waving his sword at the dog. "Move! You obscene thing, leave this place at one!"

Still hanging onto the arm, which was trailing strands of meat and flesh, the dog backed away and snarled. Sir Cecil lunged at the creature with his sword, slicing through one of its hind legs. The dog instantly yelped and dropped the arm, before rushing past the man and running out into the clearing. Hurrying to the door, Sir Cecil was just in time to see the dog racing across the clearing, although the animal stopped for a moment and looked back. When it set off again, it was limping from the wound on its leg.

"What is it, Sir?" the coachman asked with a shocked expression. "Is everything alright?"

Sir Cecil turned and looked back down at the gruesome sight. It was clear to him that the dog had been feasting on the corpse for some time, since most of its torso had been completely torn away. The body was wearing what remained of a tattered dress, and when Sir Cecil rolled it over with his right foot he was just about able to recognize the bloodied and discolored face.

"Who is that?" the coachman asked, having reached the doorway.

"Sarah Clarke," Sir Cecil muttered. "Or it was, at least. She appears to have been dead for at least a week."

"What could have done that?"

"It's hard to be sure," he replied, before spotting some cuts on the woman's chest. "I can just about make out some stab wounds. Twelve, I think." He turned to the coachman. "Something must have happened here, something truly awful. Something ungodly. We must search for the -"

Suddenly hearing the sound of footsteps, he rushed back to the door. Looking out across the clearing, he spotted a young boy hurrying away behind the chapel, trying desperately to get out of sight.

***

"Stop!" Sir Cecil said, hurrying through the forest after the boy ahead. "You there! Halt immediately!"

Stumbling for a moment, William Merriman bumped against a tree and then turned just as Sir Cecil caught up to him with his sword still drawn.

"Are you one of the boys from Hardlocke House?" Sir Cecil asked, shocked by the child's emaciated appearance. "What's going on here? You will talk to me, damn you! What happened to your teacher?"

"Please, Sir," Merriman replied, "we tried to

help her. Then we tried to get away, but..."

His voice trailed off.

"But what?" Sir Cecil asked.

"It wasn't our fault," Merriman sobbed. "The thing that was in Ms. Clarke got into Thomas, and then into Edward, and then..."

His voice trailed off. He looked past Sir Cecil, toward the house in the distance, and for a few seconds he seemed gripped by fear.

"It got into all of them," he explained finally, "one by one, until I was the only one left."

"What do you mean by that, boy?" Sir Cecil snapped. "Where are the rest of the children?"

Merriman turned and looked the other way into the forest.

Following his gaze, Sir Cecil spotted a series of dark shapes on the ground. He hurried past the boy and stopped at the edge of a small clearing, and to his horror he saw several small corpses, all of them bloodied and bruised. A few more bodies lay a little further off, and flies were buzzing in the air. After a moment, slowly, Sir Cecil turned back to look at Merriman.

"What did you do?" he asked.

"I didn't do it," Merriman cried. "It entered each of them in turn, but it said none of them were good enough. It killed them all, and then it came for me. I think the only reason it didn't get into me was..."

He reached into his pocket and pulled out the necklace.

"I was the one holding it," he whimpered. "It was Ms. Clarke's. It didn't protect her, but I think somehow it protected us. I think because she was the one who gave it to us."

"What nonsense is this?" Sir Cecil snarled, grabbing the necklace and looking at it for a moment, before throwing it aside. "There were twelve here, were there not? How many boys are left?"

"Only me," Merriman sobbed, hurrying over to try to retrieve the necklace. "Please, I need -"

"Where do you think you're going?" Sir Cecil shouted, grabbing him by the arm and forcing him to turn around. "Enough with these tales of fancy. What happened to Ms. Clarke?"

"I told you, she -"

"Did you do this?" he continued, not letting the boy finish. "Did the spirit of Satan compel you to murder all these poor souls?"

"No!" Merriman cried, twisting around in another attempt to get free from his grip. "Please, you don't understand, it can get to me if I don't have Ms. Clark's cross! It's all around, it's in the air!"

"How long have you been all alone out here like this, boy?" Sir Cecil asked. "Stop struggling and answer me! You're in a great deal of trouble, do you understand? I saw Ms. Clarke's body, it was being eaten by a scavenger. If you don't start answering my questions immediately, I swear I shall -"

"You'll what?" Merriman snapped, suddenly looking up at him with black eyes. "What will you do, pathetic man?" he continued with a grin. "You're no match for me. I can feel the lack of faith in your heart, you're nothing but a liar!"

Sir Cecil opened his mouth to reply, but for a few seconds he could only stare in horror at the child.

"Do you think I haven't met your kind before?" Merriman snarled, as the darkness began to spread through veins across his face, cracking the skin open in places. "The hypocrisy of the righteous sickens me. You remind me of someone, but I can't quite... Oh, that's right, I know who it is now. You remind me of the bastard who killed me all those years ago! God is just a crutch you use to explain away your many failings. What's wrong? Are you too scared to live a moral life instead?"

"Be silent," Sir Cecil whispered, his eyes wide with shock. "You do not speak like a young boy."

"You will make a fine vessel for me," Merriman continued. "Why not let down your defenses and allow me to enter immediately? Or, failing that, stick around for a while and let me peel away the edges of your soul so that I can force my way inside!"

He took a step forward.

"I am hungry for -"

Before he could finish, he let out a pained gasp and looked down to see that he'd been run through by Sir Cecil's sword. He stared for a moment, and then he looked up again and smiled.

"The children were no use to me anyway," he groaned. "I am very specific about the vessel that is worthy of taking me away from here. Even you do not, after all, appear to be good enough. I don't mind being patient. I've waited this long, I can wait a little -"

Suddenly Sir Cecil pulled the sword out, before slicing it through him again, this time straight into his heart. Merriman let out a pained cry and the darkness disappeared from his eyes. His lips twitched slightly, as if he was trying to say something, and then he slid back, falling off the sword and landing on the ground. For a moment, aware of what was happening but not remembering exactly how he'd been hurt, Merriman tried to crawl to safety. Spotting the silver cross nearby, he reached over, but in that moment he let out one final gasp and slumped down dead.

"May the Lord have mercy on the souls of all those who died here," Sir Cecil said, his voice trembling with shock, before turning as he heard the coachman approaching.

"What happened?" the coachman asked, spotting Merriman's body.

"Something I doubt we will ever understand," Sir Cecil replied. "We must get away from this awful place, but first..." He paused, thinking back to Merriman's black eyes. "First we must dig a grave for these boys," he continued, "and then we must leave and let someone know about Ms. Carter's death."

"Yes, Sir," the coachman said, turning to go back to the carriage.

"And one more thing," Sir Cecil added. "I don't want any mention of the dead boys," he explained. "I don't want to have to answer questions about that. We shall say that they simply were not here, is that understood?"

"Of course, Sir."

As the coachman left, Sir Cecil saw that Richard had come over to see what had occurred.

"Do not look, boy," Sir Cecil said, stepping over to him and forcing him to turn around. "You must wait in the carriage while we attend to a few matters here. Then I shall find some other place to deposit you." He paused for a moment. "And I shall make sure that no other soul ever comes to this place. I shall spread tales about it, such that anyone would go to great lengths to avoid ever setting foot on this land."

As he led Richard away from the clearing

and the dead boys, Sir Cecil inadvertently stepped on the necklace, pushing it down into the dead leaves.

CHAPTER THIRTY-NINE

SLOWLY, JESSIE'S EYES BEGAN to flicker open. For a moment she had no idea where she was or what had happened, but the last trace of an intense dream was quickly fading and finally she realized that she was on the floor in the chapel. Her head was throbbing, and a sharp pain was radiating across her temple.

"What..."

She groaned, trying to sit up, only to feel something tight pulling on her right wrist. Looking down, she was shocked to find that she'd been handcuffed to one of the pews.

"What the hell?" she stammered, trying to pull free, only to find that there was no way to get loose. She shifted around, onto her knees, and tried again, but without any luck.

For a few seconds, driven by a growing sense of panic, she could only pull on the handcuffs in a desperate attempt to get them to somehow fall away. She couldn't remember what had happened to her, but she figured that there'd be time to figure it all out later.

"That isn't going to do much good."

Startled, Jessie turned and saw Diana sitting on the steps next to the altar. After a moment, the older woman winced as she got to her feet.

"Arthritis," Diana muttered, clearly in pain. "That much was always true. I just exaggerated the extent to which it crippled me."

Jessie could only stare in shock as Diana took a couple of shuffling steps forward.

"Surprise," Diana added, before waving away a fly that was buzzing near her face. "You have no idea, young lady, just how long I have spent planning my return to Hardlocke House. One part of that included making myself seem weak and unable to do the entire job alone. Believe me, it was no fun being pushed about by you while I was in that wheelchair. You weren't exactly gentle. Still, I suppose I shouldn't complain really. You were doing the best you could."

"What are you doing?" Jessie asked, pulling once more on the handcuffs. "You have to let me out of these!"

"I don't have to do anything," Diana replied.

"Forty years ago, I tasted something – just for a moment – that I haven't been able to forget since. I told you that I sensed some kind of presence here at Hardlocke House, but I wasn't entirely honest. What I sensed was so intoxicating, so powerful, that ever since I've been trying to find a way to get it back. Unfortunately, I don't think I was quite what it was looking for. It sampled me and it passed, preferring to wait for a better subject. Who knew that spirits could be so picky? I have spent a long time considering just who might fit the bill."

She took a couple of steps forward, as Jessie stared at her, unable to believe what she was seeing.

"You asked me why I chose you to come out here with me," Diana continued. "The truth is, I needed someone fairly young, fairly stupid, and fairly naive. You seemed perfect in all three categories. I don't know exactly what I sensed here forty years ago, Jessica, but I know enough to want to serve it. If I can give it what it wants, it'll reward me. I don't know how, not exactly, but I'm willing to find out. Believe me, once you've felt that presence, anything else feels so weak and pointless."

"You..."

Jessie tried to respond, but she was starting to shake with fear.

"You *planned* this?" she continued after a moment.

"For forty years, I've kept up the pretense,"

Diana explained. "It took me all that time to work out what I should do, and what the presence wanted. Lizzy Malone ended up helping me, in her own pathetic way. Her miserable suicide convinced me that this thing should be approached with great care."

Jessie shook her head.

"There's something here, you see," Diana continued, "something powerful and ancient, something that's trapped here. It wants to leave, but it has a very specific set of criteria. It has tasted and discarded so many bodies over the years, but I think I've worked its criteria out now. It needs someone who believes in it, and someone who will willingly take it off the estate. Forty years ago, I *didn't* believe, that's why I was rejected. There are no second chances, but I've got a feeling that you're a lot more credulous than I was, especially after your experiences in this chapel."

"Help!" Jessie shouted, turning and looking back across the chapel. "Somebody help me!"

"There's nobody within ten miles of this place," Diana muttered. "You should save your breath."

"Please!" Jessie screamed, as she frantically pulled on the handcuffs. "Get me out of here!"

"The irony is," Diana continued, stepping around her, "that the presence stays out of the chapel. It's Sarah Clarke who haunts this place, while the presence mostly remains in the house. Two ghosts, keeping well clear of one another." She made her way along the aisle, heading toward the door. "*This* will be the culmination of my work," she added. "I will learn more about the presence. Not so that I can write another dull academic paper, but so that I can live and breathe the strength that the presence is able to bring to the world once it is free of this place. I think I'm old enough now to kick back a little."

Opening the door, she stopped and turned to look back at Jessie.

"I needed you to experience something before you entered the house itself," she said with a faint smile. "Something that would make sure you understood the nature of what we're dealing with. I can't risk having you fail to believe what you see once you encounter the presence, so consider this to be a little primer. After all, I don't want you to make the same mistake that I made forty years ago."

"No!" Jessie yelled, but Diana slammed the door shut, leaving her trapped inside with only the light from one candle. "Get back here! You can't do this!"

She immediately set to work trying to free herself from the handcuffs. No matter how hard she tried, however, she was unable to slip her hand out, and the pew was far too solid for her to break. She looked around, hoping to find something that she might be able to use, and finally she spotted her bag. Although she couldn't think of anything in there that might come in handy, she began to drag the heavy pew across the floor. Reaching the bag, she started frantically searching through its contents, but there was nothing.

"Come on," she muttered, hunting for her phone, only to find that Diana must have hidden it away, "there has to be some way to -"

Suddenly she heard a shuffling sound. She spun around and looked back along the aisle, but there was no sign of anyone. She was sure that she'd have heard if Diana had opened the door and stepped back into the chapel, but a moment later she heard the sound again, accompanied this time by a brief, faint bump. Something had tapped the side of one of of the pews, and after a few seconds she heard the same thing again, this time from a little closer.

Trying not to panic, she dragged the pew over to the foot of the steps. She could still hear the series of little taps, as if someone was slowly walking along the aisle and touching their fingers against the top of each pew in succession.

Reaching up onto the altar, she grabbed the candle and held it out so that she could see a little more clearly, but there was still no sign of anyone. The tapping sound continued, however, until it reached the nearest pew and came to an abrupt stop.

Jessie waited, holding her breath as the candle continued to flicker.

"Hello?" she said finally. "Is there..."

She swallowed hard, and she couldn't help but wonder whether some invisible figure might be towering over her. She tried to remind herself that there was no such thing as ghosts, but the events of the previous two nights had left her shaken. She still couldn't explain the appearance of the strange children.

"Is there anyone there? If someone's here, please just show yourself, okay? It's not fair to hide like this. Please, if you're in here..."

Her voice trailed off.

Slowly, leaning forward, Jessie waved her hand in the air. She felt nothing, although she quickly noticed that the air between the two pews felt much colder than the rest of the chapel. A specific cold patch seemed to exist right in front of her.

"Okay, get a grip," she said to herself, setting the candle down and turning to start working again on the handcuffs. She tried to focus on finding some way to break free, but the pew was far too solid and eventually she twisted around and started trying to kick the wooden panels out of the way.

After several minutes, exhausted, she stopped for a moment and tried to come up with a better idea. And then, slowly, she realized she could sense someone standing just a few feet away, right over her shoulder. She began to turn, convinced that she once again would see no-one, and then she let out a gasp as she spotted the legs of a figure wearing a tattered, bloodstained dress.

Despite the fear in her chest, Jessie forced herself to look up, and she felt her heart skip a beat as soon as she saw the dead eyes of Sarah Clarke.

CHAPTER FORTY

"NO," JESSIE WHISPERED, unable to move an inch as she continued to look up at the dead woman. "No, you... you can't... I mean... you..."

She blinked, and in an instant Sarah was gone.

Panicking, Jessie turned and looked all around. She tried to convince herself that she was imagining things, but a moment later she turned the other way and saw Sarah again, this time a little closer to the altar.

"What are you?" she stammered. "You're not a ghost. I know you're not a ghost, ghosts aren't real, so what are you really?"

The fly landed on the altar. Sarah looked down at it, and then she watched as it buzzed away again. She paused for a moment, before turning back to look at Jessie again.

"Where are my boys?" she asked.

"What?" Jessie stammered.

"Where are my boys?" she asked again. "It's been so long. Did they make it? Did they get away?"

"I don't know what you're talking about," Jessie replied, before remembering the children she'd met in the forest. "Who are you?"

She stared at her for a moment.

"You can't be who I think you are," she added, shaking her head slowly. "Please, you can't be her. You just can't be..."

"It didn't get them, did it?" Sarah continued, with fear in her eyes. "I know I should go out there and check, but I'm too scared. Just tell me that they all got away, and that they lived long, happy lives."

"If you mean... I don't know, but if you mean the orphans who lived here, I saw them outside." She paused, before remembering the necklace. She slowly reached into her pocket and pulled the necklace out, holding it up for Sarah to see.

"Where did you get that?"

"It was outside," Jessie explained, "on the door handle. I think... I'm not sure, but I think they brought it here, they..."

She paused as she realized that she was starting to accept the existence of the ghostly boys.

All her doubts were fading away as she stared up at the horrific sight of Sarah Clarke.

"That's impossible," Sarah said, her voice trembling now with emotion. "If they brought it to the chapel, that means they're still here, which means..."

Her voice trailed off, and she slowly began to reach out toward the necklace. As she was about to take it, however, she hesitated.

"How long?" she whispered.

"I'm sorry?" Jessie stammered.

"How long have I been in here?"

"I think..." Jessie paused, and then she swallowed hard. "Maybe... almost... three hundred years."

Suddenly Sarah screamed, and in that moment she disappeared.

"What the hell?" Jessie gasped, scrambling up the altar steps before the handcuffs pulled tight and held her in place. Looking around, she tried to figure out how the strange figure had managed to vanish. "She's not a ghost," she said out loud, even though she could think of no other possible explanation. "She can't be a ghost, because ghosts aren't real, because ghosts -"

Stopping, she realized she could hear a sobbing sound. She turned and looked toward the side room, and she realized that was where the sound was coming from. Not daring to move, she listened as the pitiful sobs continued, and after a moment she remembered the nightmare in which she'd seen the boys surrounding Sarah Clarke during her final moments. She paused, and then slowly she began to drag the pew across the room until she reached the door that led into the side room.

She looked around, but in the darkness she could see no sign of Sarah.

"I -"

Instantly, the door slammed shut, and Jessie took a startled step back. She could hear the sobbing again, louder this time, and she realized that the woman seemed utterly brokenhearted. She wanted to open the door again, but at the same time she was worried that she might make the woman even more angry. Although she was still struggling to accept what she'd experienced, she realized after a moment that she had to at least acknowledge what appeared to be happening right in front of her.

"I've met them," she said, hoping she could be heard. "Out in the forest, I mean. I found their skulls. I'm so sorry, but they died. I think they..."

She thought back to the moment in the nightmare when she'd seen Sir Cecil Etheridge kill little William Merriman, and to the sight of the other boys dead in the forest.

"You did your best," she continued, before crouching down and carefully slipping the necklace through the gap under the door. She was still wondering whether she might simply be hallucinating. "I don't know if they ever could have made it away from here. Whatever that thing was, the thing that seemed to be possessing you, it might have been too powerful."

She waited as the sobbing continued.

"They're here, though," she added. "They're right outside. I think for some reason they're scared to come in here, or they can't come in. If you just go out there, though, you can see them again. All twelve of them are out there, and I think..."

She paused as she remembered the moment when the necklace had been left on the handle.

"I think they're waiting for you," she explained. "Don't ask me to explain it all, because I can't, but I think they're waiting for you and I think they've been waiting for a long time. I don't think they blame you for what happened. I think they miss you. Why else would they have been coming to that door? I don't think they were knocking for me at all, I think it was you they were trying to see."

She listened as the sobbing went on and on, and she began to fear that she was losing her mind. She took a deep breath as she tried to figure out what she should do next, but a moment later she froze as the sobbing sound ended abruptly.

"Hey," she continued, "are you still in there? Are you alright?"

She waited, before getting to her feet and reaching for the handle. She hesitated, however, since she was worried about how the woman would react if she tried to go into the room. Although she tried to remind herself that there was no such thing as ghosts, some part of her still thought that she was somehow speaking to the spirit of the real Sarah Clarke. One moment she was convinced that ghosts were real, the next that they weren't, and she found herself constantly switching between the two viewpoints. Finally, slowly, she turned the handle and pushed the door open.

There was no sign of Sarah in the room. Spotting the necklace on the floor, she reached down and picked it up, and then she turned to go back out into the chapel.

At that moment, she found Sarah Clarke standing right behind her. Screaming, the woman grabbed Jessie by the throat and pinned her against the wall.

"Why are you lying about my boys?" she snarled. "They escaped! I know they did! They had to!"

"I'm telling the truth!" Jessie gasped, reaching up with her free hand and trying desperately to get free. "Why would I lie to you? They're out there and they're waiting for you! All you have to do is -"

"Liar!" Sarah screamed, squeezing her

throat tighter and leaning toward her face. "If I let them down, that would mean that I condemned them to the same fate that I suffered! Don't you understand? When that thing entered my body, I became unholy, condemned to a miserable existence here and unable to ascend to join the Lord! If you're telling me that the same thing happened to my boys, to those beautiful souls I was trying to protect, then you're saying that I failed them!"

"I'm so sorry," Jessie gasped, "but I saw them!"

She let out a pained groan as she felt Sarah's grip tighten, and then she cried out as she was thrown down from the wall. Landing hard on the side of the pew, she felt a cracking sensation in her ribs as she rolled onto the floor. Her right hand was still caught in the handcuffs.

"I'm sorry," she stammered, barely able to get any words out at all. "I don't know what's happening here, I'm only telling you what I saw. I was out there in the forest and I found their little bones, and it was one of the most awful things I've seen in my life. Someone buried them, but they're still running around out there. I don't even know what's real anymore. I don't know what's happening. I just want to go home."

Sitting up, she saw that Sarah was once again towering above her, staring down with an expression of furious disdain.

"I'm begging you," Jessie continued breathlessly, "don't hurt me. I'm not even supposed to be here. Diana brought me here as bait for some kind of thing that I don't even understand."

"*I* understand it," Sarah sneered. "It was inside me all those years ago. And while it was in there, I could feel its memories spreading through my mind. I know what the presence is, and I know *exactly* how it ended up trapped here at Hardlocke House."

CHAPTER FORTY-ONE

ALMOST FIVE HUNDRED YEARS earlier, three men stalked through the forest, dragging a fourth man whose body had been wrapped in chains. The man on the ground coughed and spluttered as he tried to get free, but finally the other men stopped and turned to look down at him.

"You," Sir Thomas Clarke sneered, "whose name shall not be spoken. Do you lack the strength even to get to your feet?"

Naked and covered in cuts and bruises, the man managed to kneel. The chains hung heavy around his neck and shoulders, and some of his wounds had split again after having begun to heal during his time in confinement. Smeared in dirt and fecal matter, and with long straggly hair, he finally managed to lift his face and look at his captors. He eyed each of them in turn, and then he allowed himself a smile that revealed two rows of rotten teeth.

"You find something amusing?" Sir Thomas asked, raising a skeptical eyebrow. "You, who have caused so much suffering, seem unable to grasp the gravity of your situation."

"On the contrary," the man replied, as blood ran from his lips, "I recognize only too well that I seem to be at a distinct disadvantage to you honorable gentlemen."

He held his hands up, and more chains weighed down on his wrists. Several of his fingers, broken long ago during his first bout of torture, were twisted and gnarled.

"Pray, relieve me of this burden," he continued, "so that I might make a better account of myself."

"We all know that your strength comes not from such mortal things," Sir Thomas said, and the other two men nodded their agreement. "We were at your trial, remember? Your villainy was demonstrated beyond doubt, as was your familiarity with certain dark arts."

"I do not recall," the man replied, tilting his head a little. "That so-called trial was so hard to follow, at least for those of us who were being tortured throughout its duration. I am sure, however, that I cannot have been condemned for anything, since I am but a simple, innocent traveling doctor."

"You are a liar and a heretic!" one of the other men snapped angrily, reaching for his sword.

"Patience, Sir Harold," Sir Thomas said, holding up a hand to stop him. He turned back to the man on the ground. "We have brought this wretched fellow out here so that he might pay for what he has done. It is not, however, for us to enact the sentence." Turning to look over his shoulder, he glanced across the clearing and saw that a carriage was arriving. "The executioner is here," he added. "All that is wrong, is about to be put right."

The man on the ground turned and watched as the carriage came to a halt. Two men stepped down from the front and walked around to open a door on the carriage's side, and they then helped a figure down. This figure was dressed all in black, its face covered by a dark veil, but already the man could tell that the supposed executioner was a woman. He watched as she was handed a dagger, and his smile faded a little as the woman began to make her way closer.

"What is this?" he whispered. "Am I to be cut down by the fairest hand in all the land?"

"You are to suffer according to your own arts," Sir Thomas replied calmly. "You have been brought to this place, because this place is known to contain certain qualities. Once your soul has been extinguished here, it shall not be able to ever leave.

Not unless someone were to willingly transport you away, but I think we can be satisfied that no such thing will ever happen. Your punishment is not so much death, as the opportunity to contemplate for eternity the mistakes you have made. Even Satan will not be able to save you."

"I am honored," the man said, looking the new arrival up and down as she stopped next to him. He peered up at the veil that covered her face, but he was not able to make out any of her features. "Truly," he added, bowing slightly, causing his chains to rattle. "I was born a lowly commoner. Never did I think that I should be raised up to the level I am at now. I am a simple man and -"

"You practice witchcraft and that is a fact," Sir Thomas said firmly.

The man turned to him.

"Witchcraft? You seem rather superstitious."

"Plenty spoke at your trial," Sir Thomas reminded him. "If you were to be simply killed, your soul would fly to that dark place where Satan resides, and there you would receive your rewards. We cannot allow that to happen. By binding your foul heart to this place, we can make sure that you are trapped forever between worlds. We will make sure that this forest remains empty, and that all good people know to keep away. That way, your mischievous games will end for good."

"What games?" the man barked, suddenly

overtaken by a fit of anger. "Healing the sick? Providing for those in need? I helped end their pain! I did what the Lord would not, I -"

Suddenly his throat was grabbed from behind by a hand clad in black silk, and he let out a gasp as his face was tilted up to meet the ominous darkness of the veiled woman.

"Might I not even see your saintly features?" he asked her. "Oh, that I could gaze upon your face in this, the moment of my death. Am I to be denied even that solace?"

He waited, but the figure merely stared down at him, and a moment later he felt the dagger's tip pressing against his back.

"How high I have risen," he whispered, "from a peasant's cradle to this most exalted position in the land. If my dear parents could see me now, they would be so proud. But you know, whatever you might do to me, I have a few little tricks that are beyond the realm of ordinary men. I bear you no ill will for what is about to happen, but I must say that I find this Thomas Clarke fellow to be mighty irritating. I warn you, then, that I might not be finished with him and his line, not even in death."

Again he waited, although he knew deep down that he would receive no reply.

"Do it, then," he added. "If it makes you feel better, Your Majesty."

At that moment, the figure plunged the dagger into the man's back and twisted hard. Letting out a gasp of pain, the man shuddered slightly before falling forward, sliding off the dagger and slumping to the ground. Immediately, the three other men rushed forward and crouched down, turning him over and holding him down as the black-veiled woman slowly got to her knees.

The man tried to say something, but all that emerged from his mouth was a rush of blood.

"Hurry!" Sir Thomas said to the figure. "If he slips away before you have done it, he might yet escape."

The figure hesitated, before placing one hand on the dying man's chest and then digging the blade between his ribs. The man shook violently, but he could do nothing as the figure cut carefully and methodically. The sound of splintering bones caused the watching figures to flinch, but the woman showed no hesitation as she pulled away several chunks of meat. Blood was bursting between her fingers.

"He is not trying to get away from us," Sir Thomas reminded the others. "He is trying to die before the final part of his sentence is carried out."

The man's ribs cracked wider as the dagger cut through his chest, and a moment later the figure reached deeper and began to pull more shards of bone out of the way. Glistening blood coated the figure's black gloves as she pushed her fingers deeper into the man's chest, but finally she was able to find his beating heart. She turned the dagger and used it to cut in a few more places, before slowly lifting the heart up. Blood poured down, but the man was able to stare with a horrified expression as his own heart was raised up, still beating for a few more seconds before falling still.

"It is done," Sir Thomas noted, as the life faded from the man's eyes. He looked at the heart for a moment, unable to hide his contempt. "Is it me," he continued, "or is some foul quality visible in that thing?"

"It is the heart of one who turned to worship evil," one of the other men suggested.

"It is nothing now," Sir Thomas said, correcting him. "It is powerless."

Reaching out, he carefully took the heart from the woman's hands. His own hands were bare, and he soon had blood smeared around his fingers. Setting the heart down, he made a point of stamping on it with the heel of his boot, grinding it into the forest floor.

Getting to her feet, the woman slowly removed her black gloves and let them fall to the ground. She looked at the dead man for a moment.

"At least this piece of scum is gone now," Sir Thomas told her. "You have done the right thing."

"Experience tells me," the woman replied, from beneath her veil, "that these evil creatures can never be killed. Nor can they be cured of their wickedness. Fortunately, they have a habit of becoming trapped in looping circles, constantly striving to achieve some aim but also failing and having to start again. In this way, their conniving natures serve to work against them. Therefore, I hereby decree that this area should be marked off limits for all time. We would not want any of our poor, innocent subjects to stumble upon the place and be drawn into the miscreants' desperate ploys. See that this is done."

"His foul spirit no doubt will linger," Sir Thomas pointed out.

"No matter," the woman said. "Let it linger. Let it blow about between the trees as the wind wishes, that is no concern of ours. So long as the evil is not concentrated within a living body, it shall lose much of its power. The most important thing is that we must keep others away from the area. No word of this matter must leave this place, nor any scrap of flesh."

She looked at the corpse for a few seconds longer, before turning and making her way back toward the carriage.

"Your Majesty," Sir Thomas said, calling after her, "you can rest assured that the rest of this matter will be dealt with in accordance with the law.

Our land is now short one wretch. We must, however, be on the lookout for others. I shall inform you if more are found."

Once the woman was back in her carriage, Sir Thomas stood and turned to the other two men.

"Let us leave this corpse to be consumed by beasts of the forest," he muttered darkly, as he took water from a flask and rinsed his hands. "The heart, too. Come, we have a long ride ahead of us."

As he and the other men made their way back across the clearing, past the dead body and the still heart, a few flecks of blood remained beneath his fingernails.

AMY CROSS

CHAPTER FORTY-TWO

"YOUR MAJESTY," A VOICE said from the far end of the gloomy chamber, ten years later, "I bring you the papers you requested."

"Make haste, then," the new king replied, his features picked out by the light of a candle that flickered on a nearby desk. "I am tired of being told that I should not see these things. I cannot sleep tonight, so I would rather make good use of my time. Why do so many people here seem to delight in finding fresh ways to hide matters from my attention?"

"I know you have a particular interest in the activities of witches in this realm," the man said, making his way across the room. "The late queen shared that interest, although she preferred to keep such matters from becoming public knowledge.

Nevertheless, she took part in several executions, along with men such as Sir Robert Marlton and Sir Thomas Clarke. She thought it her duty to intervene wherever possible."

"She did not do nearly enough," the king muttered, snatching the papers from the man as soon as he was close enough. "I sense that so many of these details have been deliberately kept from me. Is it the case that witchcraft is more common in this land than I had been led to believe?"

"Your Majesty will have to make his own mind up on that matter."

"I certainly shall," the king said as he began to look through the papers.

"Your predecessor was keen to make sure that ordinary people could not become caught up in these things," the man explained. "To that end, she declared certain areas – mostly in woodlands – to be completely off-limits. To this day, there are several places that nobody can visit without permission from the crown."

"That rule must remain in place," the king said firmly, "but I fear that Elizabeth was not strict enough when she set off to track these beasts down. She waited for them to become apparent, whereas what is needed is a campaign to root out these monstrosities wherever they fester on this island. Their malign influence must be ended, and we must not rest until this task is complete."

"You are correct, of course," the man replied. "I myself was a witness to one execution carried out by your predecessor. In a forest far from here, she cut out a man's beating heart and showed it to him before he had a chance to expire. Ever since, that forest has been left alone by the locals, who have been told all manner of tales that have served to scare them out of their wits. But more must be done and I believe that you, Your Majesty, are the only man who can make sure that the correct steps are taken."

"I shall require your assistance," the king said. "Gather a group of like-minded men and bring them to me."

"At once," the man replied, turning to leave the room.

"And what is your name?" the king called after him. "It seems to have slipped my mind, and you have impressed me. I believe I shall soon have cause to give you greater responsibilities."

"My name?" The man stopped in the doorway and turned back to him. "Freeman, Your Majesty. Nykolas Freeman, at your service. And I assure you that I shall not rest until this land has been cleansed of this terrible scourge."

***

Several hundred miles away, as night fell across

Hintern Forest, two young boys kept low as they hurried home with the rabbits they'd caught in neighboring fields. As a light rain began to fall, however, one of the boys slowed and then stopped to look to the right.

"What are you doing?" the first boy asked, turning back to him. "This rain's only going to get worse. We must get home!"

"I agree, so why do we persist in going the long way round?"

"What do you mean?"

"I mean that it would certainly be quicker to cut through this part of the forest."

"We can't do that."

"Why not?"

The first boy stepped closer to him and put a hand on his friend's shoulder.

"You don't know the area very well," he explained, "but I do. Trust me, everyone around here understands that the forest west of this point is not to be visited. In the name of King James, and Queen Elizabeth before him, that part of the forest is said to contain an evil that no man must ever encounter."

"You mean that there is some murderous villain out there? Is there some man who keeps the forest empty?"

"Not a man, exactly. At least, not a man now. He might have been one, once."

"What superstitious nonsense are you trying to get me to believe?" the second boy asked with a smile. "Am I supposed to be afraid of some will-o'-the-wisp or fairy? Do I look like a frightened old maid to you?"

"I agree that the idea is somewhat fantastical," the first boy replied, "but I beg you to trust me on this matter. We lose barely half an hour by taking the preferred route, and there is no risk out that way."

"There is no risk this way, either," the second boy said, pulling away from him and starting to make his way across the forbidden part of the forest. "You can take the long path if you wish, but I shall get home before you and I shall be sure to tell everyone the reason for your tardiness."

"Come back!" the other boy shouted, but he was too late.

Marching through the forest, the second boy allowed himself a smile as he realized that he'd show everyone else in the village just how foolish they'd been. He'd only arrived in the area a few weeks earlier, and he'd been hoping to find some way of proving his mettle. As he looked around, he saw nothing but tall, thin trees stretching off in very direction, and he found it difficult to believe that so many people had allowed themselves to live in fear. He was going to show them that they had been horribly mistaken.

"Please!" his friend yelled, from much further away now. "Don't do this!"

"You're welcome to join me!" the second boy replied, turning and waving at him as the rain intensified. "Come on, what's the worst that can happen?"

He watched for a moment as the other boy gesticulated wildly, and then – with several rabbits hanging from a branch slung over his shoulder – he turned to continue his progress.

And then he froze as he saw a figure kneeling a little way up ahead, or at least something that had taken the approximate form of a figure. A pile of leaves stood in a small clearing, and after a moment this pile shifted slightly, as if some hidden entity was starting to move.

Opening his mouth, the boy considered calling out, but something about the figure's appearance made him reconsider. The air all around was getting colder by the second as the figure began to raise its head, which was concealed beneath more dead leaves.

Although he wanted to take a step back and wait to see exactly what he'd encountered, the boy forced himself to stand his ground. The last thing he could afford was to run, making himself look like a fool in the process, so he decided to wait until he could be sure that the figure was just some harmless fool who happened to be out in the forest. Yet as the figure continued to raise its head, the boy felt a growing sense of fear starting to build in his chest, until finally he could help himself no longer.

He stepped back, just as the figure's face become visible beneath the leaves, revealing pale features and a broad grin.

"I wonder," the figure said, reaching up and parting the layer of leaves that covered his body, "whether you might be able to help me. I'm trying to find something that was taken from me."

He pulled more and more leaves aside, finally revealing a huge, bloodied hole in his chest.

"Have you by any chance spotted a heart anywhere on the ground?" he sneered. "It was cut away from me by a mad old woman who really should have known better. If you don't believe me, come closer and get a better look. Don't worry, I won't do anything to you, I'm far too weak! Look at me, I'm really nothing more than a pile of old leaves."

The boy stared at the horrific sight for a moment, before finally turning and running. As laughter ran out through the forest, he bumped against several of the trees but somehow he managed to keep going until finally – out of breath and filled with panic – he slammed into his friend and then turned to look back the way he'd just come.

The figure was nowhere to be seen. The

forest floor was blanketed by a thick cover of dead leaves, but they lay innocuously enough.

"What's wrong?" the first boy asked. "Did you see something?"

"Didn't *you* see it?" the second boy replied, turning to him.

"See what? You just stopped for a few seconds and then you ran back this way. Tell me what happened! Did you see some kind of spirit out there?"

"I saw..."

For a moment, the second boy tried to work out how he could possibly finish that sentence, but the last thing he wanted was to make himself seem like a fool. How could he possibly admit that he had been fooled by something that had amounted to nothing more than a bunch of leaves? He continued to look out across the forest for a few more seconds, before turning and shoving his friend hard in the back, forcing him to set off again.

"Come on," he muttered as they resumed their journey home, taking the long route. "I can't let you walk all alone. I know how scared you get."

"You saw something, didn't you? Please, you have to tell me, was it -"

"I didn't see anything!" he snapped angrily. "Now will you just walk with me? This rain is getting worse!"

The first boy slowed for a moment and

watched as his friend hurried on ahead. Turning, the first boy looked out at the forest, but he saw nothing untoward, just trees separated by piles of leaves. Finally, supposing that his friend had merely allowed himself to get spooked by the shadows, he turned and hurried after him.

"Wait for me!" he called out. "Slow down! What did you see in the forest? Why won't you tell me?"

CHAPTER FORTY-THREE

TWO HUNDRED YEARS LATER, Sarah Clarke stood in the chambers of her uncle's firm and tried to understand exactly what he had just told her. Her mind was racing, and although she tried several times to ask him whether he was sure of his facts, she could not quite bring herself to speak the words.

"You look rather pale, my dear," Walter Clarke said, eyeing her with a hint of amusement. "I know this has all come as rather a shock, but I assure you that there is no word of a lie in these papers. The money you have come into is considerable, and since you are unmarried I suppose that you yourself will have to decide what to do with it."

"Yes," she stammered, before taking a seat next to his desk. "I confess, when you asked me to come here today, I had no idea that you intended to tell me such a thing."

"You must be careful with this money," he told her. "It is sufficient to make you a free woman, but it is not so much that you can afford a life of idleness. Not that I would ever expect such a thing of you. I am sure your parents would be proud if they could see the fine, upstanding young woman you have become, but first tell me... Have you considered taking a husband?"

"A husband?"

She looked at him with a bewildered expression, as if the idea had never even crossed her mind.

"It's not a weakness," Walter told her. "The right husband could be very useful to you. As a woman alone in the world, you will face certain... challenges."

"I know this," she replied. "My name has been blackened several times already. All I have ever wanted is to do good work that pleases the Lord."

"It's not the Lord's opinion that I'm worried about," he said. "It's the men of this town, who see an unmarried woman and assume that there must be something wrong with her. Every conceivable barrier will be placed in your way, my dear, and there are some matters that even I cannot help you with. Would you not consider taking at least a meek, compliant husband? He would really only have to be for show."

He waited for her to reply, but he could tell now that she was lost in thought.

"I can advise you," he continued. "As I have explained, I fear I have little time left in this world, but I can certainly help you come up with a plan. I am -"

Before he could finish, he began to cough violently.

Sarah immediately took a handkerchief from her pocket and held it out for him. He took the handkerchief and held it against his lips until the coughing fit subsided. By that point, the white fabric was dotted with spots of blood.

"The point I am trying to make," he said, once he'd got his breath back a little, "is that this is a moment that will change your life. The money comes from your parents, and I admit that its arrival in your hands is rather unlikely and could even prove to be controversial. I would suggest that you think long and hard before you decide what to do with it and -"

"I already know what to do with it."

"There are many -"

It took a moment before Walter realized what she had just said.

"You do?" he asked cautiously.

"I don't know how, or why," she continued,

with a faraway look in her eyes, "but I have often dreamed of a particular place where I think I could help people. I know that I am easy to dislike, and that this money will only make me even more unpopular, so I propose to surround myself with the only people who might actually see me for who I really am." She paused, before turning to her uncle with a smile. "My mind is set. I am going to open an orphanage. And I know exactly where it must be built."

***

"Are you really sure about this?" Walter asked a few weeks later, as he followed Sarah through the forest. He coughed into his hand for a moment and wiped away more blood. "Why here, of all places? We are miles from anywhere!"

"Any time I have ever looked at a map," she replied, keeping her gaze fixed on the clearing ahead, "or thought of the breadth of our land, I have felt drawn to this particular place. I do not know why, but I am starting to wonder whether the Lord has been trying to guide me here. What if the money is part of the Lord's plan? What if I was always supposed to start this orphanage?"

"The land was surprisingly easy to purchase," he admitted. "It's said that the locals are rather superstitious about this place. I couldn't quite get to the bottom of what they think is wrong with it, I'm not sure that they even know anymore. Anyway, you should be left alone. Construction will soon begin on the house itself, but -"

"And the chapel," she said, interrupting him. "Don't forget that, and a few small outhouses as well. No expense shall be spared."

"Indeed, Sarah, but I do hope that you are not rushing into anything. I'm quite sure that an existing house could have been found, somewhere closer to a town or village. Out here, you will be awfully isolated."

"It will just be me and the children," she replied, "which is how I want it to be. Children do not judge, nor do they listen to gossip and condemn a woman simply because she ruffles a few feathers. Children are pure and innocent and kind, and I am going to make sure that they stay that way. There are some in this land who suffer terribly, but here they will find a safe haven and I will nurse them to -"

Before she could finish, her uncle launched into another heavy coughing fit. This time he had to stop and lean against a tree, and Sarah took a moment to support him.

"I am so sorry," she said, "I have been pushing you too hard. This journey was unnecessary. I let my excitement get the better of my judgment."

"I will be quite alright," he told her, although he was still in some discomfort. "I might rest here for a moment, though. Just to get my strength back."

Reaching into his pocket, he took out a silver cross attached to a necklace.

"While I remember," he continued, handing the necklace to her, "this is for you."

"It's beautiful," she replied, holding the necklace up, "but -"

"It belonged to your mother," he explained. "I found it in her possessions after she died, and I kept it because I suppose I wanted some reminder of her. Now, however, I think you should have it. As far as I know, it has been passed down through many generations on her side of the family. It's a true Hardlocke family heirloom, and I seem to recall that your mother was wearing it on the day she married your father Percy Clarke. It should be yours now."

"I will wear it always," she said, before slipping the necklace into place. "Thank you so much. It will remind me of her, and of you, always."

"I hope so. Now, stop waiting here with this foolish old man. You go ahead and take a look at the plot of land."

"No, I will stay with you."

"Don't be foolish, girl," he replied. "I can

see the excitement in your eyes, and I will not do anything to dampen that. I'll be quite alright resting here." He paused, before chuckling as he pushed her away. "Go!"

"I shall be only a short distance away," she said, before turning and making her way between the trees.

A couple of minutes later, she reached the clearing and stopped to take a look at the spot where the house would soon be built. Her heart was filled with ideas about how the orphanage would be run, and for a moment she could only look around and imagine the happiness of the children who would soon be in her care. She was certain that she was going to give them the fullest, happiest lives possible. As she set off again across the clearing, her heart was filled with hope for the future, and with the belief that -

Suddenly she felt something hard beneath her right foot. Looking down, she was surprised to see what appeared to be a fragment of bone. She crouched down and took a closer look. Although she told herself that the piece of bone must surely be from an animal, as she held it up she couldn't help but notice that it looked like part of a human rib.

She hesitated, before putting the piece of bone back down and then forcing herself to focus on the task at hand. Ahead, the far end of the clearing marked the spot where the house would be built.

"It's going to be wonderful," she said, with tears in her eyes, before turning to look back toward her uncle. "Don't you -"

Stopping suddenly, she saw that he had fallen to the ground.

"Uncle Walter?" she called out, before hurrying back over to him. "Uncle Walter, are you alright?"

CHAPTER FORTY-FOUR

FINALLY, TWO YEARS LATER, Sarah Clarke stood and looked up at the grand facade of her new home. Hardlocke House – as she had chosen to name it, after her mother's side of the family – was complete, and she felt a surge of hope in her heart as she realized that she was now on the verge of achieving her goal.

"Is there anything else I can do for you?" Mr. Arthur asked as he stood next to her.

"I think I shall be perfectly fine," she replied, wiping a tear from her cheek as she turned to him. "Thank you so much for everything you have done to help me."

"Your uncle would have wanted nothing less," he pointed out. "I feel rather as if it is wrong to leave you here all alone, however."

"Nonsense," she told him. "I have so much to do, and the first children will be arriving on Sunday. As you can imagine, I shall be so busy, I shall barely have time to rest."

"Write and let me know how you are managing," he said.

"I will. And thank you again. Hardlocke House is magnificent, and I shall never forget your role in helping me get it ready. Please, have a safe journey back to London."

As Mr. Arthur walked away, Sarah once again found herself marveling at the house. It was even greater and more stunning than she'd dared hope, but she knew that the hard work had only just begun. She had less than a week to get the place ready for the first orphans, and she told herself that she was going to make sure that the house was absolutely perfect by the time they arrived.

"This is it," she whispered, as more tears ran down her face. "This is my life's work."

***

Closing the door on the front of the stove, Sarah held her hands close and tried to get warm. Now that darkness was falling outside, she was preparing for her first night at Hardlocke House, but her mind was already racing with thoughts of everything that would have to be done in the morning.

Turning, she looked up at the grand portrait on the far wall. It had been her uncle, the late Walter Hardlocke, who had commissioned the picture. Sarah had not been keen, but she had acquiesced to her uncle's wishes and now she felt that it would be wrong of her to hide the portrait away. She supposed that she would get used to it with time, and that it might help her to establish her authority whenever she received a visitor, although she couldn't help but wish that the painter had made her look a little happier.

She got to her feet, but at that moment she heard a single distinct thudding sound coming from elsewhere in the house. She turned and looked toward the doorway, and for a moment she couldn't help but worry. She tried to tell herself that there was no reason to be concerned, but then she heard the sound again and she hurried out into the hall and looked up the stairs.

She waited, and a few seconds later she heard the sound yet again. This time, she was certain that it was coming from somewhere on the upper floor.

"Hello?" she called out, worried that one of the workmen might have stayed behind.

After fetching a candle from the next room, she began to make her way up the stairs. She told herself that the most likely cause of the sound was a stray window that must have been left open, perhaps one that allowed a breeze to enter the house and move a door. By the time she had reached the top of the stairs, she was certain that this was indeed the cause of the noise, although the house had now fallen silent and she was beginning to wonder whether the sound might in fact have come from outside after all.

"What silliness," she muttered under her breath, as she turned and looked at all the closed doors that led away from the landing. "I simply cannot allow myself to react in this way to every little sound."

She took a deep breath, and then she turned to go back down the stairs.

At that moment, however, she froze as she heard a creaking sound coming from the far end of the main corridor. She looked over her shoulder and held the candle up, and she saw to her surprise that the farthest door was swinging open. She felt no breeze, no hint that an errant window had been left askew, and as she looked toward the open door she couldn't help but worry that something seemed to be staring back at her from that far room. No matter how hard she tried to tell herself to stop worrying, she could feel a gaze burning into her soul.

"Who's there?" she called out finally, before she could stop herself. She reached out and grabbed the railing at the top of the stairs, but she already knew that turning and running back down wasn't an option.

She took a few seconds to compose herself, and then she forced herself to start walking along the corridor, making for the room at the far end. Whatever had caused the noise, it seemed to have come from the large dormitory that was set to welcome the first boys a few days later. That was the room where the orphans were supposed to feel completely safe and secure, and as Sarah reached the open door she couldn't help worrying that somehow some creature might have broken into the house.

Stopping, she held the candle up. She could see the nearest beds, all stripped down and ready to be made, but there was no sign of anyone or anything.

Although she was tempted to simply turn and walk away, she knew that she had to take a closer look. She stepped into the room, and she immediately noticed that the air was icy. She turned and looked around, holding the candle a little higher, but its flickering light exposed only the bare beds and – a little further off – the walls.

Her footsteps rang out as she made her way to the middle of the room. She turned all around, but the only movement came from shadows cast by the candle's light.

"If there's anyone here," she said, trying – but not particularly succeeding – in her attempt to hide the fear from her voice, "you must show yourself at once, do you hear me? I won't tolerate bad behavior here in my house. The Lord will..."

Her voice trailed off, and after a moment she reached up and touched the silver cross that hung from her necklace.

"The Lord will protect this house," she continued. "Be in no doubt about that, the Lord -"

Suddenly an immense force slammed into her from behind. Screaming, she was thrown through the air and sent crashing into one of the walls. The candle fell from her hand and was extinguished as it hit the floor, and Sarah slithered down in absolute darkness until she could only sit breathless on the wooden boards and try to pull herself together. She began to sit up, but her mind was racing and she had no idea what had just hit her. When she turned and looked back across the room, she saw only darkness.

She reached up to touch the cross again, and she felt a little strength from the sensation of its metal edges against her fingers.

After a few seconds, she let go of the cross and got to her feet, although she kept her back pressed against the wall as she listened for any sign of movement in the dormitory.

"Who..."

Unable to get any more words out, Sarah simply waited. At first, the calm and peace all around allowed her to believe that perhaps the tempest was over. She had no idea what had hit her, but she supposed that something might have fallen, perhaps a panel from the roof. She looked up and saw no sign of the night sky, yet still she tried desperately to believe that she had been struck by something entirely explicable.

And then, very slowly, she realized she could feel her necklace moving.

She tried to ignore the sensation, but then she reached up and to her horror she found that some force in the darkness had taken hold of necklace and seemed to be pulling the cross forward, as if to examine it more closely. She began to move her fingers along toward the cross, at which point she found that it was somehow holding itself up in the air.

"How?" she whispered. "Lord, if this is a message, I am but your humble servant and I confess that I do not understand. I am..."

Realizing she could hear a faint, rumbling laugh coming from directly ahead, she froze.

"Lord," she stammered after a few more seconds, "I..."

Again her voice trailed off, and this time she was able to hear the sound of somebody else breathing in the darkness.

"Oh, you pretty thing," a man's voice purred suddenly. "You give me strength. How you are going to suffer for your misplaced faith."

Sarah turned to run, but a force instantly pinned her hard against the wall, and she could only scream as she felt a cold, dead hand pressing against her face.

CHAPTER FORTY-FIVE

"WELCOME TO HARDLOCKE HOUSE."

Standing at the top of the steps, Sarah Clarke looked down at the two young boys who stood in the clearing. She took in their scared, tired, dirty little faces, and then she turned her gaze to the man who had arrived with them.

"Joseph and Michael, I believe?" she asked.

"That's right, Ms. Clarke," the man replied, doffing his hat at her. "Two wayward young men without parents. They were living on the streets of York for some time before we managed to drag them kicking and screaming here. Joseph's seven years old and Michael's only six. They're good healthy boys, but you might find that they're a bit of a handful at first." He hesitated. "To be honest, Ms. Clarke, they've both been placed in homes before, but it's not gone that well. We're hoping that they'll do better out here, away from distractions."

"I'm sure we'll get along just fine," she said, looking at the boys again. "My name is Ms. Clarke and I am in charge of the house. I shall be your teacher, as well as your guardian, and we shall all have a splendid time just as long as you are willing to listen to instructions. Are you willing to do that, boys?"

She waited, but the two children seemed too nervous to say anything.

"I've got to get going," the man said, taking a step back, "but I'll be leaving them with you now. And if you want my advice, Ms. Clarke, you'll be tough with them right from the start. You don't want to show any weakness, not with boys like this. You need to set them to work."

"I shall take that into consideration."

The man hesitated, looking around.

"Are you..." He turned to her again. "Are you here all alone, Ms. Clarke?" he asked. "Do you not have a man with you?"

"I do not need anyone else," she replied. "The house mostly runs itself, the boys will have jobs to do, and we are going to be growing most of our own food. What little we need from outside can be acquired without too much difficulty, since I have made arrangements with some people from the nearest village. The house has been waiting so patiently for its first boys, and now they are here." She looked down at Joseph and Michael. "I assure you," she continued, "that we are all going to have the most wonderful time."

"Do you think it's proper that you don't have help?" the man asked.

"I believe I have already answered that question," she said firmly. "Please, if you don"t mind, the boys and I have some work to be getting on with."

***

Once the man had gone, Sarah took the boys inside and showed them around, and then she did indeed set them straight to work scrubbing the floor in the hall. While they worked, she made her way through to the office and stopped at her desk, at which point she felt a flicker of fear in her chest.

Standing completely still, she tried to listen to her own thoughts. Several days had passed since her terrifying experience in the dormitory, and she had begun to believe that it had all been in her head. Although that idea was somewhat difficult to accept, she was coming around to the possibility that the excitement of opening Hardlocke House up had simply become too much for her, and that the pressure had caused her to suffer some sort of episode.

"You mustn't be too hard on yourself," she remembered her uncle telling her, shortly before he'd died. "You're like your father in that regard, Sarah. You expect so much of yourself and you barely give yourself time to rest."

She missed her uncle so much, and she dearly wished that he might have been around to help her as she finished setting up the orphanage. In truth, he was the only person she would have trusted to help on a more long-term basis, since he had been her guiding light ever since the deaths of her parents many years earlier. The Clarke side of her family, in particular, had experienced so much tragedy and bad luck, stretching as far back as anyone could remember, that Sarah sometimes wondered if there would ever be any peace for any of them. Reaching up, she touched her necklace again and she told herself that she, finally, was going to break that cycle.

"Ms. Clarke?" a voice said cautiously, and she turned to see that Joseph was standing in the doorway. "We're done."

"Are you, indeed?" she replied, stepping over to take a look at the hall floor, which proved to be very clean. "You've both done a wonderful job, and I think you should now have a little time to play. Why don't you go outside and explore a little? Don't go too far, though, and be careful not to go into any of the other buildings."

"Yes, Ms. Clarke," Joseph said, turning to walk away.

"Wait," she said suddenly, surprising even herself. "You look sad, Joseph. Why is that? Are you not settling in well here at Hardlocke House?"

He looked back up at her.

"You look ungrateful," she continued, although she was not entirely sure where the words were coming from. She had noticed no such thing. "I think perhaps you do not understand the nature of the responsibilities that you face here. You have both done a good job with the floor, but now I want you to clean the stairs as well before you take a break."

Joseph turned to Michael, and then to Sarah again.

"Please," he said, "can we not do that tomorrow? The floor took so long, and my arms are aching. So are my knees."

"You won't get stronger if you don't push yourself," she told him. "Stop complaining. The stairs require your attention."

"But they look clean already," he said, turning and looking over at the staircase. "Please, I'm so tired, I think -"

Before he could finish, Sarah grabbed him by the arm and pulled him closer. He let out a shocked cry, but she was already squeezing his arm tighter as she leaned down to him.

"Are you whining about the fact that you have to work?" she sneered. "Are you such a pitiful little creature that you can't even do some basic cleaning?"

"I want to go!" he sobbed. "I don't want to be -"

Suddenly she slapped him hard, and then she shoved him back so firmly that he fell and landed with a jarring thud on the floor. He immediately started crying loudly, as did Michael.

"Stop making that miserable noise!" Sarah snarled.

Ignoring her, the boys turned to run, but in that moment Sarah grabbed them both and pulled them back. She opened her mouth to tell them to get to work, only to feel something cold rush through her body. For a moment, her eyes seemed to be burning and she could taste blood in her mouth, and she could only listen helplessly as she heard her own voice screaming at the children and calling them the foulest names imaginable. She tried to stop herself, but it was as if her entire body had momentarily been taken over by some other force and she was unable to contain the anger. Finally, after what felt like an eternity, she let go of the boys and took a step back, and she felt herself returning to normal as the burning sensation faded from her eyes.

To her horror, she saw that both Joseph and

Michael had soiled themselves.

"I don't know what..."

She paused, but she quickly realized that she couldn't be seen to have lost control.

"Go and clean yourselves up!" she barked, trying not to panic. "I don't care where, just go and do it! And then put your clothes in a pile so that I can wash them!"

The boys stared at her, as if they didn't dare move.

"Go!" she screamed, pointing to the stairs, and they both raced up toward the dormitory.

Stumbling back through to the office, Sarah collapsed into a chair and tried to work out exactly what had happened. Never in all her life had she felt such anger bursting through her own body, yet for a moment it was as if she'd been entirely seized by some other power. Reaching up and touching her forehead, she found that it was caked in a cold sweat, and a moment later she spotted her own reflection in a nearby mirror. She was momentarily horrified by the sight of her pale face and heavy, tired eyes, but she quickly sat up and tried to regain her composure.

Finally, getting to her feet, she realized that the strange moment was over. She felt like herself again, so she made her way to the hall and then she headed up the stairs, determined to find Joseph and Michael and make sure that they were being looked after properly. And she told herself that no matter what happened, she would never ever strike them – or any other child – again.

Somewhere in the back of her mind, however, another voice was laughing.

CHAPTER FORTY-SIX

"FROM THAT DAY ON," Sarah Clarke's ghost continued, still standing over Jessie in one corner of the chapel, "I was afflicted by a great evil that grew stronger and stronger. It was an evil that had been trapped here many years earlier by a member of my own family, and I truly believe that this presence – whose name I have never learned – found some way to reach out and steer me here. As a descendant of the great Sir Thomas Clarke, I was deemed to be the one who must pay."

Starting to sit up a little more, Jessie tried to figure out how she was going to escape. She looked at her wrist, which was still handcuffed to the pew, and then she looked up at Sarah again.

"I tried to fight it," Sarah sobbed, "but I couldn't. That *thing* had become a part of me, and death was my only way out. I hoped that at least I had saved my children from the presence. I was too afraid to stay anywhere near the house after I died. Once I realized that I was doomed to remain here for eternity, I chose to hide away here in the chapel. I heard noises outside sometimes, but I assumed they came from the presence in the house."

"The children are out there," Jessie stammered. "I told you, I've seen them. They're right outside that door and I swear they're waiting for you."

She paused, before holding the necklace out to her.

"So this belongs to *you*, right?" she continued. "The children brought it here. They don't hate you. They don't blame you, either. What happened to them is not your fault."

Sarah slowly took the necklace and held it up.

"I think they just want to be with you again," Jessie explained. "I think they understand, better than either of us, what really happened here."

She waited, hoping that she might finally have made the woman understand. A moment later, however, Sarah turned to her and screamed. In that instant she vanished, and the necklace fell to the floor.

"Okay," Jessie muttered, turning around and starting to kick at the pew, hoping that brute strength might help her get away, "I'm out of here. I don't know how, but I'm not sticking around for any more of this!"

For a couple of minutes, she worked furiously, kicking the pew over and over. Sometimes she felt as if she was making progress, as if the wood was buckling slightly at one of the joins, although she still wasn't entirely confident that her plan was going to work. Since she had no other ideas, however, she figured that she'd just have to stick to brute force, and eventually she began to let out a series of angry grunts as she kicked and kicked and kicked and -

Suddenly one of the wooden panels broke away. Jessie frantically tried to move another panel, and finally she was able to loop the handcuff over the damaged end. Scrambling back, she realized she was free, and she stumbled to her feet before starting to limp along the aisle, heading toward the chapel's main door.

"I have had enough of this place," she muttered under her breath, "and -"

Before she could finish, Sarah Clarke appeared right in front of her and snarled, before grabbing Jessie by the arm and slamming her down against the side of the one of the nearest pews. Letting out a gasp of shock, Jessie rolled down onto the floor before immediately trying to haul herself up. This time she could feel an ever sharper pain in her right side, and she only managed to get onto her knees before having to stop for a moment to get her breath back.

After a few more seconds, she somehow found the strength to stand. She took a stumbling step away from the pew, before turning and seeing that Sarah Clarke was once again standing in her way.

"Please," Jessie said, "what did I ever do to hurt you? Why won't you let me leave?"

"You're just like all the rest," Sarah replied, her voice filled with anger. "The world thought that I was a monster. Even after I showed you what happened to me, you think that I was weak for letting that thing into my head."

"No! I don't think that at all! I don't know exactly what that presence was, but it overpowered you, and I'm sure there was no way you could have fought back. I only -"

"I wanted to protect the children!" Sarah screamed, lunging at her and knocking her once again to the ground. "They were all I cared about and they were taken from me!"

Jessie tried to crawl away along one row of pews, only for the nearest pew to topple over and land on her. Struggling to get up, she scrambled over to the far wall and turned to look back across the chapel. In the moonlight, Sarah Clarke's ghost was still standing in the central aisle, although after a moment she faded into the shadows.

"It's not my fault!" Jessie shouted, hoping against hope that she was still being heard. "Whatever happened to you, it happened three hundred years ago! I get that you're angry. I'd be angry too. But you can't take it all out on me. That's not fair."

She looked around, but now she couldn't see Sarah at all. She turned toward the door, and she realized that she could get over there in just a few seconds. If she could just get outside and escape the chapel, she'd be able to keep away from Sarah's ghost.

She hesitated for a moment, and then she began to run along one of the rows. After just a couple of seconds, she saw Sarah ahead, but this time she was prepared; jumping up onto the pew, she hurried over into the next row, then the next, before finally managing to reach the door. She grabbed the handle, pulling the door open, but in that moment she heard a loud scream in her ear, and she was pulled back with such force that she accidentally pulled the handle off. A fraction of a second later, she was almost knocked unconscious as she hit the floor.

"Damn it!" she muttered, rolling onto her side. She'd come so close to getting outside, and when she looked over her shoulder she saw that the front door was now wide open.

Before she could react, the door slammed shut. The broken handle, however, meant that the door quickly began to open again.

Feeling another sharp pain in her ribs, Jessie tried to sit up. She threw the handle aside and tried to figure out how she was going to get out of the chapel, just as the door swung shut. A gust of wind began to blow it open again as Jessie tried to get to her feet.

"You're going nowhere!" Sarah hissed, suddenly grabbing her head from behind and pulling her back. "I've waited three hundred years to make someone pay for what happened to me! Now you tell me that my boys died too, and I can't let that go unpunished!"

"Please," Jessie gasped, as she felt Sarah's hands tighten around her throat. "I wasn't... the..."

"Three hundred years is such a long time," Sarah continued. "I felt every moment, and I had plenty of chances to think about what happened to me. I was only trying to do the Lord's work, I was trying to provide a place for those poor boys, but the world wouldn't let that happen, would it? No, the world saw fit to cut me down, and my boys and I all suffered at the hands of that *thing*! Even in death, I am abandoned by the Lord, so why should any other living creature be spared the pain and misery that was visited upon me?"

She leaned even closer, as Jessie struggled

harder and harder to breathe.

"My revenge on the world," Sarah sneered, "will be complete and -"

"Ms. Clarke?"

Sarah froze, still gripping Jessie's throat, as soon as she heard her name. She couldn't quite believe that the voice was real, but then the door bumped open again and she slowly looked up, only to see the twelve dead little boys standing outside in the forest, staring into the chapel.

"Please!" Jessie gasped, barely able to stay conscious. "Don't -"

Suddenly Sarah let go, leaving Jessie to fall to the floor. Stepping over her, Sarah slowly stepped forward, and finally she saw that all the boys from the orphanage were waiting for her.

"We tried to find you before," Edmund said, "but we couldn't get in there to you."

"We've been waiting for so long," Thomas added. "Please, Ms. Clarke, we don't know what to do. We don't know where to go."

Making her way cautiously along the aisle, still not quite believing what she was seeing, Sarah finally reached the doorway and stepped out into the forest. She walked over to where the boys were standing in a semi-circle, and then she looked down as William Merriman stepped closer and reached out, taking her hand.

"Please, Ms. Clarke," he said, staring up at

her, "can you come with us? Can you help us find the way?"

"Of course," she replied, as tears streamed down her face. "My boys, I had no idea you were out here all this time! You must forgive me!"

"We don't have to forgive you," Merriman replied. "We know it wasn't really you. But it gets cold out here, and we've been searching for so long. We don't know where we're supposed to be now."

"I shall..." She hesitated, and then she wiped her tears away. "I shall help you. Of course I shall. We'll find it together."

"We think it's away from the house," Merriman said, as he and the others led Sarah off through the forest. "We think once we find where we're supposed to be, we won't ever have to come back here."

They continued to talk, but within seconds they were lost from sight. Their voices remained for a moment longer, drifting through the cold night air, and then the forest fell still and silent. The thirteen ghosts of Sarah Clarke and her orphan children were gone forever, lost among all the leaves that littered the forest floor.

CHAPTER FORTY-SEVEN

"DAMN IT" JESSIE GASPED, rolling onto her front and then starting to sit up. She could feel pain everywhere now, but she'd just about managed to get her breath back as she looked toward the open door.

She hadn't seen Sarah leaving with the children, but she was pretty sure that was what had happened. Spotting the silver necklace on the floor, she picked it up and then limped to the door, but when she looked outside there was no sign of anyone. She briefly considered going back into the chapel to search once again for her phone, before realizing that she had no time. Diana didn't know yet that she'd escaped, so she turned and began to limp out into the forest.

"And where do you think you're going?" a

voice asked.

Spinning around, Jessie was shocked to see Diana standing about twenty feet away.

"Such a lovely look of pure fear in your eyes," Diana continued with a smile. "Why, I do believe my little plan is working. You're almost ready."

Panicking, Jessie turned and limped the other way around the chapel. She wasn't sure where she was going, but she told herself that she had to get as far away from Doctor Diana Moore as possible. She soon found herself at the foot of the steps at the front of Hardlocke House, but she knew she couldn't go inside so she turned to find some other way. At that moment, however, she saw Diana stepping around the chapel and heading closer.

"Do you not think it's a bit late to run now, Jessica?" she called out. "You agreed to help me with my work. Well, we've reached the final stage. I really hope you're not thinking of dropping out of the study now."

Looking around, Jessie desperately tried to figure out which way to run. The pain in her side was getting worse, and she'd hurt her right ankle in the encounter with Sarah, so she wasn't even confident that she could outpace Diana. Finally, realizing that she had to buy herself some time, she did the one thing that just moments earlier she'd written off: she turned and hobbled up the steps and into Hardlocke House, and then she turned and slammed the door shut. To her immense relief, she found the key was still in the lock, so she turned it before taking a few steps back.

Seconds later, the handle turned as Diana tried to follow her inside, but the lock held.

"Oh Jessica," she heard Diana saying outside, "what's this all about? I'm so glad you made it out of the chapel. You were always supposed to. In fact, I'm surprised it took you so long."

"Screw you!" Jessie yelled, although she was shocked to hear the fear in her own voice.

She grabbed the key from the lock and slipped it into her pocket, just in case Diana found any way to turn it from the outside.

"You must forgive my methods," Diana continued, "but I had to be sure that you believed in ghosts by the time you reached Hardlocke House on your third night. I knew that poor Sarah was haunting the chapel, that's why I made you sleep in there. I assume you got a good look at her in the end, did you not? There can't be any doubt in your mind, not anymore. You saw her ghost, and the ghosts of all those sad little children as well. You can't claim to be incredulous now. You know there was a ghost in that chapel, so now you won't find it difficult to believe when you encounter the presence that has been lurking for so long in Hardlocke

House."

"You're lying!" Jessie snapped angrily. "Everything you've told me has been a lie!"

"Sometimes a lie is the only way to get to the truth."

"Go to hell!" Jessie replied. "When I get out of here, I'm going straight to the police. You're going to go to jail for what you've done! Do you hear me? You won't get away with this!"

She waited, but Diana didn't reply, and after a moment Jessie realized she could hear footsteps walking away from the door, trampling across the leaves. She hurried to the nearest window and looked out, but there was no light outside and she couldn't make out which way Diana had gone.

Stepping away from the window, she turned and looked across the hall. The stove was burning in the office again, offering just enough light for her to be able to see the staircase nearby. She limped over and looked up, and then she turned and hobbled into the office. Feeling certain that Diana must be lying in wait somewhere outside, she figured that she needed to find some way to defend herself. She wasn't even sure whether there were any other ways for Diana to get into the house, so she started desperately looking for something, anything, she could use as a weapon.

Finding nothing, she grabbed a burning candle from the side and headed back out into the hall. For all she knew, Diana could be entering the building through a back door at that moment, so she headed past the stairs and over to one of the other rooms.

Entering what turned out to be some kind of library, she limped over to a cabinet and pulled the door open. All she found inside, however, were some books, and she was already starting to realize that the library might not be her best hunting ground. She headed over to a table and briefly searched for something, and then she hurried to the hall, only to stop suddenly as she heard a distant rattling sound.

She listened as the sound continued for a few seconds, and then the house fell silent once more.

For a moment, Jessie felt too scared to move. She quickly realized, however, that she could hear another noise coming from somewhere on the ground floor, as if somebody was trying to get a window open. She briefly considered using the opportunity to go out the front door, but then she reminded herself that she might be mistaken and that Diana might be out there. Besides, she was also starting to worry that Sutton, the guy who'd driven them out to Hardlocke House a few days earlier, might secretly be involved with the deception. She tried to figure out what to do next, and then she heard the unmistakable sound of somebody walking across one of the nearby rooms.

She ducked around the corner and stopped at the foot of the stairs. Peering back at the corridor, she was just about able to make out the sight of Diana Moore stepping into view. Realizing that she only had a few seconds in which to make a decision, Jessie looked around and then began to creep carefully up the stairs.

By the time she reached the landing, she couldn't help thinking that she'd made a terrible mistake. Still, she knew it was too late to back down now, and she looked over her shoulder just in time to see Diana stepping into the darkened hall. Pulling back, Jessie dropped down so that she could see through the gaps in the railing, and she watched as Diana walked over to check the office.

"Jessica?" the older woman called out. "Are you in here? I understand your reluctance to show yourself, but you're only delaying the inevitable. You're been primed, seasoned if you will, to now take part in the most important study of all time."

The light from the stove was catching Diana's face as she stepped into the office, and a moment later she disappeared from view.

"Forty years ago I was rejected by the presence that lives in this house," she continued. "I was rejected for one reason and one reason only. I couldn't bring myself to believe that it was real. Now I've brought you here to do what I could not.

Don't be angry that I had to manipulate you a little. Instead, be grateful that I gave you this opportunity."

She stepped back out of the room, and Jessie immediately pulled back so that she wouldn't be seen.

A moment later, however, she heard Diana starting to make her way up the stairs.

Turning, Jessie crawled on all fours along the nearest corridor. She knew she couldn't risk making any noise at all, so when she found an open doorway at the corridor's end she slipped through and moved out of the way. She waited, and then she turned and looked back the way she'd just come.

Suddenly Diana switched on a flashlight.

Jessie pulled out of the way, and she felt fairly sure that she hadn't yet been spotted.

"I know you're up here somewhere," Diana said calmly. "There's really nothing you can do now to change what's going to happen. I have exposed you to the truth, and now you're ready to encounter a truly extraordinary presence. You will feel the same wonder that I felt all those years ago, but the difference is that you will be ready to accept it. You will be the perfect vessel to carry it away from this place."

Her footsteps rang out as she began to make her way slowly along the corridor.

As the flashlight's beam reached the room,

Jessie turned and saw that she was in some kind of large, high-ceilinged dormitory. There were various bare beds all around, and she realized after a moment that somehow – impossibly – she'd seen the room before. It was the same room where she'd seen the children in her dream, even though she was certain that she'd never been shown any photos of the inside of the house. She tried to figure out what had really happened, and then she crawled around one of the beds and ducked down behind, just as Diana entered the room.

Feeling something crunching beneath her feet, Jessie reached down and felt wet, mulchy leaves. Looking up, she was just about able to spot a hole in the roof.

"I'm getting closer, aren't I?" Diana said, as Jessie squeezed down in a desperate attempt to keep from being seen. "I can almost smell you, Jessica. And the presence certainly knows that you're here. It's known since you arrived on Friday."

Realizing that at some point she was going to have to try to get away, Jessie told herself that she just had to be quick. If Diana attacked, then... She didn't want to have to hit a seventy-year-old woman, but she told herself that she might not have a choice.

And then, as the flashlight's beam danced at the far end of the room, Jessie suddenly realized she could feel something breathing against the back of her neck.

AMY CROSS

CHAPTER FORTY-EIGHT

FILLED WITH PANIC, Jessie sprang to her feet and pulled back, only to fall over the bed and topple to the floor. She let out a cry of pain as she hit her ankle hard, and then she scrambled into the corner of the the room. She turned, just as the flashlight swung around and caught her, almost blinding her in an instant.

Holding her hands up, she tried to protect her eyes.

"There you are," Diana said, quickly walking over to her. "It's okay, my dear, you've been through a lot but you don't have to worry. Just submit yourself to the inevitable and you'll be fine."

"You're insane!" she screamed.

"Poppycock," Diana replied. "My mind is as sharp as ever, and I'm in full control of this situation. You're about to be filled by the most wonderful and powerful presence that anyone can ever experience. If you think that I brought you here to hurt you, or to sacrifice you in any way, you're wrong. In fact, as I stand here now, I am supremely jealous of you, young lady. You're about to become -"

Stopping suddenly, she furrowed her brow slightly. She began to reach up to touch her face, but something seemed to be wrong and after a moment she tilted her head slightly. As she did so, her eyes began to fill with the same darkness that had once infected Sarah Clarke.

"No," Jessie whispered, "this can't be happening..."

Diana winced, as if in pain, and then she stepped forward and reached out to support herself against the wall. She hesitated for a moment, and then slowly she turned to Jessie and smiled.

"I can feel it," she gasped. "It's in me now, spreading through my body and mind. I've waited forty years for this, and yet it's still so much better than I ever could have anticipated. I was too young before, I was immature and I wasn't capable of recognizing true power. I shrank away from it when I should have embraced it, but now I have the chance to put everything right and I must..."

She froze for a few seconds, as if consumed by the splendor of whatever she was feeling. At the same time, black veins began to spread from her eyes, reaching across her cheeks as she opened her mouth and let out a faint, low rasping sound.

"It's so much more," she managed to stammer finally, as Jessie looked to the door and tried to pick the perfect moment to run. "I was too young to appreciate it before, but now I feel the glory." She took a couple of stumbling steps back. "Wait!" she shouted. "Forget her! Take me again, give me another chance! I know I'm old now, but I've learned so much and I can serve you properly! I'll welcome you, and I'll do whatever it takes to get you away from this place. That's what you want, isn't it? A vessel who'll willingly carry you across the threshold and back out into the world. I know the rules, you need someone who accepts that you're real, someone who's willing to help you, and I -"

In that moment, Jessie jumped up and tried to rush to the door. Before she'd made it even half a step, however, Diana grabbed her and threw her back against the side of one of the beds with impossible strength.

"Leave me alone!" Jessie screamed.

"I'll do everything you want!" Diana gurgled. "I -"

She froze, and half a second later she began to laugh.

Too scared to make a move, Jessie pulled back into the corner as she tried to figure out what she should try next.

"Why would I want the body of an old woman," Diana continued, slurring her words slightly as a broad smile spread across her face, "when I could have something so much younger? Why would I want to be rancid and infirm, when I could be strong and powerful?"

She turned and looked down at Jessie again.

"The old woman had her chance many years ago," she added, "and she turned me down. I do not forgive insults, and I do not settle for anything but the best. Even after just a few minutes, I can feel that her body is so much weaker than before. I can feel the pain in her knees, and in her back, and I can feel the feebleness of her mind. Her body might get me away from this place, but I would soon be in need of a replacement. And why go to all that trouble, when I could just start with something so much younger?"

She took a single, limping step toward Jessie and then stopped again.

"She told me that I would be pleased with you," she continued. "These past two nights, she has been trying to draw me out and converse with me. She told me I had to be patient, that you would come on the third night, and now here you are. I am ready to take you, but first I must shed this old woman's form so that she pays for rejecting me."

"Diana?" Jessie stammered. "Are you -"

Suddenly Diana tilted her head back and let out a pained gasp. Her whole body seemed stiff and tense, and a moment later her throat began to split open. Jessie could only watch in horror as blood began to gush down onto the old woman's chest, and a moment later she realized she could hear the sound of bones cracking. Diana seemed to be whimpering slightly as her arms pulled back and snapped at the shoulders, and slowly something was pushing out from beneath the front of her dress. Jessie realized after a moment that the woman's ribs were peeling out from her body, tearing through the fabric with their bloodied tips. It was as if Diana's body was being broken open from the inside.

"Please," Diana managed to gasp, as a torrent of blood rushed out from her split belly, "why are you..."

Her legs snapped out to the sides and she dropped to her knees, but some force was holding her torso upright. She slowly tilted her head forward, revealing a heavy split that had cracked straight down through her forehead and nose, forcing her eyes partially out of their sockets as blood streamed from the wounds. She tried again to speak, but her jaw had already splintered into two halves and all that emerged was a frantic rasping groan. Still, somehow, the sound of laughter was breaking out from somewhere deep inside her body with such force that she continued to shake violently until – finally – she slumped forward and landed dead just a few feet away from Jessie.

And still the corpse shook with a low, rumbling laugh.

Too horrified to even know how to react, Jessie could only stare at what was left of Diana. Only when she saw that a pool of blood was about to reach her feet did she scramble up and pull back against the wall. Diana was dead, of that there was no doubt, but her body was still shaking and a consistent laugh was still rippling out from somewhere deep within what was left of her. Although she knew that what she was seeing was impossible, Jessie could only stare in wide-eyed shock until finally she looked over once more at the door.

She paused, and then she began to pick her way slowly around the edge of the room, taking care to not make any noise. A moment later she stepped into the doorway, and then she stopped as she heard the crunching sound of broken bones grinding together in Diana's wrecked body.

"Hey," a spluttering voice said. "Where do you think you're going?"

Jessie forced herself to turn and look. Diana's head had lifted from the floor and had partially turned to look at her.

"Good news," the head said after a moment, as Diana's jaw twitched. "I'm not done with you yet.

In fact, I haven't even started!"

Turning, Jessie raced out of the dormitory and along the pitch-black corridor. All she knew was that she had to get out of Hardlocke House as fast as possible, so as soon as she reached the top of the stairs she began to rush down. Just as she'd reached halfway, however, she felt something pull on her feet and she tumbled forward. She tried to reach out and save herself, but she was too late and instead she fell and crashed down the remainder of the staircase, landing with a thud at the bottom. Without even stopping to make sure that she was uninjured, she stumbled to her feet and tried to reach for the door, but in that moment she felt a heavy cold force rush into her body and she dropped to her knees.

She reached a hand toward the door, but already her eyes were starting to fill with darkness as she felt laughter in the back of her mind.

CHAPTER FORTY-NINE

"NO..."

The door's handle was so close, just a few inches from the tips of her fingers.

"Please..."

The laughter was getting louder, roaring into her thoughts like an oncoming train, shaking her mind and jolting her so hard that she could barely move a muscle. Her eyes, meanwhile, were starting to burn.

She tried to reach forward, but something still seemed to be holding her back.

"I could get used to this," a voice purred in her mind. "You're young, so that's the first of my criteria met. You're fit and healthy, which means you'll make a good home for me for many years. It's so nice to feel a heart beating again. I can't wait to see how the world has changed while I've been trapped here. Are the descendants of that wretched harridan Elizabeth still on the throne? I hope so, because I've been plotting my revenge for a very long time. Once that's taken care of, I rather think that I shall try to master more of the powers I was learning when that bastard Sir Thomas Clarke saw fit to have me killed. At the time, I thought I'd been cut down in my prime. Now I realize that my prime is only just beginning."

"What are you?" Jessie gasped through clenched teeth.

"I am the thing that is coming with you, out into the world again."

"No!"

Somehow fighting back, Jessie hauled herself to her feet. She stepped toward the door, but then she froze as she realized she could feel a strange heaviness on her back, weighing her down. Although she desperately wanted to pull the door open, she instead took a couple of steps back and looked through into the office.

She froze as soon as she saw her own reflection. Her eyes were black, and dark little veins were spreading across her face. At the same time, she was able to make out a faint shadow, and a moment later she realized that a rotten man was resting on her back.

Spinning around, she pulled away and

bumped against the doorway that led into the office. She reached up and touched her face, and she realized she could feel the dark veins throbbing beneath her cheeks. Shocked, she stumbled through into the office and stopped next to the desk, inadvertently knocking several of the skulls to the floor.

"Why are you resisting?" the voice asked, as the figure still clung to her back. "You're almost as bad as the last woman. Diana Moore refused to believe that I could be real. I'm glad that she finally came around to the truth, but it was far too late. You, on the other hand, are perfect. Let's leave now, so that I can see the dawn far from this miserable house."

"You're not real," Jessie whispered. "None of this is real."

"Come now," the voice replied, "Diana told me all about her plan. How was poor Ms. Clarke out there in that chapel, anyway? Was she as pathetic in death as she was in life?"

"Please leave me alone," she sobbed. "I just want to go home."

"And I want to come with you. See? We're after the same thing, so don't delay. Let's go."

Feeling something pulling on her shoulders, Jessie somehow managed to stand her ground. After a moment she turned and saw the portrait of Sarah Clarke, and she realized that she was grappling with the same presence that had attacked Sarah and Diana and all the children. Gripping the side of the desk, she tried to pull herself together, but there was still a part of her that refused to believe what was happening.

"I'm dreaming this," she said firmly, trying to convince herself, "or I'm hallucinating."

"Were you hallucinating those ghosts in the chapel?" the voice asked. "Were you hallucinating the moment I tore my way through Diana Moore's pathetic body? Are you hallucinating the strength and power you feel from me right now?"

Jessie opened her mouth to reply, but at that moment she realized she *could* feel immense strength surging throughout her body. Along with the strength came a sensation of power, of potential, and she found herself anticipating everything that she and the presence could do once they left Hardlocke House together. Although she had no specific ideas about what might happen, she felt certain that she could be part of something that would change the world.

Reaching into her pocket, she fumbled for a moment before pulling out Sarah Clarke's silver necklace. She pressed her fingertips against the cross and she squeezed her eyes tight shut as she tried to find some source of protection.

"I recognize that thing," the voice said. "If you think it will help you, you are mistaken."

Feeling a force pulling the necklace away, Jessie gripped it as tight as she could manage. Even when the cross began to twist in her palm and cut the flesh, she refused to let go, until a moment later the entire necklace was yanked away with such speed that the cross dug into her hand. She let out a pained cry as she looked down, and as the necklace hit the far wall she saw that it had ripped a thick cut straight past the base of her thumb. Already blood was running down to her wrist.

"You're too smart for petty trinkets," the voice told her. "You feel my power. You know our potential together. It's time for you to willingly carry me away from here."

Finally, slowly, she turned and began to walk toward the hall. A part of her was screaming that she should stop, but she couldn't ignore the sense of true strength that was filling her soul. She'd always led a fairly meek, unadventurous life, and now that was all about to change; now she felt that she could *be* somebody, that she – with the presence as a guide – could make everyone notice her. For a moment, nothing seemed to be beyond her grasp.

"That's right," the voice continued. "We can do this. We're a team."

Reaching the door, she took hold of the handle, but then she hesitated. Black tears were running down her face, and when she looked over her shoulder she saw herself reflected once again in the mirror in the office. The creature on her back seemed larger, as if it was growing by the second, and after a moment the creature turned and grinned at her.

"Just a few more steps," it reminded her. "Don't stop to think now."

Although she felt the pull of the outside world, Jessie couldn't help staring at her reflection. After a moment, she turned and made her way back into the office, heading all the way over to the mirror and stopping to take a closer look. She saw her own black eyes staring back at her, as well as the dark veins that were already spreading down her neck. A moment later she spotted something moving in the darkness behind her, and she watched as a scarred, angry face leaned over her shoulder and began to whisper in her ear.

"There's no time to waste," it told her. "You will take me away from here. Now!"

She opened her mouth to reply, and then she hesitated for a moment before finally answering.

"No."

"Don't be foolish, you -"

"You're not real."

"You're looking right at me," the face replied, before leaning even further forward, until Jessie could just about see it out of the corner of her left eye. "Forget the reflection. Look at me."

"You're not real," she said firmly, "because

you *can't* be real."

"You've seen enough to know the truth."

"I also know that certain things just don't happen," she told it. "No matter how real you might seem, it's just not possible. You look like something that came out of a nightmare, because that's exactly where you're from. I'm imagining you and -"

"No!" the creature shouted.

"I'm imagining you and I refuse to believe that you're real!" she snapped angrily. "I'm not going to start believing in ghosts and demons and monsters just because of one night! No matter what I can see right now, I know the truth and I won't let this happen! Doctor Moore was right, only weak minds believe in ghosts!"

"Liar!" the creature screamed, leaning even further forward.

Turning, Jessie found herself face-to-face with the twisted face of a man who had been dead for half a millennium, a man who – in what she realized now could only have been a nightmare – she'd seen being executed by Queen Elizabeth. And no matter how real the creature seemed, she was somehow able to cling to the belief, the knowledge, that such things simply did not exist in the world.

"You're not real," she said firmly. "You'll never convince me that you are, because I know that things like you *can't* be real. I won't believe in you even if..."

She paused for a moment, as she felt her heart pounding in her chest.

"Even if you kill me," she added finally. "Even then, I'll never believe in you."

The creature opened its mouth, revealing bloodied gums and sharp, broken teeth. And then, in the blink of an eye, it disappeared entirely.

As the sense of heaviness fell from her shoulders, Jessie let out a gasp of relief and leaned forward, putting her hands on the mantelpiece beneath the mirror. For a moment she'd actually felt herself believing that all the things at Hardlocke House – the ghostly figure in the chapel, the boys in the forest, and the creature in the main house itself – had been real. She'd felt the lure of believing in something so fantastical that its very existence had threatened to shatter her understanding of the world. Somehow, however, she'd managed to hold on to a glimmer of sanity.

The entity in the house.

The children in the forest.

Sarah Clarke in the chapel.

None of them had been real.

Taking a step back, she realized that she needed to do one last thing. She needed to go up to the dormitory and see what had really happened to Diana Moore. Perhaps she was really dead, but that didn't mean that some kind of monster had killed her. She looked around for a moment at the dark office, and she felt her pounding heart finally starting to return to normal.

"It's just a house," she said out loud, to remind herself. She even forced herself to shrug, before turning and limping toward the hallway. "It's just a big, empty, admittedly slightly spooky house."

Suddenly a powerful force gripped her by the shoulders and slammed her against the wall. The painting of Sarah Clarke shuddered and almost fell, but Jessie had no time to react. The same force lifted her up and turned her around, before flinging her through the air, sending her crashing straight through one of the windows. As the wood and glass shattered, all she could do was scream.

AMY CROSS

CHAPTER FIFTY

1601...

"YOUR MAJESTY, IT IS DONE," Sir Walter said, kneeling before the throne. "No word shall ever be spoken of the wretched creature whose corpse was burned in that forest. Word has been put around that the entire area is to be avoided."

"And what of the next such creature?" Elizabeth asked wearily. "And the next? And all that ones who follow? When will this scourge on our land ever end?"

"I fear we have done all that we can. We must trust in God to protect us."

"Some say that my father brought this about," she replied. "That this is some form of punishment for the schism that he brought about.

Are you of that view?"

"I am certain that is not the case," Sir Walter said firmly. "Your father, the king, was a most righteous man. He would not have done anything that might draw this realm into danger. And the latest monstrosity *has* been destroyed. We know that."

"Not destroyed," she said, with a hint of fear in her voice. "Trapped. That is all that one can do with these things. They are most vexatious, but this is a weakness for them as well as a blessing. We trap them, we let them chase their own tails, and we pray that they will defeat themselves and never find a way to get free."

***

1611...

"We ride on the orders of King James," Nykolas Freeman said as he marched across the yard and prepared to mount his horse. "We are to meet Harold Connaught in York, and from there we are to advance toward any house that is suspected of harboring evil or wickedness."

"And what are we to do when we reach those houses?" one of the other men asked.

Freeman took a moment to climb onto the horse, and then he turned to the others.

"Is that not obvious?" he said after a moment. "We drive them out. Every ghoul, every trickster. We cleanse England of any scourge that tries to take root here. By the time we are done, England shall be the purest nation of them all!"

***

1738...

"It looks perfect," Sarah Clarke said as she stopped at the desk and looked down at the drawings for the new house. "Please, you must start work at once on its construction."

"And there's nothing you'd like to change?" the architect, John Pilton, asked.

"Nothing at all." She paused for a moment. "I often think that a house is like a tree. Even when dead leaves fall to the ground, they're still all around. They rot into the ground, but they still leave behind traces." She paused. "I believe Hardlocke House will be a very fine tree indeed."

"I wanted to ask you one thing," he said. "There is a site not five miles from the one that you have specified, and I think that this other site would be a far more suitable place for -"

"No," Sarah said firmly, her eyes filled with wonder as she continued to gaze at the drawings. "I cannot explain why, but somehow deep in my heart

I know that Hardlocke House must be built in the exact location that I have commanded. It is as if..."

She paused for a moment, before turning to him.

"It is as if," she continued, "something there is calling to me. To my blood!"

***

1980...

"This is going to be perfect," Andy Malone said as he stopped and put an arm around his wife. Looking up at the facade of Hardlocke House, he took a deep, satisfied breath. "We're going to make a mint off this place."

"It looks pretty creepy," Lizzy muttered.

"Exactly! Think of all the idiots who'll come flocking through the front door for the chance to spend a night in a real haunted house! We can charge double what they'd pay at some ordinary dive."

She looked at the windows, and for a moment she couldn't help but feel that something was staring back at her. She watched each window in turn, half expecting to spot some face gazing back out; she saw no such thing, of course, yet still she couldn't shake the sense that something malign lurked within the house. With every fiber of her being, she wanted nothing more than to turn around and leave, but she knew that wasn't a possibility. Andy had put all their money into the house, so they had no choice but to try to make it work.

"Come on!" Andy said, stepping away from her and hurrying up the steps, while pulling the key from his pocket. "Let's take a look inside! The future starts now. I swear, Lizzy, this house is going to change our lives forever!"

***

1982...

Standing in the front room of her flat, Diana Moore stared down at the stain on the carpet. She'd scrubbed for hours, but she'd never really expected to get all of the blood out. Now she knew that she'd have to get a brand new carpet, which would mean taking a trip into town the following day. Which, in turn, would mean dealing with people.

She let out a heavy sigh.

"Stupid girl," she muttered as she thought back to the final moments of Lizzy Malone. "Such a weak mind."

Turning, she made her way through to the bathroom. She washed her hands, and then she froze as she saw her own face staring back at her from the mirror. Although she tried to tell herself that nothing was wrong, she realized that something about Lizzy's visit had stirred a deep memory. She thought back to her time at Hardlocke House, and to that moment when she'd felt a presence in the house. She'd tried so hard to convince herself that the presence had been a figment of her imagination, but something Lizzy had said kept echoing in her thoughts.

"It's almost like it was probing me," she heard Lizzy's voice saying. "Like it was testing me, trying me out to see if it could use me in some way."

She tried to put such thoughts out of her mind, but a moment later she heard Lizzy again.

"After that presence was inside me in the house, I can still feel it now. It's like it's somehow still attached to me even from all this distance. I feel like it's never going to let me go."

Taking a deep breath, Diana told herself not to fixate on the woman's feeble rambling, but at the same time she was once again thinking back to her own experience at the house. Slowly, despite her best efforts, she was starting to realize that the thing she'd felt had been real, and she felt an irresistible force pulling on her soul, trying to get her to return. The idea was terrifying, although after a few seconds she realized that the experience at Hardlocke House had given her a momentary sense of extreme power. Of potential.

"I'm going back," she whispered finally, still looking at her own reflection. "Not yet, but one day. When the time is right and I have everything prepared, I'm going back to Hardlocke House and I'm going to -"

Suddenly the mirror cracked straight down the middle, and in a flash Diana saw another face staring back out from the glass.

***

Today...

Morning sunlight streamed through the treetops as Jessie – shattered and bloodied, and limping heavily on a damaged leg – slowly made her way along the path that led away from Hardlocke House.

Her face was covered in cuts. One of her eyes was swollen shut, and smeared blood was caked all around her mouth. A heavy gash marked one side of her forehead, where she'd had to painfully slide out a piece of glass once she'd woken up about an hour earlier. Her right arm was agonizing, and she was fairly sure it was at least fractured, if not broken; she certainly couldn't move the fingers of her right hand at all. She was certain that she'd broken some ribs, not only after crashing through the window and landing outside, but also in the chapel. There were sharp pains in her right hip and leg, and her right ankle kept clicking with a faint murmur of discomfort.

The handcuffs were still hanging from her right wrist.

As she rounded the next corner, she finally saw the van parked a little way ahead. Sutton was leaning against its side, smoking, and it took a moment before he glanced in her direction. He stared for a moment, as if he couldn't quite believe what he was seeing, and then he dropped the cigarette and rushed over to her.

"Jessie?" he said, reaching out to grab the sides of her arms, catching her just as her knees buckled and she dropped to the ground. "Where's Doctor Moore? What happened back there?"

***

Six months later...

"And how are the nightmares now?" Doctor Richardson asked as he made a couple more notes on the chart. "Would you say that they're occurring more frequently, or less?"

Sitting opposite him, in a large leather armchair, Jessie thought about the question for a moment.

"Less," she said finally.

"You're sure?"

She thought some more, and then she nodded.

"Not by much," she added. "I still have them every few nights. But that's better than *every* night, right?"

"It certainly is," he said, turning to another page and continuing his notes. "And what would you say about the intensity? I know some of the ones you've described have been pretty horrific, and you mentioned waking up covered in sweat and not immediately remembering where you were. Are you still experiencing flashbacks while you sleep?"

"They're about the same," she told him, and then she watched as he wrote. "They finally closed the case on Doctor Moore's death. I wasn't much help, but they said the injuries were consistent with her maybe having been attacked by some kind of wild animal."

"Do you want to talk about that?"

She paused. For the most part, she was simply worried about giving the wrong answer. She was fully aware that many people thought she'd lost her mind out at Hardlocke House, and the last thing she wanted was to give them any more ammunition.

"Sure. I don't mind, but I still don't remember very much about that last night. I mean, I remember *some* things, but they're not things that really happened. Do you think that the false memories, the ones about ghosts and all that other stuff, are my brain's way of covering up the truth?"

"That's certainly one possible interpretation," he told her. "Your brain might consider the real memories to be too horrific, so in a way it's protecting you."

"So how do we get past that?" she asked.

"I don't know that we can," he replied. "And I'm not sure that we should."

"But I want to help clear up what really happened."

"The police absolutely don't consider you to be a suspect in any way," he reminded her. "They believe that whatever killed Doctor Moore also attacked you, and that you're very lucky to have escaped. They've had men combing the woods near Hardlocke House, in case some kind of animal is roaming the area, but -"

"They haven't found anything," she said, interrupting him.

"Indeed not."

"But that doesn't mean it didn't happen," she added. "If you take away the impossible things, whatever's left has to be the truth."

"That's a very mature way of looking at it."

He made some notes.

"But the fake memories..." She paused. "About the ghosts and all the other stuff... Will the fake memories ever start to fade? They still feel so real."

For a moment, she thought back to the sensation of the creature on her back, and to the sight of Sarah Clarke walking off into the forest with the twelve dead children. She reminded herself that none of those things had actually happened, but there was still a lingering part of her mind that couldn't help replaying those images over and over again. Every time she felt a nagging urge to consider the possibility that she'd encountered ghosts, however, the rational and logical part of her brain took over and reminded her of one simple truth.

There's no such thing as ghosts.

"You're making excellent progress, Jessie," Doctor Richardson said as he set the chart aside. "I think we should continue our weekly sessions for now, but I hope you feel that there's some light at the end of the tunnel. And the report from Doctor Sedgewell indicates that your physical injuries are clearing up nicely. Before you head off today, is there anything else you'd like to ask me?"

"No," she replied. "Thank you."

As Doctor Richardson showed her out to the next room, where her parents were waiting, Jessie focused on keeping her thoughts calm. Her mother started fussing over her, as usual, but Jessie had long since accepted the inevitability of that so she was able – somewhat – to tune her voice out as they all headed to the car. Ever since she'd ended up in the hospital six months earlier, she'd focused on staying as calm as possible, and she'd tried not to talk about the events at Hardlocke House too much. Sure, people asked, but she hadn't yet found a way to explain those three days without making it all sound like a ghost story.

And it wasn't a ghost story.

She knew that, deep in her heart, with absolute conviction.

"I'm just going to go and fetch the car," her father said once they were out at the front of the building. "You girls stay right here."

Jessie almost asked to go with him, but she knew there was no point. She didn't like being treated as if she was fragile, but she knew that there was no point picking pointless arguments. A moment later, turning to her mother, she flinched slightly.

"You're so brave," Karen told her, with tears in her eyes. "You know that, don't you?"

"You've said it a million times."

"I just don't know how you manage it." She paused. "I know what you've said to everyone, sweetheart, but I was reading online last night about haunted house cases and -"

"Mum, do we have to do this?"

"Just hear me out," Karen continued. "You've been so quick to dismiss the idea that anything supernatural or paranormal happened out there at that house, but you still haven't quite explained how you ended up with so many injuries."

"I told you, I don't remember, but obviously something totally rational and normal happened."

"You don't know that for sure!"

"I do," she said firmly, "because I know that anything else is impossible!"

"Honey, just..." Karen's voice trailed off for a moment. "I suppose I should focus on the fact that we got you home. Whatever happened to you out there, it looks like..."

She paused, and then she stepped over and hugged Jessie tight.

"Just because I don't know how I got these injuries," Jessie said, "doesn't mean that I'm going to jump at the easiest explanation. If my time with Doctor Moore taught me anything, it's that you have to stay firm and hold onto your convictions, even if you're tempted to start believing in things that are completely impossible." She paused for a moment. "And I know, without a shadow of a doubt, that ghosts aren't real. Nothing's ever going to change my mind about that."

"Well, it's good that you know your own mind," Karen said, as Dom parked the car in front of them and she opened the door so that Jessie could climb inside. "So who's for ice cream on the way home?"

As the car pulled away a couple of minutes later, Jessie stared out at the world and felt more sure of her beliefs than ever. Whatever had happened out at Hardlocke House had been a hallucination, mixed with something that must have been too horrific for her mind to process. She knew it might take a while longer for the nightmares to pass, but she was willing to wait. All that mattered was that she'd managed to cling to the truth, to the simple mantra that she kept running through her mind during her every waking moment, a mantra that was just about keeping her sane.

Ghosts aren't real.

EPILOGUE

Twenty years later...

"OH HEY," JANEY SAID as she rounded the corner and almost bumped into the woman in the aisle, "sorry, I totally wasn't looking where I was going."

"It's fine," the woman replied, stepping out of her way. "Please."

"Thanks," Janey said, slipping past her and heading toward the section she was after, before slowing and then turning to look over her shoulder. She paused, as if she couldn't quite believe what she was seeing. "Are you..."

Her voice trailed off for a moment.

"Are you Doctor Banks?"

"I am," Jessie replied, clearly a little

uncomfortable.

"I've read, like, everything you've ever written," Janey continued, unable to hide her excitement. "Sorry, I don't mean to fan-girl all over you, but we studied some of your work on a first year module and it was, like, so intense. I'm a first year student, I'm doing some psychiatry stuff. You really inspired me to get started."

"That's great," Jessie said, before turning back to look at the shelf. "I wish you the best of luck with your studies."

"I especially loved that paper you wrote on Hardlocke House," Janey added.

As she reached out for one particular book, Jessica froze.

"The one about how you went there with Diana Moore, I mean," Janey continued. "It was a really interesting examination of the way the human mind responds to unclear stimuli. I thought you handled it really sensitively, too. You didn't make Doctor Moore out to be some kind of lunatic, it was more like she had this kind of..." She paused, searching for the right words. "It was like a major breakdown," she added finally. "You really chronicled how this giant of the academic world went from complete skepticism to just..."

Again, her voice briefly trailed off.

"Well, you covered it all, I guess is what I'm saying," she added. "You really unraveled how

Doctor Moore's mind... well, unraveled."

"I think I see what you mean," Jessica replied. "Thank you, I'm glad you appreciated that particular piece of work. As I'm sure you can imagine, it was quite a sensitive topic. It's always important to take the emotion out of these pieces, even when one was directly involved. I *did* consider stepping back and letting a colleague write the report, but in the end I trusted myself to have the necessary discipline."

"You totally did it justice."

An awkward silence fell for a moment, before Janey suddenly realized that this was probably her cue to leave. She'd heard that Doctor Jessica Banks preferred to be left alone when she wasn't teaching, and the last thing she wanted was to be a pest.

"I'm sorry," she added, taking a step back, "I'm totally getting in your face. It's just that as someone who *does* kinda believe in all that stuff, I was fascinated to see an outsider's perspective. But I'll leave you alone now."

She turned to walk away.

"You believe in ghosts?" Jessica asked.

Janey stopped and turned back to her.

"Well, yeah," she explained, "like, totally. Sorry, I know you probably think that makes me a complete moron, but I've believed in them most of my life. I actually saw one once, you see, which pretty much cemented it in my mind." She put her hands briefly on the sides of her head. "I know. Crazy, right? Yeah, probably, but when something like that gets, like, lodged in your heart and your soul, nothing can really get it out. Not that I let this stuff conflict with my studies, of course. I'd never talk about ghosts in a professional setting."

She paused, and another awkward silence began to stretch between them.

"Sorry again," Janey added, before turning away. "I'll be -"

"Are you looking for some extra credit?" Jessica asked suddenly.

Janey turned back to her.

"I'm sorry?"

"The holidays are coming up," Jessica continued, "and sometimes students like to pick up some extra credit for a little work outside the curriculum. I was just wondering..."

Janey stared at her, not quite able to believe what she was hearing.

"Me?"

"It's not compulsory."

"No, I mean... Don't you have students on your own courses who could do it? I'm only in my first year, and you don't even know me!"

"I have a good impression so far," Jessica told her, "and all my students are either busy or... unsuitable. What I'm proposing is a short residential project, taking place over, say... three nights."

"What kind of project?"

"An important one," Jessica told her. "To be honest, I've been planning it for a number of years, but for one reason or another I've kept putting it off. And seeing as you just started talking about Doctor Moore, you made me think that perhaps I should get myself into gear. After all, there's no time like the present."

"I'm sorry," Janey replied, "but I still don't quite get what you're asking."

Jessica hesitated, before reaching into her pocket and pulling out a single, rusty old key. It was the same key that, twenty years earlier, she'd slipped away after using it to lock the front door at Hardlocke House. She'd not meant to take it with her when she'd left, but after one thing and another she'd later found it in her possessions, and she'd never quite got around to seeing if anyone would like it returned. In the back of her mind, perhaps, she'd always known that she might need it again one day.

"I'm thinking of going back to Hardlocke House," she explained, "and I need an assistant."

"Hardlocke House?" Janey's eyes widened with shock. "Why? I mean... I thought your work on that place was complete years ago."

"So did I," Jessica replied, "but one eventually learns that some work never really ends.

More questions always arise, and there's no harm in going back and raking over the coals, so to speak."

"What exactly do you want to *do* at Hardlocke House?" Janey asked cautiously. "I thought your report made it pretty clear that you considered the case closed."

"Oh, I've got it all worked out," Jessica said. "Would you like to come to the cafeteria with me? I'd love to buy you a coffee and explain things properly. That way, you can make an informed decision about whether or not you want to participate."

"Totally," Janey said, as they started walking away together along the aisle. "Wow. Thank you for even considering me, Doctor Banks. I can't believe something like this could be happening, all because I just happened to drop into the library this afternoon."

"Serendipity strikes," Jessica replied. "And, please, call me Jessica. In fact, call me Jessie."

"Okay, Jessie. I can't wait to tell everyone about this in class. They're all going to be so totally jealous!"

"Let me explain the project to you first," Jessie said as they headed out through the double doors. "Before you commit to anything, I want you to understand *exactly* why I'm proposing to go back to Hardlocke House. You see, I've been thinking that I can improve on Doctor Moore's approach. I've had twenty years to think about what really happened over that weekend. The truth is, I want to do what she did, but better. The fact that you already believe in ghosts makes you the perfect person to assist me, Ms. Szozak. I really think that together we can put right what went wrong with Doctor Moore's work. I've really come around to some of her ways of thinking."

"Huh." Janey hesitated. "That's weird, I didn't know I told you my surname."

"You must have," Jessica replied as the doors swung shut. "So, are you available from Friday to Monday this weekend?"

***

Hundreds of miles away, in the gloomy office of Hardlocke House, dust drifted through the air near the large mirror above the fireplace. The house had stood empty for two decades, locked up and abandoned once again following its most recent tragedy. Outside, more dead leaves had fallen, and while some remained fairly fresh on the top layer, others had rotten down to become nothing more than foul-smelling mulch.

Suddenly the mirror in the house's hallway cracked straight down the middle, accompanied by an angry, hungry snarl.

Also by Amy Cross

The Devil, the Witch and the Whore
(The Deal book 1)

"Leave the forest alone. Whatever's out there, just let it be. Don't make it angry."

When a horrific discovery is made at the edge of town, Sheriff James Kopperud realizes the answers he seeks might be waiting beyond in the vast forest. But everybody in the town of Deal knows that there's something out there in the forest, something that should never be disturbed. A deal was made long ago, a deal that was supposed to keep the town safe. And if he insists on investigating the murder of a local girl, James is going to have to break that deal and head out into the wilderness.

Meanwhile, James has no idea that his estranged daughter Ramsey has returned to town. Ramsey is running from something, and she thinks she can find safety in the vast tunnel system that runs beneath the forest. Before long, however, Ramsey finds herself coming face to face with creatures that hide in the shadows. One of these creatures is known as the devil, and another is known as the witch. They're both waiting for the whore to arrive, but for very different reasons. And soon Ramsey is offered a terrible deal, one that could save or destroy the entire town, and maybe even the world.

AMY CROSS

Also by Amy Cross

The Soul Auction

"I saw a woman on the beach. I watched her face a demon."

Thirty years after her mother's death, Alice Ashcroft is drawn back to the coastal English town of Curridge. Somebody in Curridge has been reviewing Alice's novels online, and in those reviews there have been tantalizing hints at a hidden truth. A truth that seems to be linked to her dead mother.

"Thirty years ago, there was a soul auction."

Once she reaches Curridge, Alice finds strange things happening all around her. Something attacks her car. A figure watches her on the beach at night. And when she tries to find the person who has been reviewing her books, she makes a horrific discovery.

What really happened to Alice's mother thirty years ago? Who was she talking to, just moments before dropping dead on the beach? What caused a huge rockfall that nearly tore a nearby cliff-face in half? And what sinister presence is lurking in the grounds of the local church?

AMY CROSS

Also by Amy Cross

Darper Danver: The Complete First Series

Five years ago, three friends went to a remote cabin in the woods and tried to contact the spirit of a long-dead soldier. They thought they could control whatever happened next. They were wrong...

Newly released from prison, Cassie Briggs returns to Fort Powell, determined to get her life back on track. Soon, however, she begins to suspect that an ancient evil still lurks in the nearby cabin. Was the mysterious Darper Danver really destroyed all those years ago, or does her spirit still linger, waiting for a chance to return?

As Cassie and her ex-boyfriend Fisher are finally forced to face the truth about what happened in the cabin, they realize that Darper isn't ready to let go of their lives just yet. Meanwhile, a vengeful woman plots revenge for her brother's murder, and a New York ghost writer arrives in town to uncover the truth. Before long, strange carvings begin to appear around town and blood starts to flow once again.

Also by Amy Cross

The Ghost of Molly Holt

"Molly Holt is dead. There's nothing to fear in this house."

When three teenagers set out to explore an abandoned house in the middle of a forest, they think they've found the location where the infamous Molly Holt video was filmed.

They've found much more than that...

Tim doesn't believe in ghosts, but he has a crush on a girl who does. That's why he ends up taking her out to the house, and it's also why he lets her take his only flashlight. But as they explore the house together, Tim and Becky start to realize that something else might be lurking in the shadows.

Something that, ten years ago, suffered unimaginable pain.

Something that won't rest until a terrible wrong has been put right.

AMY CROSS

Also by Amy Cross

American Coven

He kidnapped three women and held them in his basement. He thought they couldn't fight back. He was wrong...

Snatched from the street near her home, Holly Carter is taken to a rural house and thrown down into a stone basement. She meets two other women who have also been kidnapped, and soon Holly learns about the horrific rituals that take place in the house. Eventually, she's called upstairs to take her place in the ice bath.

As her nightmare continues, however, Holly learns about a mysterious power that exists in the basement, and which the three women might be able to harness. When they finally manage to get through the metal door, however, the women have no idea that their fight for freedom is going to stretch out for more than a decade, or that it will culminate in a final, devastating demonstration of their new-found powers.

Also by Amy Cross

The Ash House

Why would anyone ever return to a haunted house?

For Diane Mercer the answer is simple. She's dying of cancer, and she wants to know once and for all whether ghosts are real.

Heading home with her young son, Diane is determined to find out whether the stories are real. After all, everyone else claimed to see and hear strange things in the house over the years. Everyone except Diane had some kind of experience in the house, or in the little ash house in the yard.

As Diane explores the house where she grew up, however, her son is exploring the yard and the forest. And while his mother might be struggling to come to terms with her own impending death, Daniel Mercer is puzzled by fleeting appearances of a strange little girl who seems drawn to the ash house, and by strange, rasping coughs that he keeps hearing at night.

The Ash House is a horror novel about a woman who desperately wants to know what will happen to her when she dies, and about a boy who uncovers the shocking truth about a young girl's murder.

Also by Amy Cross

Haunted

Twenty years ago, the ghost of a dead little girl drove Sheriff Michael Blaine to his death.

Now, that same ghost is coming for his daughter.

Returning to the small town where she grew up, Alex Roberts is determined to live a normal, quiet life. For the residents of Railham, however, she's an unwelcome reminder of the town's darkest hour.

Twenty years ago, nine-year-old Mo Garvey was found brutally murdered in a nearby forest. Everyone thinks that Alex's father was responsible, but if the killer was brought to justice, why is the ghost of Mo Garvey still after revenge?

And how far will the real killer go to protect his secret, when Alex starts getting closer to the truth?

Haunted is a horror novel about a woman who has to face her past, about a town that would rather forget, and about a little girl who refuses to let death stand in her way.

AMY CROSS

Also by Amy Cross

The Curse of Wetherley House

"If you walk through that door, Evil Mary will get you."

When she agrees to visit a supposedly haunted house with an old friend, Rosie assumes she'll encounter nothing more scary than a few creaks and bumps in the night. Even the legend of Evil Mary doesn't put her off. After all, she knows ghosts aren't real. But when Mary makes her first appearance, Rosie realizes she might already be trapped.

For more than a century, Wetherley House has been cursed. A horrific encounter on a remote road in the late 1800's has already caused a chain of misery and pain for all those who live at the house. Wetherley House was abandoned long ago, after a terrible discovery in the basement, something has remained undetected within its room. And even the local children know that Evil Mary waits in the house for anyone foolish enough to walk through the front door.

Before long, Rosie realizes that her entire life has been defined by the spirit of a woman who died in agony. Can she become the first person to escape Evil Mary, or will she fall victim to the same fate as the house's other occupants?

AMY CROSS

Also by Amy Cross

The Ghosts of Hexley Airport

Ten years ago, more than two hundred people died in a horrific plane crash at Hexley Airport.

Today, some say their ghosts still haunt the terminal building.

When she starts her new job at the airport, working a night shift as part of the security team, Casey assumes the stories about the place can't be true. Even when she has a strange encounter in a deserted part of the departure hall, she's certain that ghosts aren't real.

Soon, however, she's forced to face the truth. Not only is there something haunting the airport's buildings and tarmac, but a sinister force is working behind the scenes to replicate the circumstances of the original accident. And as a snowstorm moves in, Hexley Airport looks set to witness yet another disaster.

AMY CROSS

Also by Amy Cross

The Girl Who Never Came Back

Twenty years ago, Charlotte Abernathy vanished while playing near her family's house. Despite a frantic search, no trace of her was found until a year later, when the little girl turned up on the doorstep with no memory of where she'd been.

Today, Charlotte has put her mysterious ordeal behind her, even though she's never learned where she was during that missing year. However, when her eight-year-old niece vanishes in similar circumstances, a fully-grown Charlotte is forced to make a fresh attempt to uncover the truth.

Originally published in 2013, the fully revised and updated version of *The Girl Who Never Came Back* tells the harrowing story of a woman who thought she could forget her past, and of a little girl caught in the tangled web of a dark family secret.

AMY CROSS

Also by Amy Cross

Asylum
(The Asylum Trilogy book 1)

"No-one ever leaves Lakehurst. The staff, the patients, the ghosts... Once you're here, you're stuck forever."

After shooting her little brother dead, Annie Radford is sent to Lakehurst psychiatric hospital for assessment. Hearing voices in her head, Annie is forced to undergo experimental new treatments devised by a mysterious old man who lives in the hospital's attic. It soon becomes clear that the hospital's staff, led by the vicious Nurse Winter, are hiding something horrific at Lakehurst.

As Annie struggles to survive the hospital, she learns more about Nurse Winter's own story. Once a promising young medical student, Kirsten Winter also heard voices in her head. Voices that traveled a long way to reach her. Voices that have a plan of their own. Voices that will stop at nothing to get what they want.

What kind of signals are being transmitted from the basement of the hospital? Who is the old man in the attic? Why are living human brains kept in jars? And what is the dark secret that lurks at the heart of the hospital?

AMY CROSS

BOOKS BY AMY CROSS

1. Dark Season: The Complete First Series (2011)
2. Werewolves of Soho (Lupine Howl book 1) (2012)
3. Werewolves of the Other London (Lupine Howl book 2) (2012)
4. Ghosts: The Complete Series (2012)
5. Dark Season: The Complete Second Series (2012)
6. The Children of Black Annis (Lupine Howl book 3) (2012)
7. Destiny of the Last Wolf (Lupine Howl book 4) (2012)
8. Asylum (The Asylum Trilogy book 1) (2012)
9. Dark Season: The Complete Third Series (2013)
10. Devil's Briar (2013)
11. Broken Blue (The Broken Trilogy book 1) (2013)
12. The Night Girl (2013)
13. Days 1 to 4 (Mass Extinction Event book 1) (2013)
14. Days 5 to 8 (Mass Extinction Event book 2) (2013)
15. The Library (The Library Chronicles book 1) (2013)
16. American Coven (2013)
17. Werewolves of Sangreth (Lupine Howl book 5) (2013)
18. Broken White (The Broken Trilogy book 2) (2013)
19. Grave Girl (Grave Girl book 1) (2013)
20. Other People's Bodies (2013)
21. The Shades (2013)
22. The Vampire's Grave and Other Stories (2013)
23. Darper Danver: The Complete First Series (2013)
24. The Hollow Church (2013)
25. The Dead and the Dying (2013)
26. Days 9 to 16 (Mass Extinction Event book 3) (2013)
27. The Girl Who Never Came Back (2013)
28. Ward Z (The Ward Z Series book 1) (2013)
29. Journey to the Library (The Library Chronicles book 2) (2014)
30. The Vampires of Tor Cliff Asylum (2014)
31. The Family Man (2014)
32. The Devil's Blade (2014)
33. The Immortal Wolf (Lupine Howl book 6) (2014)
34. The Dying Streets (Detective Laura Foster book 1) (2014)
35. The Stars My Home (2014)
36. The Ghost in the Rain and Other Stories (2014)
37. Ghosts of the River Thames (The Robinson Chronicles book 1) (2014)
38. The Wolves of Cur'cath (2014)
39. Days 46 to 53 (Mass Extinction Event book 4) (2014)
40. The Man Who Saw the Face of the World (2014)

AMY CROSS

41. The Art of Dying (Detective Laura Foster book 2) (2014)
42. Raven Revivals (Grave Girl book 2) (2014)
43. Arrival on Thaxos (Dead Souls book 1) (2014)
44. Birthright (Dead Souls book 2) (2014)
45. A Man of Ghosts (Dead Souls book 3) (2014)
46. The Haunting of Hardstone Jail (2014)
47. A Very Respectable Woman (2015)
48. Better the Devil (2015)
49. The Haunting of Marshall Heights (2015)
50. Terror at Camp Everbee (The Ward Z Series book 2) (2015)
51. Guided by Evil (Dead Souls book 4) (2015)
52. Child of a Bloodied Hand (Dead Souls book 5) (2015)
53. Promises of the Dead (Dead Souls book 6) (2015)
54. Days 54 to 61 (Mass Extinction Event book 5) (2015)
55. Angels in the Machine (The Robinson Chronicles book 2) (2015)
56. The Curse of Ah-Qal's Tomb (2015)
57. Broken Red (The Broken Trilogy book 3) (2015)
58. The Farm (2015)
59. Fallen Heroes (Detective Laura Foster book 3) (2015)
60. The Haunting of Emily Stone (2015)
61. Cursed Across Time (Dead Souls book 7) (2015)
62. Destiny of the Dead (Dead Souls book 8) (2015)
63. The Death of Jennifer Kazakos (Dead Souls book 9) (2015)
64. Alice Isn't Well (Death Herself book 1) (2015)
65. Annie's Room (2015)
66. The House on Everley Street (Death Herself book 2) (2015)
67. Meds (The Asylum Trilogy book 2) (2015)
68. Take Me to Church (2015)
69. Ascension (Demon's Grail book 1) (2015)
70. The Priest Hole (Nykolas Freeman book 1) (2015)
71. Eli's Town (2015)
72. The Horror of Raven's Briar Orphanage (Dead Souls book 10) (2015)
73. The Witch of Thaxos (Dead Souls book 11) (2015)
74. The Rise of Ashalla (Dead Souls book 12) (2015)
75. Evolution (Demon's Grail book 2) (2015)
76. The Island (The Island book 1) (2015)
77. The Lighthouse (2015)
78. The Cabin (The Cabin Trilogy book 1) (2015)
79. At the Edge of the Forest (2015)
80. The Devil's Hand (2015)
81. The 13th Demon (Demon's Grail book 3) (2016)
82. After the Cabin (The Cabin Trilogy book 2) (2016)
83. The Border: The Complete Series (2016)
84. The Dead Ones (Death Herself book 3) (2016)

85. A House in London (2016)
86. Persona (The Island book 2) (2016)
87. Battlefield (Nykolas Freeman book 2) (2016)
88. Perfect Little Monsters and Other Stories (2016)
89. The Ghost of Shapley Hall (2016)
90. The Blood House (2016)
91. The Death of Addie Gray (2016)
92. The Girl With Crooked Fangs (2016)
93. Last Wrong Turn (2016)
94. The Body at Auercliff (2016)
95. The Printer From Hell (2016)
96. The Dog (2016)
97. The Nurse (2016)
98. The Haunting of Blackwych Grange (2016)
99. Twisted Little Things and Other Stories (2016)
100. The Horror of Devil's Root Lake (2016)
101. The Disappearance of Katie Wren (2016)
102. B&B (2016)
103. The Bride of Ashbyrn House (2016)
104. The Devil, the Witch and the Whore (The Deal Trilogy book 1) (2016)
105. The Ghosts of Lakeforth Hotel (2016)
106. The Ghost of Longthorn Manor and Other Stories (2016)
107. Laura (2017)
108. The Murder at Skellin Cottage (Jo Mason book 1) (2017)
109. The Curse of Wetherley House (2017)
110. The Ghosts of Hexley Airport (2017)
111. The Return of Rachel Stone (Jo Mason book 2) (2017)
112. Haunted (2017)
113. The Vampire of Downing Street and Other Stories (2017)
114. The Ash House (2017)
115. The Ghost of Molly Holt (2017)
116. The Camera Man (2017)
117. The Soul Auction (2017)
118. The Abyss (The Island book 3) (2017)
119. Broken Window (The House of Jack the Ripper book 1) (2017)
120. In Darkness Dwell (The House of Jack the Ripper book 2) (2017)
121. Cradle to Grave (The House of Jack the Ripper book 3) (2017)
122. The Lady Screams (The House of Jack the Ripper book 4) (2017)
123. A Beast Well Tamed (The House of Jack the Ripper book 5) (2017)
124. Doctor Charles Grazier (The House of Jack the Ripper book 6) (2017)
125. The Raven Watcher (The House of Jack the Ripper book 7) (2017)
126. The Final Act (The House of Jack the Ripper book 8) (2017)
127. Stephen (2017)
128. The Spider (2017)

AMY CROSS

129. The Mermaid's Revenge (2017)
130. The Girl Who Threw Rocks at the Devil (2018)
131. Friend From the Internet (2018)
132. Beautiful Familiar (2018)
133. One Night at a Soul Auction (2018)
134. 16 Frames of the Devil's Face (2018)
135. The Haunting of Caldgrave House (2018)
136. Like Stones on a Crow's Back (The Deal Trilogy book 2) (2018)
137. Room 9 and Other Stories (2018)
138. The Gravest Girl of All (Grave Girl book 3) (2018)
139. Return to Thaxos (Dead Souls book 13) (2018)
140. The Madness of Annie Radford (The Asylum Trilogy book 3) (2018)
141. The Haunting of Briarwych Church (Briarwych book 1) (2018)
142. I Just Want You To Be Happy (2018)
143. Day 100 (Mass Extinction Event book 6) (2018)
144. The Horror of Briarwych Church (Briarwych book 2) (2018)
145. The Ghost of Briarwych Church (Briarwych book 3) (2018)
146. Lights Out (2019)
147. Apocalypse (The Ward Z Series book 3) (2019)
148. Days 101 to 108 (Mass Extinction Event book 7) (2019)
149. The Haunting of Daniel Bayliss (2019)
150. The Purchase (2019)
151. Harper's Hotel Ghost Girl (Death Herself book 4) (2019)
152. The Haunting of Aldburn House (2019)
153. Days 109 to 116 (Mass Extinction Event book 8) (2019)
154. Bad News (2019)
155. The Wedding of Rachel Blaine (2019)
156. Dark Little Wonders and Other Stories (2019)
157. The Music Man (2019)
158. The Vampire Falls (Three Nights of the Vampire book 1) (2019)
159. The Other Ann (2019)
160. The Butcher's Husband and Other Stories (2019)
161. The Haunting of Lannister Hall (2019)
162. The Vampire Burns (Three Nights of the Vampire book 2) (2019)
163. Days 195 to 202 (Mass Extinction Event book 9) (2019)
164. Escape From Hotel Necro (2019)
165. The Vampire Rises (Three Nights of the Vampire book 3) (2019)
166. Ten Chimes to Midnight: A Collection of Ghost Stories (2019)
167. The Strangler's Daughter (2019)
168. The Beast on the Tracks (2019)
169. The Haunting of the King's Head (2019)
170. I Married a Serial Killer (2019)
171. Your Inhuman Heart (2020)
172. Days 203 to 210 (Mass Extinction Event book 10) (2020)

173. The Ghosts of David Brook (2020)
174. Days 349 to 356 (Mass Extinction Event book 11) (2020)
175. The Horror at Criven Farm (2020)
176. Mary (2020)
177. The Middlewych Experiment (Chaos Gear Annie book 1) (2020)
178. Days 357 to 364 (Mass Extinction Event book 12) (2020)
179. Day 365: The Final Day (Mass Extinction Event book 13) (2020)
180. The Haunting of Hathaway House (2020)
181. Don't Let the Devil Know Your Name (2020)
182. The Legend of Rinth (2020)
183. The Ghost of Old Coal House (2020)
184. The Root (2020)
185. I'm Not a Zombie (2020)
186. The Ghost of Annie Close (2020)
187. The Disappearance of Lonnie James (2020)
188. The Curse of the Langfords (2020)
189. The Haunting of Nelson Street (The Ghosts of Crowford 1) (2020)
190. Strange Little Horrors and Other Stories (2020)
191. The House Where She Died (2020)
192. The Revenge of the Mercy Belle (The Ghosts of Crowford 2) (2020)

AMY CROSS

For more information, visit:

www.blackwychbooks.com

AMY CROSS

Made in the USA
Las Vegas, NV
16 March 2025